BLACK RIVER

An account of Christmas Preacher, a slave freed

By

Myles Ojabo

DAFEL BOOKS
Auckland

First published in 2018
Published by Dafel Books, Auckland, New Zealand
www.dafelbooks.com

ISBN: 978-0473411756

SOME IDOMA WORDS AND THEIR MEANINGS

Inu: Room
Ugwu: Chicken
Alekwuafia: Resurrected Ancestor
Oli'doma: Idoma Home
Ole: House
Alichebe: Royal gown
Enyi: Water
Ikwu: Death
Ano: We
Cha: Ride
Wa: Come
Nyo: Go
Onihi: Pounded Yam
Olo: Soup
Ole'gbo: Home of the Igbos
Oligra: Home of the Igala tribe
Ihi: Yam
Onyilo: Male
Achadu: Prime Minister
Ayi'doma: Children of Idoma tribe
Ufi: fear
Otubiobi: Evil mind
Jeje: Dance
Owu: Wind
Ewo: Dog
Owoicho: God
Ugwugwu: Masquerade
Eyi: Blood
N'ya: I did
N'je: I know
Aah gei je: You will know
Gwo: Fall
Adam: My father
Ikwu: Death

Enyo 'nobi: Black river
Awo 'lila: You are a fool
Onya: Woman
Ekemgbe: Lie
Ofu: Power
Onye: Who
Okoho: A sort of soup
Njangada : Dry okra
Adou: Your father
Eje: Beans
Agbou: Banana
Eche: Existence
Ko chow: Please
Aa: You
Kela: Talk
Ano nyo'le: Let's go home
Odi yaa la'America?: What is happening in America?

Until the lions have their own historians, the history
of the hunt will always glorify the hunter.
- Chinua Achebe

In liberty or bondage, the African could not be
separated from the American.
- Colson Whitehead

PART ONE

ODA'NYAA

FROM A REALM OF FOREBEARS, a set of eyes searched the foreign land for a descendant. These eyes belonged to the one born out of the union of a leopard and a beautiful woman. On this winter night of 1790, thunder roared and the lightning stretched its form to touch diverse places in Virginia. The boy, sprawled over the hard earth, woke. It snowed the previous night. And now, the cloud appeared heavy. Oda'nyaa, the mermaid, stood in front of all the sleeping bodies. He saw her in the dark, and she offered her hand to him. He took it and she dragged him into her embrace. The tapping of the rain on the roof intensified. *Ochigbo*, his name before his slave days, seemed to fade away. Now they called him Christmas. The other slaves were named Christmas too – since they all arrived in Virginia in Christmas of the year before. He remembered the first time he saw Oda'nyaa. The three-year-old Ochigbo swam alongside his mother in the Opialu black river. He saw a frog dive into the water and felt his breath stop. He began to slap the surface of the water. His mother couldn't reach him in time before he drowned.

The dust in Opialu's air increased, and residents remained indoors most of the time. The village thought him dead. His father sent a message to the great coffin-maker, and headed to the river with three youths known to be good swimmers to find his body. The beautiful woman named Oda'nyaa took him to the bottom of the black river, to show him her greatness. He felt the golden walls of her kingdom. He found the caudal fins of the other mermaids in the kingdom fascinating. He played and cuddled them. Oda'nyaa's smile always seemed welcoming. On this day, carrying her alluring smile, she tried hard to convince him to enjoy the beautiful land of the white man.

In his state of prodigious intoxication, she drew closer to his body and whispered, 'We could become clouds.'

His body craved for her. One of the sleeping bodies in the room shook. Christmas saw their bodies dissolve. He and Oda'nyaa. They vanished into the thin air like dust. They soared toward the sky. Christmas felt cold. His vision blurred. Air blocked his ears. They became the omniscient clouds. He could now see far. He could read the minds of every slave he slept amongst. He saw the fear of the tall skinny Christmas woman, and even the greed of the robust old Christmas man. He saw the hatred and rebellious plot of another. A teenager plotted suicide, desiring to find a river to jump into.

Through the sense of the clouds they saw, felt and smelt the future. Many little houses and a lot of people dominated this future. The place felt hot, and people sweated severely on merely walking short distances. A fuzzy smell drifted in the air of this place. They encountered his future being, wrinkled at sixty-six years of age. Old Christmas levitated through the sky with his body drenched in sweat and steamy fragments of cloud.

Sixty-six-year-old Christmas, floating through the comfort of the sky, heard a shout. He looked down and saw the black ocean. He slept. His body floated. He could only mumble, Opialu, Opialu, Opialu. His strength weakened. His wrinkled body floated into Opialu. The divine ability fulfilled its part. He remained still in the middle of the dark Opialu clouds. Lightning hit the village, stretching out to different areas. This couldn't wake him. At the sound of thunder, the older Christmas fell swiftly and landed on the thatched roof of a hut. His skinny body tore the roof and landed in the middle of a woman's room. The sound woke people. A very young woman, naked and asleep, lurched out of her mat.

'Wizard! Wizard!' both Christmases, the watchful clouds and the one in the woman's hut, heard people screaming from outside the hut. The young woman clasped a big earthen pot and shook in fright.

The clouds, young Christmas and Oda'nyaa, gathered and glared in awe through the hole in the roof. The unclothed woman took the cloth hanging on the wall and covered herself. She ran out, and he followed. She ran into the arms of a big man in the midst of a growing gathering of bare-chested men. The men, all armed with machetes, glowered at the older Christmas in fear.

'I'm not a wizard!' he tried to explain to them.

The young woman with a plain cloth around her whispered into her father's ear. The man whispered back.

They welcomed Old Christmas in Opialu, and gave him a wife in the young woman whose body he almost crushed, for custom required this of any honourable man ever to set eyes on a nude virgin. Village women exclaimed, and young men danced ogrinya. The dust went up to the ancestors. The cloud roared in delight. They offered Old Christmas a land on which he could build his huts.

The clouds that the younger Christmas and the greatest of mermaids became began a conversation.

'I am coming back here an old man,' Christmas said.

'It could be averted,' Oda'nyaa replied. 'Home is America. And in America you are betrothed to me and me alone.'

'But... I would like to come back.'

'It is not wise.' She sighed.

'Why?'

'You will die a terrible death if you come back,' she whispered.

Back in the large hall with the other slaves, he prayed to his alekwuafia to have a kind master. He truly wanted a good master He wanted good food and a spacious room. He wetted a tip of his finger and touched his forehead.

* * *

The wagon wobbled in its movement through the scanty village of Richmond. The lawns looked patchy, and the rising sun seemed lazy. Christmas's heart began to pound heavily.

His seller started a conversation, 'You know what year it is?'

'Seventeen-ninety,' Christmas replied.

'You know who the president of America is?'

'George Washington,' Christmas said.

'You are to act smart. I don't want no buyer regretting this purchase.' The man snorted. 'You know what to say if tested in this regard.'

They stopped seven miles after the city hall, and there the Preacher residence stood. Christmas jumped down from the wagon. So did the seller. A tall and slender man, perhaps in his mid-twenties, stood in front of the white house.

'That would be your master,' the seller said to Christmas. He looked up at the man and shouted, 'Hey, Mr. Preacher.'

'I can see you got a negro there,' said Mr. Preacher approaching.

'You would be lucky if you purchase this one. Fresh good, about fifteen years old,' shouted the seller.

The seller's horse became unsettled and tried to hop forward. This could be bad luck, Christmas thought. This man, Mr. Preacher, could be a bad man. Christmas felt the man's stare on him. It felt warm. He noticed the smile.

'A handsome African,' Mr. Preacher said.

Christmas looked down, at the brown-reddish leaves masking the soil. This Mr. Preacher could be a good man. He sounded firm and cultured.

'What is your name, boy?'

Christmas felt the cold palms of Mr. Preacher over his shoulder.

'Speak up boy,' the seller raised his voice.

'Christmas,' he said. 'They calls me, Christmas.'

Mr. Preacher looked at the seller and asked 'How much?'

'Twenty hundred.'

'I can give you fifteen hundred,' Mr. Preacher bargained. 'You know you have been unfair to me in the past.'

'I should charge you even more, considering what your Quaker friends been doing recently, petitioning the congress for the abolition of slavery,' the seller drawled. 'Make it eighteen.'

'Come see me tomorrow and I give you cash.' Mr. Preacher sighed.

'Good, Mr. Preacher. Will write you a receipt after cash is received.'

'Why do you call him Christmas?' Mr. Preacher asked.

'All of them – the slaves that arrived in my last shipment before Christmas Day of 1787 are named Christmas, Mr. Preacher,' the seller said before jumping on the seat between his wagon and his horse to drive away.

The sound of a gunshot echoed in the woods. Richmond's air stank. Perhaps a lot of fish in the black river died and were starting to smell.

'Tell me, boy. Where are you from in Africa?'

'Oli'doma.'

'I heard of the Hausas, Fulanis, Igbos and Zulus. Never heard of Oli'doma.'

'My folks comes from Kwararafa country,' Christmas said proudly.

'Come on in Christmas. You must be hungry,' Mr. Preacher said leading the way into the white big house.

An elegant and pregnant white woman in a colourful dress arranging some plates on the dining table, looked up and smiled. She might be in her mid-twenties, Christmas guessed.

She smiled. 'And who have we here?'

'His name is Christmas. Randy brought him,' Mr. Preacher said.

The woman approached Christmas, held him by the sides of his shoulders. 'You can take a seat and I will dish you some bird nest pudding.'

Christmas hesitated. He and his fellow slaves used to watch the seller and his brothers eat. They prayed in their hearts for the Randy brothers to spare them some leftovers. The brothers often left something, and the slaves and the dogs owned by this seller struggled and fought to have a share. Once, Christmas kicked one of the dogs in the belly. The dog cried so loud and tussled over the floor. The premises became quiet, like an Oli'doma shrine. The seller and his brothers appeared.

'Who did this?' the seller asked quietly looking at the wailing dog and taking off his hat.

Two slaves looked at Christmas.

His hands were tied and his body, suspended, hanging from a tree. The clouds in the sky gathered over Richmond. Christmas's skin broke on every lash. The rain started and washed away the blood spilled out of his back. Night came, fellow slaves listened to him moan in pain. They listened to hopeless words about fleeing back to Oli'doma. They listened to him speak of how great his people in Oli'doma were. How his people became crocodiles and migrated from the great Kwararafa country.

Mr. Preacher and his wife took their seats. They watched him. He struggled to use the spoon to fetch pieces of apple in custard.

Christmas soon emptied his bowl.

* * *

He got a big *inu* to himself. Mrs. Preacher mentioned that once Mr. Preacher built a cabin for him behind the house, he would leave the big house. Christmas knew the real reason for this. He pried on the couple's conversation earlier on, during breakfast, and he bit his lower lip in displeasure over all he heard. He reconsidered running away. The mistress thought he stank and recommended that cabins be built for him and the other slave in the house.

Christmas acquainted himself with the only slave woman in the house. She seemed big, and perhaps halfway between her thirtieth and fortieth year. She frowned all the time. Her smile, even though rare, appeared sullen. She often cleaned the big house, using lime soap on the floors, the wide mahogany stairs and the windows. She swept away dead moths and spider webs in corners.

She said to him in the kitchen house, 'I loves cookin'. Before Massa Preacher buys me, I lives in a farm white folks force us to eat roaches. Here we eat really good. Lucky you here.'

Antonia went on to tell him about her history. 'My grandma say her own mama was from Africa. She got this massa who is knowed for the name, "Five-hundred-dollar Massa". He done sold grandma for five hundred dollars. And she ain't the first to be gone for the price. He done these deals durin' Easter and it called "Easter Specials". He got his slave womens pregnant and got them to stand in the market at the start of Easter and by end of the day business over. He knowed business like no white fella in North Carolina. My grandma got pregnant with my mama in the time the massa decided to sell her. Five-hundred-dollar Massa told customers that there was twins in my grandma history. He told them to buy her for five hundred dollars and look forward to ownin' twins.'

'And your mama born twins?' Christmas asked.

'No. She born no twins. My mama came out alone like a skinny little girl. And life for grandma and mama be hell after. They live with the new massa until I was born.'

She showed him around the house – Mr. Preacher's bedroom, the wash room and the visitors' rooms. She showed him the stores, the spring house, Mr. Preacher's study, the kitchen house, the stable and the carriage house. She told him the new massa and his wife used to be Quakers who spoke to other Quakers and their God in a dignified manner, using 'thee' or 'thou' instead of 'you'.

'You a slave so they would refer to you and all other poor people as "you"', she said and further advised him about his roles which involved tending to the horses, hogs and chickens. She said her great-grand mother, a Yoruba, got captured from the centre of Africa. She wanted to know if he came from Yoruba land.

'I from one of the greatest peoples in Africa,' Christmas proclaimed.

'What they call them?'

'The people of Oli'doma.'

'Never heard about them folks.'

'We is the crocodile people,' he said.

'You sure could be a crocodile,' she said with sarcasm, pushing her lower lip out. 'I be an alligator if you be a crocodile. Ain't got no time for this.' She left him alone.

He lay down to sleep. The pallet felt warm. He could see the slender moon through the window. He longed for a beautiful dream but got a bad one. He saw himself in the slave ship that brought him to Virginia. He lay underneath the pile of bodies with excessive odours and could hardly move. He woke up almost breathless and felt glad to be in 1790 and not in the year of his capture. He remembered how they, the males, were heaped up beneath each other. He remembered the stench of his own body and, worse, the stench of others. He remembered the poisonous gases emitted out of the anuses of some of the slaves above his face. He remembered the taste of urine and watery shit washed over his body. He went through this torment. He, of a great tribe, once of the Okolofa Kingdom of Kwararafa origin.

Two slave women died of suffocation and were left unattended to for a fortnight. For this reason some slave women around the dead began to fall sick. The slavers got rid of the dead rotting bodies, shoving them into the sea. Prior to the intense cleaning of the section, they took out all the women alive and placed them all up amongst the men. A pregnant slave girl roughly thrust over Christmas birthed her dead baby over his body the following night. And for the rest of the journey, he never again looked forward to the bread forced into their mouths daily.

Christmas couldn't sleep. He thought about his family. Christmas remembered how he and his brother scrambled over gory chickens with their heads all severed. He and Abah always competed in their pace of picking one *ugwu* each time to hand to their father, seated over the rock at the edge of the Opialu black river in moments like this, and casting the birds received from them each time into the river. The sacrifices were in honour of their great alekwuafia, Orinya, and their very first forebear, Abutu, the one fathered by a leopard. Daybreak came and Christmas didn't realise this until Antonia came knocking hard on the staircase leading into the attic. She entered and he sat up.

'Don't be lazy, boy? Get up and go join Massa in tendin' to them damn hogs.'

Christmas walked into the hog house and Mr. Preacher frowned.

A chicken wailed from afar and could be heard flapping its wings. The hogs started grunting.

'You ought to rise before dawn and be here early. I don't like to whip negroes, but might be forced to if you put me to the test again.'

Christmas nodded, eyes lowered.

'Come, I will show you how to feed the hogs onwards.'

Mr. Preacher poured feed over the feeders. The hogs wailed. Their bodies brushed against each other. The morning didn't last. The master taught Christmas to identify the signs of the female swine being on heat – a good time for the most fertile boar in the farm. But this morning, the females were kept away in different pens. He still wasn't sure of his new owner. He wanted to be liked by Mr. Preacher. No slave wanted to be hated by his master.

They tended to the chickens and goats. They finished on time, and Christmas requested to clean Mr. Preacher's galoshes.

'I don't follow,' Mr. Preacher said.

'I want to clean your shoes...' Christmas repeated, pointing at Mr. Preacher's galoshes.

'You are doing well with the language, boy,' Mr. Preacher replied, taking off his galoshes.

The clouds gathered but it didn't rain. The sun gently rose instead. Christmas sat in front of the big house thinking of Oli'doma. On one Eke Market day, he remembered coming across Ochi'Oche's father on the market ground, and the chatty old man wouldn't leave his side. The man wouldn't stop talking about how the gods favoured Ochigbo's hardworking father. The man could be right. His father owned great acres of land scattered around Opialu. Ochi'Oche's father blamed his own poverty on his ill health – the venom warring against his scrotum. He showered abuses on the village doctor whose concoctions made him so weak he couldn't farm anymore.

'It has been a long time since you saw your cousin, Ochi'Oche. *Ano nyo'le* so you can spend some time with him.'

'You are right but...'

'Don't turn down my invitation, Ochigbo. Didn't your mother tell you I was her closest sibling? As cousins, you and Ochi'Oche should spend more time together.'

He didn't want to disappoint his uncle and so followed him home and, shockingly, Ochi'Oche wasn't home. None of his wives were home either.

'I don't think he is far away,' the uncle said offering him millet drink.

He drank it and life went out of him. He woke and saw himself in chains among a number of slaves. They were surrounded by some Hausa people with a couple of white men.

* * *

He entered the stable and moved a heap of hay into an empty pen. Rain started. It stopped and started again. But it didn't last. Christmas saw Antonia fetch water from the well, situated a few feet away, and head off to the big house. Oda'nyaa appeared. Her entire body wet. He trembled and dropped the saddle in his hands. She disappeared in a blink. One of the horses grunted. The apparition took over his mind. He walked back to the big house. She looked like a fair African woman. He didn't want the leftover Antonia kept for him, and headed straight for the attic. He continued to think about the mermaid. Sometimes she appeared with legs.

Antonia's movements got him standing. Quietly, she climbed up to his dwelling.

'I hear you talkin'. You got a woman in here?'

'No.'

'Evil soul, Christmas... You want a woman, you talk to Massa. How old you is again?'

'They say I'm sixteen,' Christmas said.

'You crazy, Christmas?'

'I ain't crazy,' he replied.

'But you talkin' to yourself. Look here. Why you leavin' the leftover in the kitchen house? I tells you boy, you lucky white fella like Massa buys you.'

He said nothing.

'You done seen any woman?' she asked.

He shook his head.

Antonia shut the door and left. Christmas sighed and covered himself with the quilt lying on the ground. He glanced at his side and caught the figure of Oda'nyaa. She wasn't naked this time. She wore a transparent long gown, an *alichebe*, with some shiny gold coated spots.

'Oda'nyaa, the woman of my dreams,' he called and stared in awe. 'What are you doing here?'

'I have always visited from the greatest of black rivers... You are now accustomed to me...'

'What do you really want from me?'

'I am here to help you, Ochigbo... To reveal the unknown to you,' she said and walked toward him. She placed her fingers over his eyes. He heard her meditation. The words were like the wind, and in little time they were transported into the dark.

(echoes)
In the enyi we live
In the enyi we cherish
Let ugwu lay eggs of the past...

He sensed light taking over the dark, and the dark became Opialu. Christmas and Oda'nyaa walked along an Opialu bush path. Sunset arrived. The sun soon grasped the colour of the udala fruit. Some children, naked to the waist, ran past them raising a lot of dust into the air.

'You bring me back here.'

'Your spirit is here with me. We are back in time.'

They were now in front of his uncle's house. She went in through the mud wall without opening the door. He got in just like she did. To his astonishment, he saw himself, his embodiment in the past, in conversation with Ochi'Oche's father.

'Do they see us?' he whispered.

'No, they can't even hear us,' Oda'nyaa said.

Christmas saw his younger self fall to the floor clutching his stomach after drinking the millet drink.

A smile of relief settled on his uncle's face. He walked across the unconscious body and out of the hut.

'Where is he going'?' Christmas asked Oda'nyaa.

'Let's go after him,' she said.

They followed him past the black river to a small hut. A bulky man came out to meet him. Christmas recognised the man to be one of the Hausa men behind his capture and journey out of Opialu.

'Oh no...' Christmas's spirit lamented. He turned around and couldn't find Oda'nyaa. 'Where are you?'

'Christmas, are you speaking to somebody?' he heard Mrs. Preacher call out. He looked around and found himself back in the attic in Richmond.

* * *

In three months, many changes occurred. Mrs. Preacher birthed a boy and named him Marcus. There were more hogs and hog houses. The slave cabins were now finished and standing. Christmas got a dwelling of his own. Although the walls of his dwelling seemed ugly, he appreciated having them to shutter him from prying eyes. He shifted the straw bed to a corner, and hammered nails on different parts of the walls so he could hang his clothes. He looked around and appraised his arrangements. He thought of Oda'nyaa. To her, he didn't stink. He wouldn't be running away anytime soon.

He headed for the big house to carry the load of used dishes to the kitchen house. He entered the kitchen and saw Mrs. Preacher salting some fish.

Antonia, rocking the baby near the fire, cleared her throat and said, 'I love this infant.'

'God will give us another boy,' Mrs. Preacher said. She kept the fish aside and poured some soda water into the bowl of used dishes.

'We gon have more boys to run them businesses of the house when Massa old,' Antonia said.

'You mean girls don't work hard like boys, Antonia?' Mrs. Preacher asked.

'You gets me wrong, Mrs. Preacher,' Antonia replied. 'Good if you done born more, but I'm afraid I gon spoil them girls.'

Christmas laughed.

Mrs. Preacher glanced at him. She said, 'I have good news. My husband will buy a beautiful young mother with two strong boys.'

'She gon make a good wife for Christmas?' Antonia asked.

Christmas's heart skipped.

'Antonia,' Mrs. Preacher said. 'I suppose she may be too old for Christmas. Her main task is to come help in looking after my baby so you can concentrate on the work of the house.'

'Christmas be shoutin' all night 'joyin' hisself with some damn spirit woman, Mrs. Preacher. He sure need a woman.'

'She lie, Mrs. Preacher,' Christmas almost yelled before catching himself.

'Stop it, Antonia! Christmas is still a child. And no one talk that way around here,' Mrs. Preacher said, washed her hands and took her baby from Antonia.

Antonia, with hands on her waist, stared deeply at Christmas. 'Tell me to my face that I lie, boy.'

Christmas remained quiet and looked away.

'My dear lord,' Mrs. Preacher exclaimed. Her infant began to cry. She nodded her head and left for the big house with her child. It didn't take long for Mr. Preacher to call.

Christmas's heart started to pound. He walked out of the kitchen with Antonia following.

Mr. Preacher waited with a whip in hand under the oak tree. He dropped the whip and dragged Christmas to tree trunk. He tied Christmas's body firmly to the tree. Christmas searched the cold tree for solace.

'Carnal behaviours are not allowed in this residence, Christmas. It is dirty and unspoken of in this family,' Mr. Preacher said.

The first lash hit his back. Tears gushed out of his eyes. He cried without screaming. More lashes broke his skin. In the end, Antonia loosened him and he fell on his knees and desperately longed for the hold of his real mother. Antonia led him back to the kitchen house. He sat on a stool. She gathered some ginger roots, cut them in small beats and pounded them in a wooden mortar. She applied the crushed roots and its juice on his back. He felt like screaming.

* * *

During one of the dying days of winter, Mr. Preacher drove home the woman named Esther along with her sons. The new woman, perhaps a year older than Antonia, looked thin and beautiful. Christmas considered marrying her. Christmas helped unpack their things from the wagon to the cabin next to Antonia's.

The older son, Black John, said he recently turned sixteen. Esther's younger son, Moses, was about twelve. Attentive to the new woman's movements he noticed a tear rolling down her cheek and through this tear he found an invisible passage through which he slipped into her mind. He didn't stay there for long, but he could see the dark memories of lost babies she carried with her.

One evening, just before bedtime, Christmas heard Moses crying out. Christmas ran into the sitting room in the big house, and found the new woman holding Moses firmly over a bench. Mrs. Preacher, in fury, whipped the child's behind.

'What you do that for?' Esther cautioned her son. 'You don't peep underneath at nobody as they undress.'

Christmas felt sorry for Moses. He committed the same offence several times, but no one ever caught him.

* * *

He lay on his pallet and started to think of Esther. He thought of Antonia, comparing their features. He preferred the former though. He kept wondering how beautiful Esther looked in her younger days. She looked a hundred times more beautiful than Antonia. He wanted to call the woman's name but ended up calling Oda'nyaa's.

He heard the sound of a sudden but brief wind outside. Her voice came in echoes. 'You want me and I am here.' Oda'nyaa appeared beside him.

'I want you in my life forever,' he whispered and stood up to embrace her.

'Let us spend some time in my kingdom,' she said.

'I want to hold you and...' He noticed her troubled look. 'What is the matter?'

'It's what you said... that you want me forever.'

'Isn't that going to happen?'

'You are human. And will die one day. You cannot have me forever.'

'How old are you?'

'You really want to know?

He nodded.

'Five-hundred and sixty years of existence.'

Christmas reasoned. She could be right – he couldn't have her forever. *Ikwu* couldn't be avoided in life. This scared him. 'Let us go and see what you want me to see.'

She placed her fingers over his face and began to sing:

> *Into the black river ano nyo*
> *Black ocean, ano wa*
> *On black water-horses ano cha...*

And darkness scooped the two of them into a grubby passage littered with rags and small pools of muddy water. A dying candlelight lit the passage. Christmas saw a very weak old man seated by the edge of the wall.

Oda'nyaa whispered, 'Ignore the wretched man.'

Christmas couldn't look away.

'Don't listen to her. She is no good for you,' the man said. 'I'm your alekwuafia captured by her spell. You and I are under her spell and need to be free from her.'

'Don't listen to him. He is the one who is no good for you,' Oda'nyaa insisted and Christmas pretended to listen to her. They found the waters and Oda'nyaa's legs became a caudal tail. Christmas swam underneath the waters with profound pleasure but his heart remained with the old man. Could it be Orinya, his great ancestor? Whom his father, back in Opialu, often tossed severed chickens at in sacrifice?

Oda'nyaa showed him her shrine, a place fellow mermaids gathered to worship her. She showed him various mirrors which she used to see earthly affairs. Whatever and wherever she wanted to see – in Oli'doma, in Virginia. They swam past tilapias and salmons. Passed sharks. They encountered other mermaids. These mermaid bowed their heads in acknowledgement. Oda'nyaa showed him her throne, the royal seat she sat and made vital decisions regarding all black rivers and oceans.

Back in Christmas's cabin, she shared his pallet until the early morning. She cuddled him. He moved. A strange bird squealed loudly outside. The clouds gathered. They laughed and held each other closely. They heard Marcus's cry vaguely coming from the big house.

'You shouldn't listen to that old man we encountered on our way. It is true – he is your ancestor. But he doesn't mean you good. He has never been of any use to the Ogah family. Under his chiefship, your people, the crocodile people, became refugees in their own land. The land, at that time, wept,' she said and sighed. 'Orinya still dwells in wretchedness, even in death.'

'You say he is my forefather, Orinya?'

She shook her head, saying yes.

'No one in my lineage ever spoke bad of Orinya,' he said.

She stared deeply into his eyes.

He stared back. He saw fury and almost got up from the pallet in alarm. She smiled.

He felt good most of the time Oda'nyaa remained around him. He felt so good except for the moment he met his ancestor. The strong urge to flee America came with the forebear.

* * *

Christmas, awakened by a loud bang on the cabin door, sprang out of bed. 'Open up Christmas! Massa wants you!' Antonia yelled.

He opened the door; his eyes wide open.

'You little son of a whore. See the damn stench of sex comin' out this room. What you spendin' your whole night playin' with yourself for?'

'I ain't doin' nothin',' Christmas replied.

'Of course you is. See the look on your face.'

'Please, Antonia. I don't wants Massa whippin' me crazy.'

She sighed. 'Somethin' gone wrong in the hog house. Massa wants you,' she repeated and walked away.

He headed to the hog house. Mr. Preacher, Black John and Moses were shoving out the bodies of dead hogs. The big surviving boar kept grunting amidst the dead quietness in place. Christmas felt the lump come up his throat. His eyes couldn't contain his tears. He blamed himself for this, and for a moment he wished his master died like the hogs. If Oda'nyaa didn't visit, perhaps he might have checked on the animals and tried to save some of them.

'Hey, Christmas, when was the last time you checked on the hogs?'

'Not long,' he lied. 'They fine when I check, Massa. They eatin' and lookin' strong just after Black John led the horses to the field.'

'This disease I long dreaded almost wiped them all out,' Mr. Preacher said raising his voice. Later in the night, on transporting the load of dishes from the big house to the kitchen house he heard Antonia tell Esther, 'Massa regrets buyin' you and them boys.'

'Why that is?' Esther asked.

Antonia looked at Christmas. 'Tell her what done happen in the hog house.'

'Them hogs all dead,' Christmas said.

'Massa done lost a fortune,' Antonia added.

'He gon sell us back?' Esther asked, wiping her wet hands over the dress she wore.

Antonia nodded her head in agreement.

Christmas saw tears fill Esther's eyes. He knew Antonia to assume many things and circulate them like chaffs. Somehow she sounded believable this time. In the coming days, butchers stopped coming to the farm. The eggs from the chicken house brought little money. Strange people began visiting the house. Two or three men, at times. Sometimes, a man and a woman.

'Them Quakers,' Antonia said. 'I wonder what they here for.'

Christmas took some fruits to the sitting room for the visitors before returning to the kitchen house. Antonia walked in afterwards with some woods for the fire.

'I told you Massa use to be part of them Quakers,' she said. 'But he left when they try to force him to free me.'

'What they want that for?'

'Them Quakers say slavery ain't no good,' Antonia whispered. 'Quakers, in those days when they own slaves, never flog no slave.'

'But Massa whip us,' Christmas said.

'How many times Massa whip you, boy?'

Silence.

'No nigger better than a well-disciplined slave,' she said. 'Where you gon go if Massa asks us to leave? How we gon survive?' Antonia asked. 'Gon be better if he sells us to some other white folk who be good as he be.'

They took trays of roasted pork and mashed potatoes to the dining room.

'I know I'm still worthy of God's presence in my household,' Mr. Preacher said. He led the visitors into the dining area.

'Thou act as thy typical fellow southerner. Free thy slaves and rejoin the society, Mr. Preacher,' one of them advised. 'The status of being a slave is unacceptable to God, and it is our desire that thee yield to the light.'

'I do not treat them cruelly. I'm not a doer or proclaimer of iniquity. I discipline them with the whip which is good – the bible encourages this. I can let thee talk to them.' He dragged out a couple of seats and gestured at the visitors to sit.

'Howdy,' the older visitor called out to Christmas and Antonia. 'Come, loved ones...'

Both approached.

'You all worship God?' The man stared at Antonia.

'They ain't no man like Jesus,' Antonia said. 'They says Jesus be the only way to heaven.'

'How about you?' The man looked at Christmas.

'We prays to the water and our ancestors in Oli'doma where I come from,' Christmas said.

'Mr. Banks, please ask them if I have ever been unkind to them?' Mr. Preacher interpolated.

'It's 1790 Mr. Preacher. Thou must understand that all men stand equal in the sight of God. Thou must free them.'

'I am sorry, I see no wrong in my doings and I don't feel led by the light to act in thy will.'

Antonia bowed and left; Christmas stayed in the room.

They all ate in silence. Christmas filled their tumblers with water each time they became empty. In the end, Esther came in to help Christmas clear the dishes and carry the large rug beneath the dining table and chairs, on which crumbs settled.

Mr. Preacher saw the visitors off to their horses. He soon returned, and mumbled, 'Good night.' He took the *Virginia Gazette* lying by a cushion and headed upstairs.

Night came. Christmas got to his cabin worried. He wondered what freedom in the white man's world felt like. Freedom for him waited in Opialu.

Christmas felt his spirit leave his body. His spirit walked out through the wooden planks bound together for a wall, floated hastily toward the big house and entered. He found Mr. Preacher seated in a worrisome state in his kingly matrimonial bed. His wife, also seated, knitted quietly.

'Saddened by the visit, I suppose,' the woman said.

'It is Mr. Banks, the overseer. I need to go after him.'

'He has just left here.'

'I know but...'

They heard their first child crying. She got out of the bed and left the room.

Christmas's spirit moved. Mr. Preacher trembled and looked around. He shrugged his shoulders, stood and put on his black hat. He headed out, and Christmas's spirit followed at a distance. Mr. Preacher mounted his horse and rode through the night. The energy in Christmas increased beyond the need for thirst or hunger. Richmond smelt of tobacco. He tailed the master through a detour since the puddles in the other rutted street recently increased in number. In Mr. Banks's house, Mr. Preacher pleaded with Mrs. Banks to wake her husband.

He entered the sitting room. Christmas's spirit hung by the edge of a pillar.

'What is on thy mind, Mr. Preacher?' Mr. Banks asked on coming out.

'I'm worried, Mr. Banks.'

'On account of what might that be?'

'Something my father made me believe which I doubted not until now.'

'Steven Preacher. One man instrumental to the acceptance of Quakers in Virginia.'

'It is the belief that negroes have no soul... I... have been thinking...' Mr. Preacher said.

'That was in thy father's days. He would unsay that sacrilege if he were alive today.'

'...about thy statement regarding negroes being equal to us in the eyes of God. My wife and I, living with the ones we own... we see no difference between ourselves... and them. The colour of their skin, Mr. Banks, and perhaps the little education I and my wife were privileged to acquire – makes the difference... I am confused.'

'Thou art right Mr. Preacher. Negroes possess souls and deserve salvation.'

'Is it right even to admit them into the Society of Friends, once I can give them their freedom?'

'There's nothing in the laws of God against it. But the current situation demands that free negroes have separate meetings from ours.'

'I would like some time to think about freeing my slaves. It's going to be hard for me with the finances of the estate being as they are, as I may require the hiring of some skilled hands. I will come up with a plan for the longer term, Mr. Banks.'

'How long would thee be dependent on slaves?'

'With the debt I have, I may be in need for another three, maybe four years.'

The words stung Christmas. It stung because his spirit couldn't find truth in them. The words were burdened with such reluctance.

'Thou will have to come up with a declaration in the next yearly meeting. That period in which thou will remain a master of slaves is hardly short. Thou will declare a date you will free them, and ensure the negroes can be well in society,' Mr. Banks said.

Mr. Preacher nodded.

'It is in my heart to tell thee something else,' Mr. Banks said.

'What is it, Mr. Banks?'

'The words that I would say to you now are Godly. Don't take them amiss. There's a better life in Louisville, Kentucky County, that awaits thee. Success. Riches. Do not count thy losses in Richmond. The death of hogs or the losses in thy business ain't the end of thee.'

'My father left me a lot of small houses here in this village, and the rent...'

'Sell them, Mr. Preacher. Sell them, use thy money and acquire better and cheaper houses in Louisville, and I assure thee, thou will regret not.'

Christmas thought about this place.

* * *

Christmas finished the early morning work at the hog farm. He saw Moses watching the sunrise. A cloud line blurred a section of the orange sun.

'You enjoy workin' for them white folks?' Moses asked on noticing his presence. He drew closer to Christmas and in a lower tone, asked, 'Ain't ever gon run away?'

'Don't ever ask me about that again,' Christmas replied.

You a fool,' Moses replied.

'What you say?' This provoked Christmas.

'What you gon do?' Moses stood up to Christmas.

Christmas smiled, turned around and headed toward his cabin.

He stopped. Christmas felt like hitting Moses. He continued toward the cabin. He saw the boy's mother going to the big house. She looked old enough to birth him. He couldn't understand his attraction toward her. He held this secret from the very first day she and her sons set foot in the residence. He wouldn't admit these feelings for the slave woman to Oda'nyaa either.

Christmas sat on the stool in front of his cabin, and at this very instant his spirit slipped away after Esther. He wanted Esther to have feelings for him. Her mind housed many thoughts and none were channelled toward him. The woman cherished her friendship with Antonia but couldn't get rid of the figment of jealousy Christmas couldn't understand. Christmas could now see through her eyes. She cried quietly again. He searched her mind. She feared being sold. The woman loved her children. Deep in her heart, she adored Black John and Moses. She feared the impending outcome of Mr. Preacher's decision. He could sell her and keep her boys. Christmas wondered why she believed such story coming from the strangest of all slaves – Antonia.

Esther carried baby Marcus to the room upstairs for a bath. She placed the child in the tub shaped like a big hat turned upside down. Esther bathed the infant, scrubbing him with the blue fluffy sponge in the tub. The child liked the effect and let out a laugh. She supported him in his seated posture inside the space facing the roof.

She began to talk to the child, 'All my baby daddies been scattered over the south like grains,' she started. 'Most of them mens never learned of their children. Them white folks owned every child that been in my womb.' Some black men actually raped her in the past. Black men. But some of these rapes were less unbearable compared to her total submission to white men. She could fight some of the black men off until her strength failed, but couldn't do the same to the white men.

She surpassed her own mother in terms of the number of children she bore. 'Eighteen,' she said talking to Marcus again. 'I can recall all the ways I born them children and just two is left. I was luckier than my mama. She got none of us to care for.' Esther experienced in tears three still-births, and witnessed the sale of four of her children; she saw death snatch away two. She didn't want to be sold again. No slave ever got used to being sold.

She towelled young master Marcus, dressed him in the yellow cotton pants Antonia made from muslin with lilac bands.

* * *

Christmas looked forward to showing Esther and Black John around the neighbourhood. They requested for passes from Mr. Preacher. Mr. Preacher always stressed on the importance of holding passes outside the residence. He said dubious slave catchers caught negroes without passes and took them down to Alabama to sell.

Christmas now hated his desire for Esther. His mind kept testing the edges of his self-control. They left the residence. The sun rose. Christmas noticed her staring at his arms.

'Them mosquitoes been terrible here. You should rub them molasses on your body every mornin' and evenin'.'

'I gon do that,' Christmas replied.

'Black John can fetch you some,' Esther said.

Christmas wanted to ask if she could rub the molasses on his skin. The thought excited him. It scared him too.

They came across a crowd. A negro, under the directive of a white man, lashed a fellow negro hanging from a tree.

They inquired from one negro in the crowd about the cause of the punishment.

'Chicken theft,' the negro said. 'He done steal from Mr. Vaughan.'

'Who Mr. Vaughan is?' Christmas asked, confused.

'You don't want to know,' Black John said. 'You been in Richmond longer than I been here and you don't know the owner of the Henrique Plantation. He truly terrible to them slaves.'

Some negro men and women in the crowd laughed at every sting of the whip. The slave's cry echoed across the clearing.

They walked toward the black river.

'Antonia got a lot of horror stories about the river,' Christmas said.

'She done told me a few,' Esther agreed.

'Is them stories really scary?' Black John asked.

'There was one she told me about them slaves tryin' to head across it, to escape,' Christmas began. 'White folks, whose duty it was to catch them slaves who tried to go across, trap them. These slave catchers never returned the slaves to their massa. Just drowned them.'

'No good.' Black John shook his head.

'I guess black folks still run away in these parts,' Esther asked looking at Christmas.

'Don't know,' Christmas said.

'Massa Preacher don't whip bad like old Massa,' Black John said. 'Why should we think of runnin' mama?'

'They all the same, son,' she said, stopped and looked at Christmas.

'I ain't gon say nothin' to nobody,' Christmas said looking away. 'You both seen nothin'. Before he brought y'all here, he whip me and it hurt bad that Antonia treat me with ginger.'

'I can trust you,' she said, smiled weakly and kept walking. 'Black John, tell me, no matter what gon happen – if Massa Preacher sell me, you gon look after your brother?'

'I goes wherever you go, Mama,' Black John said.

'He ain't gon risk losin' you and your brother, I knows. He got nothin' to lose gettin' rid of me,' she went on.

'You believe all Antonia put in your head, Esther? Massa ain't gon sell nobody,' Christmas said.

It came to pass after a few days that he, Christmas, got it right. Mr. Preacher summoned all of them to the sitting room of the big house. They were all lined up. She, Christmas, Antonia, Black John, and Moses.

'There will be changes in our lives very soon. It is a big change,' Mr. Preacher began, with the familiar smile the slaves were accustomed to. 'You all know the setback that has occurred lately. It is a big loss. Moving away from Richmond will do us good. We moving to Louisville in Kentucky County.'

'You ain't gon sell nobody?' Esther asked in shock.

'Who told you that?' Mr. Preacher asked.

* * *

The wagon and carriage raced through the forest. Christmas remained deep in his thoughts. With him in the wagon were Black John, Moses, their mother and Antonia. Mr. Preacher, his wife and the young master were in the carriage. Mr. Preacher drove the carriage and the house agent providing the new house in Kentucky County, handled the wagon by coaxing the horse with the whip. This same agent, before this day, brought Mr. Preacher buyers for his properties in Richmond. What was so good about this place called Louisville? Rumours were too good to be true. One jobless Irishman, a beggar, went to Kentucky County, made it big and now own some twenty slaves.

Christmas struggled to keep Esther out of his mind. He thought of Oli'doma. He tried to recall his last memory of his father. Of his mother. Of his siblings. Their faces were faint in his head. He recalled how he, along with his father and mother and brother, sat around the dish of *onihi* and *olo* for dinner. The memory of the journey from his village remained so clear. How he got captured and transported through the black forest, from Oli'doma to Ole'gbo. They walked for nearly sixty kilometres. For days they stank. They fed on small chunks of *ihi* and drank from the streams and rivers they came across. The magnitude of pain on the soles of his feet increased, and all the other slaves, with shackles around their necks, felt the same. They were all scared of being whipped like the full-breasted woman whose legs became too heavy to move. Most of their captors wore boots and just couldn't feel what they, the slaves, felt. They were made to lie on the wet grass of the forest to rest. The slavers pleasured themselves with some of the young female slaves. The one they called Mr. Garble, the worst of them all, lacked shame. He exploited different slave women each time, bleating like a goat. What sort of creature did this openly, in front of captured men? At least the other slavers carried out their acts furtively, away from downturned eyes.

Mr. Garble decided to insert his manhood between the legs of the full-breasted woman. But history changed. She truly endured all the lashings. She endured all the downpour of spittle on her. She endured the heaviness of the shackle around her neck. Her naked feet burned. The other slavers, even though flogged her, feared touching her. But Mr. Garble got the shackles off her neck, held his whip firmly and commanded her to lie on the wet grass. She vanished in response.

Fright encased Mr. Garble. The pompous shoulders deflated. Everyone including his fellow slavers watched him run in circles. The situation changed days later. Mr. Garble, leading his faction, became a baby. At first, he stayed awake along with every scheduled captor, guarding the slaves they forced to sleep. The full-breasted woman's absence became a cruel infection in his chest. Mr. Garble coughed steadily. In his first sleep after seven days, he dreamt. He screamed out of this nightmare, waking everyone asleep. Christmas felt satisfied in this helplessness. Two other slaves laughed and were brutally punished. Mr. Garble shot them point blank. Another form of spirit took control over the white man's body. A devouring spirit. He whipped the men all over their bodies. They trembled in pain and bled profusely. One of them died on the spot. They left the other slave behind in a gory state to tell his story to his descendants.

Mr. Garble shot at rabbits, lizards and bush cats, laying claims that some of the owls they saw during the course of the journey possessed the spirit of the full-breasted woman.

The slave, always in front of Christmas during the travel, predicted the full-breasted woman's return. He believed she could free all of them. On the morning they caught sight of the black river in Ole'gbo, some slaves began to shout. Evil birds clouded the sky. They said the full-breasted woman flew back in the form of an *Igwu*, and she didn't come alone. The full-breasted woman came back flying amidst an escort of other giant eagles. Slaves and slavers cried in terror. Christmas couldn't look up.

'Sprit birds!' one of the slaves shouted. Three slavers began cocking and firing their guns at the eagles. Most of the bullets were useless. Some eagles squealed in pain on being hit by a bullet, but none fell to the ground. The *Igwus* flew higher toward the sky. They fled in one direction at an incredible speed. Mr. Garble disappeared. Christmas and the other slaves lay flat on the ground. Still, no freedom.

'She only came to pour out her vengeance on Mr. Garble,' the slave in front of Christmas said.

Christmas hated the bird woman on hearing this, and hated himself even more. He noticed how shaken the slavers were, but they wouldn't give up. They continued to lead them all through the forest. They journeyed for half an hour in wonder and fear, and came across the body of Mr. Garble.

* * *

'Too far a journey,' Black John said interrupting Christmas's thoughts.

'We ain't halfway yet,' Antonia said, looking out at the green leaves by the roadside.

Christmas avoided saying anything. He avoided any conversation with her lest she embarrassed him like she sometimes did, in the presence of Esther and her boys. To them he stank. He thought of Oda'nyaa. Since she began coming to him, his spirit gained more liberty of leaving his body, to the past and future. He thanked his alekwuafia in prayers.

Two nights earlier, in his spirit form he delved into the future, many generations ahead, and discovered his reincarnation. The day of his reincarnation would surely come. In a time wagons no longer needed horses, and wheels were coated with brass, a woman rebirthed him. He watched himself being born again in life. The sparse joy in the room during this birth surprised him. The woman, a daughter of an Ogah generation, reluctantly inquired of the child's sex.

'*Onyilo*,' one midwife said almost in tears.

Why didn't she want him? His spirit eyes searched the mind of the mother but couldn't read anything.

* * *

On reaching a black river in the dark, flatboats were arranged by acquaintances of the agent in the wagon. Christmas, Esther, Antonia and Black John helped the waiting hands unpack their belongings into the flatboats with lamplights. A massive steamboat sat by the shore and Christmas stared at it in awe. It carried German immigrants. The engineer in charge of the steamboat kept the steam pressure high to prevent it from darting away from the shore.

The second phase of the journey began. The breeze steaming out of the river and the sound of low tide rocked Christmas to slumber, and in this slumber his spirit visited Opialu's future. In this future he appeared to be much older, perhaps sixty-five. An elderly Abah

Ogah, his own brother, summoned enough courage to stand in front of his compound with the support of Opialu youths.

'There's no Ogah greater than me in Oli'doma!' Abah roared. 'Where is he – he who they say flew with wings from the white man's land?'

The youth cheered. Old Christmas, seated in front of his hut, glared at them.

'Where is he who they say is so great that his spirit remained in Opialu all the years his body was in the white man's land?' Abah continued. 'I challenge you to a fight. There's always an Ogah who is the greatest.' Abah lifted his right hand up toward the sky to receive lightning, stunning Old Christmas. Abah threw the lightning toward Old Christmas. The sound of thunder followed. Lightning and thunder sent Old Christmas flying into the collapsing hut. He heard the cry of a woman.

Christmas felt the same pain in the present. The bruise of thunder. It stung all over his body in the flatboat.

* * *

The new Kentucky home looked different from the former house. The sitting room, coffee room and master's office were on the ground floor. The master's bedroom, guest rooms and children's rooms were upstairs. The rooms in the new big house were spacious unlike the house in Richmond. One could stand in front of this big house and count all the houses in Louisville. Constant sound of voyages on the black river seemed to be part of Louisville's splendour.

A three storey brick building stood behind the big house, and Mr. Preacher called it a 'slave dwelling.' This excited Christmas. This slave dwelling, a smaller mansion, turned out a blessing. The Preacher negroes wouldn't have to live in cabins any more. The rooms on the ground floor became storerooms for hay. Their rooms were on the middle floor. The women stayed on the left side of the building's sitting room, and the males stayed on the right side. The third floor became the meeting place.

It didn't take long for Christmas and Black John to discover a creek in the neighbourhood that emptied into the black river. They remained there and watched for a period before heading back home in the buggy Mr. Preacher left them. They met one of the pregnant horses, transported from Richmond, birthing a foal. Christmas helped pull out the small creature, to relieve the dam.

One summer day of 1790, Christmas returned to the residence from collecting mail to meet the suckling foal lying dead. Mr. Preacher, Black John and Moses stood around the body.

'What happened?' Christmas asked.

'Moses rode it,' Mr. Preacher said quietly, staring at the dead animal. He looked up and said, 'Christmas and Black John, tie Moses to the oak tree.'

Moses bolted into a run desperate to escape. Black John and Christmas followed. Christmas dived at Moses, pushing him to the floor. This didn't impress Mr. Preacher. The master, holding onto his whip, waited patiently.

They tied Moses's body to the trunk of the oak tree.

And Mr. Preacher said, 'You would do nothing like this again?'

Twelve-year-old Moses laughed. He felt no emotion or regret.

 Christmas feared for Moses.

'You can't do nothin' to me, white man.'

Esther arrived and began to plead, 'Please, Mr. Preacher. He ain't gon do that no more. Please.'

'No one gon kill nobody, Esther,' Black John said, trying to impress Mr. Preacher. No negro liked the sight of the whip. The first lash broke Moses's skin. Moses shook his body and held back his breath.

* * *

Christmas finished washing the horses and turned out the lamp. He heard some people talking outside. He didn't unbolt the door, but squatted quietly and peeped into the dark through a little round hole on the wooden door. He saw Mr. Preacher, standing very close to Antonia. The rays of the moon shone on their faces. To Christmas's surprise, his master caressed Antonia's behind, and she kept looking into his eyes, smiling and frowning. Christmas strained his eyes in disbelief. The stolen pleasure completely overwhelmed him. He couldn't hear what they said to each other. He watched them walk away. Christmas unbolted the door, came out of the stable, and headed toward his dwelling. His handsome master acted no different from a hog. And Antonia, a loud barking self-acclaimed saint, acted no different from a dog at its rutting.

'You done seen Antonia?' Esther asked him. He dusted his feet and entered the dwelling's sitting room.

'No,' he said, irritated. 'I don't meddle in nobody's business.'

'What you sound that way for?'

'Ain't Antonia's lover,' he replied quietly in a measured anger. He wanted to be mean to her. Perhaps due to the master's act or perhaps the fact that she didn't have feelings for him. He went into his room but his spirit stayed behind. He swanned into her, took hold of her consciousness and searched unknown places in her mind. Antonia seemed to have spoken to Esther several times of how good Massa Preacher made her feel. In their last argument, Antonia claimed she never met a black man better than a white man. In Esther's opinion, all men were snakes. Esther went into her room which she sometimes shared with her sons, and covered Moses with a quilt. He woke and turned to his side. She knew he didn't like the way she covered him up to the neck. She put out the lamp, sat on the straw bed before lying down. She heard the sound of footsteps out in the dark. Mr. Preacher must have followed Antonia back. Esther fought her thoughts. She slept, with Christmas still housing her thoughts. What was he doing? The ageless Oda'nyaa in his life meant joy, yet he kept wasting a whole lot of time in the mind of a woman too old for him. He felt like leaving but remained.

His spirit remained in Esther's mind until morning. She got out of her room, entered Antonia's, with Antonia still beneath her sheets, but alone.

'You speak bad on Christmas, and now you do worse,' Esther began. 'Don't act a fool, Antonia.'

'Who you see me with?'

Esther stared deeply at her.

Antonia sighed and struggled to sit up. 'I likes me some company from time to time. He says he loves me.'

'And you gon tell me you believe him?'

'Of course I does.'

'Come on here. You lost your mind?'

'Is you jealous?' Antonia shot back.

'Massa gon never leave Mrs. Preacher for you.'

'You gon wait and see.'

'You disgust me. Bein' with him don't make no sense.'

'You done talkin'?'

Esther sighed. She sat on the edge of Antonia's ruffled bed. 'Allow me talk my piece to you.' She paused. Christmas could feel her pain. She began, 'I was raised on a plantation where long before my mama was brought in there, negro males that worked themselves so hard lived. They was like giants. Them mens was use to matin' them horses and cattles. My mama arrived and she was treated no different by them negros... They make her sleep her behind on different pallets each night. The white fella is who I blame for this. She bore all her children on that farm, and them children was all sold. I was born last to inherit me her role. She was sold shortly, and them mens went back to their old ways on horses and cattles till I turned thirteen. Mens terrible, Antonia.'

'I thinks Massa different. Trust me.'

Silence.

* * *

Black John's boiled corn went missing and this resulted to a fight. Christmas watched Black John smack Moses on the head. Moses picked up little rocks and threw them at Black John. Their mother intervened.

'You boys stop or I go tell Massa Preacher, and he gon whip the two of you.'

The fighting ceased. Christmas got habituated to meddling in Esther's thoughts. He loved her thoughts. He loved to have her in sight when he couldn't meddle in her thoughts.

Later on, Christmas, Black John and Moses started to fill up some sacks with hay outside the kitchen house. Esther, Antonia and Mrs. Preacher were in the kitchen house. The negro women washed a large basin. Mrs. Preacher, pregnant again, fed the fire some wood. Mr. Preacher and Marcus were in the terrace of the big house. Baby Marcus, dressed in a squirrely fur cloak, could sit on his own now. Esther soon joined the mistress in feeding the fire with more wood.

'I have noticed Antonia isn't as foul mouthed as she can be,' Mrs. Preacher said looking at Esther.

Antonia placed a basin of water over the fire, but the fire kept dying. 'I gets tired of it,' Antonia said. 'Christmas, please come help me keep the fire goin'.'

Christmas gathered some of the driest of wood from the pile in there. He again prayed to his alekwuafia that she wouldn't embarrass him there.

'Maybe you done got your own spirit man to keep you quiet,' Esther added staring at Antonia.

Mrs. Preacher looked shocked.

Antonia developed an unsettled expression. 'She just jealous,' she murmured.

Silence.

The water in the pot slowly began to boil.

Esther finally broke the silence. 'Why should I be jealous of you, Antonia?'

'Something is going on, I can tell,' Mrs. Preacher said.

'I can't hide this no more,' Esther said and sighed. 'I can never be jealous of nobody. I can never be jealous of you bein' with Massa in the dark.'

Antonia used tea towels to take the pot off the fire. She wiped her hands over her dress and stared at Esther.

'Mrs. Preacher, you ought to ask Antonia what Massa done did with her – in her room.'

Mrs. Preacher said nothing at first. But Christmas could see the knuckles of her hand whitening. They clutched her knees. She sighed, got up and walked toward the steaming basin. Without warning she lifted it, turned and flung it hard at Antonia's face.

Antonia reeled back and lurched into an agonizing dance. She jumped on a single leg and fell screaming. The steaming pot truly seared the side of Antonia's face and the sight reminded Christmas of a slave whose hands were held down a hard iron grill. It horrified him to see. The searing left coal-black scum over bare red flesh. Esther jumped repeatedly like she could feel Antonia's pain.

* * *

He hardly found sleep since the incident. His spirit journeyed between the minds of Antonia, still unconscious, and Esther. The latter wept most of the time. Christmas never expected Mrs. Preacher to strike her in that manner. The white woman's mind became so fouled with jealous rage that he couldn't enter it. Mr. Preacher kept to himself. On this day Esther and Mrs. Preacher, sat by Antonia's bedside, and Christmas sank into Antonia's mind.

Doctor Fruitvale, fetched by Black John, treated Antonia's wounds. 'She needs some days, perhaps weeks, to recuperate. Her face will be scarred but the wound will close up in two or three months if her bandages are maintained,' he said.

Christmas searched Esther's mind. She worried for Antonia's life. She worried about Mrs. Preacher.

'Wretched me,' Esther cried.

Antonia moved slightly.

'I lost my temper, and that was it,' Mrs. Preacher said.

'If only I knowed, Mrs. Preacher,' Esther said. 'I would say nothin'.'

Antonia, in her oblivion, began to cough.

A week later, Christmas in possession of Antonia's mind, saw her struggle to drink some soup and eat a little piece of bread. The injury around the side of her face and neck still bit deep. She rotated her head slowly in the same rhythm she bent her head to sip tea.

Antonia's sense of smell became stronger. She still couldn't open her eyes. Christmas could tell she knew the moment Esther left the room with Marcus for the big house, leaving Mrs. Preacher alone with her. She tried to reject the milk Mrs. Preacher kept forcing into her mouth.

The white woman lost possession of her mind again, and Christmas caught sight of a whip hidden underneath her cloak. Mrs. Preacher flung the bowl of milk against the wall and lashed Antonia's body using all her strength. Christmas felt each whip sting his spirit severely. Mr. Preacher rushed in from the hallway. Esther emerged with Marcus still in her arms. Christmas trickled out of Antonia's mind, reached for Esther's. Esther trembled at the sight of the whip in Mrs. Preacher's hand. She felt like casting herself into the river. It felt like death, for Antonia to be beaten in her bedridden condition. She watched Mr. Preacher struggle with his pregnant wife, trying to wrest the whip off her. She fought her husband like a cat and managed to strike him twice before he overpowered her.

'Adulterous skunk!' she screamed at him.

He forced her into his embrace.

'I hate you! I hate you!' Mrs. Preacher went on.

* * *

The night grew cold. Christmas opened the door, and Mr. Preacher entered the room. The master asked him to narrate all the recent occurrences. Christmas thought of Antonia's scarred face. He gave his account. The night wind got stronger. Mr. Preacher swallowed hard and thanked Christmas before walking briskly toward Esther's door.

Christmas's spirit tailed Mr. Preacher. Esther opened her door.

'I will not come in,' he said calmly and led her out of the dwelling. Christmas's spirit soon transformed into the fine dust the breeze deposited on their faces. Mr. Preacher tried to shield his face. 'Did you ever see me enter her place?' He gestured at Antonia's window speaking loudly due to the wind.

She shook her head indicating no.

'Did you ever see me in carnal relations with her?'

'No.'

'Did she tell you I had relations with her?'

'I done seen you with her in the dark...'

He looked down before staring at her directly, and with an unreadable expression turned around to leave.

Christmas's spirit returned in him. It didn't take long for him to sleep. In the morning, Christmas woke up to his master's summons. All slaves apart from Antonia came to the sitting room. Mrs. Preacher walked down the mahogany stairs before Mr. Preacher spoke.

'We all have been aware of the happenings, all because I refused to be like other slaveholders. I treated you slaves well – because it was the way my father taught me. And I have been paid back with evil. Esther cooked up a lie that is about to break my family.'

Esther's expression remained the same despite the tears beginning to flow down her cheeks. Christmas couldn't believe Mr. Preacher could look them all in the eye and lie.

'I forgive you, Esther. I will not sell you. But you belong here no more. Your servitude will end on the day Antonia recovers.'

'Please Massa,' Black John pleaded.

'But Mama gon be free,' Moses said. 'No white man gon own her no more.'

'Black John, Moses is right. Your mama will be free from my service,' Mr. Preacher replied.

Mrs. Preacher could only shake her head.

The tension in the residence soon died. Antonia managed to get off her bed in the first month of winter and she walked slowly between the dwelling and the big house several times, her face shadowed in the cowl of a woolen shawl.

PART TWO

ANTONIA

THE COUNTY OF KENTUCKY became the fifteenth state of the country in George Washington's tenure. 1795 looked promising. For Christmas, nothing could changed. Perhaps his desire for women in the physical world could cease. Even for his master's wife, now a mother of two more children – Simons and Harriet. Even for Antonia. Christmas, envious of his master's exploits, always longed for the nights his ancestor mounted him into the dream world of the master. Mr. Preacher's nightmares were hardly spoken about in the residence but every resident got used to his constant howling in the middle of the night. The monster continued to visit Antonia's room and his long-suffering wife could only wish for Antonia's sale.

Night time came and Christmas, frustrated over his loneliness, metamorphosed into the rain and wandered in the past, amongst descendants of Abute Eje, the leopard man. Christmas saw his forefather, Orinya Ogah. This same Orinya shed tears for Idoma land in a time his people became refugees. Rain fell and soaked deep into the ground. Christmas felt the wet and muddy feet of people. He saw everyone under the rain. The pouring waters washed away the bitter taste of Idoma blood the war left. The crops died and their leaves were partly buried in mud. Children were still dying. Orinya's greatness shone – his decision to lead his people out of the country.

Christmas appreciated the privilege to witness the most vital history of his lineage scribbled in the heart of the land. Long before the Hausa people emerged with their swords and horses, the Country of Kwararafa idolised an *Achadu*, and Orinya attained a chieftaincy position during the regime. Before the *Achadu* became *Achadu*, the chiefs guided him into the world of the dead by suffocating him. They prepared his corpse, dressing him in royal *alichebe*. They conducted a great burial ceremony and resurrected him, letting his spirit descend back into him. The *Achadu* became a spirit among mortals, filled with the deep wisdom and intelligence of Abutu Eje and other ancestors. This great prime minister fell to defeat. The Hausas came, stole women and children, killed men and reigned over the land. Ayi'doma became prisoners in their own country.

Orinya almost yielded to weakness. He came out of hiding and consoled his people. The country kept mourning. Oda'nyaa emerged from the black river, and pronounced Orinya the *Achadu*.

'You will all leave the country,' she advised.

Twelve mermaids stood behind her. And they all spoke in rhythm, 'We will lead Ayi'doma out of Kwararafa.'

Orinya prostrated himself in front of Oda'nyaa and said, 'We are full of thanks.'

In three market days, all surviving Ayi'doma began to converge in Orinya's compound. Oda'nyaa and her maids arrived with a plan. They divided the multitudes of Idoma men and women into several groups, and a mermaid got assigned to lead each group.

'The Hausas have heard of the plot of Ayi'doma to leave the land,' Oda'nyaa spoke to the gathering. 'They do not want you to leave. They killed your prime minister. What else do they want? They have taken wives and children, leaving only a few. I will turn you all into special creatures for easy escape. The wrath of the Hausas is venomous.'

Her words were powerful. She gave them hope. The rain became intense. She and her maids maintained their legs, despite the rain – all in Oda'nyaa's power. She lifted her staff and Orinya's group transmuted into crocodiles. They began dashing for the black river, a route to their new settlement in Oli'doma. Another group of Ayi'doma all evolved to civet cats, and they ran so fast and became the first to reach the new land. A group metamorphosed into hawks, and started on a smooth sail. There were other groups in which men, women and children became black monkeys, red monkeys and even dogs.

The Hausas were alerted by their greatest witch doctor and they came to attack Ayi'doma in the heavy rain. At first, the various groups of animals and birds the Idoma people transmuted to ran faster than the Hausa people's horses, stray arrows and spears. Some black and red monkeys could not escape the arrows and died. The Hausas tried to hunt the crocodiles on the banks of black rivers. In the end, bodies of the Hausas littered the water. The crocodiles fed on them, gnashing their bones and chewing their flesh. These crocodiles, with full bellies, reached the new land. They called it Opialu, a settlement in the new country. And the rain continued to fall for many, many months. Oda'nyaa and all her maids remained with the Idoma people in their earthly feminine bodies, for a long time.

* * *

It continued to rain whenever his spirit travelled back in time. In Kentucky, it snowed and it kept Christmas busy. Since Black John reported sick, Christmas carried the entire burden. His days were full of work and his nights full of spiritual travels. Now seated on a bench in front of the dwelling, his shoes surrounded by flakes of snow, Christmas admired Louisville's thickly wooded high bank which faced the broad water. He recently accompanied Mr. Preacher to the bank. From the top of that bluff, the river lived peacefully with the Ohio falls glaring back at him and his master. He recalled the moment Esther left the residence. Long before dawn. It took time before dawn came. Moses left a bruise on Simons's chin. Simons cried running into the big house to show his father the wound Moses inflicted on him using a rock. Mr. Preacher walked out of the big house. No sign of anger. But what happened surprised everyone, even Mrs. Preacher. Her amiable but unreliable husband smacked Moses across the jaw, and blood sprinkled out of his mouth. He fell. Mr. Preacher didn't stop. He kept kicking Moses on the sides of his belly. Moses rolled on the ground. The residence became very quiet in the days that followed and even the usual noises of the children playing reduced. Mrs. Preacher until this day refused tea or food from Antonia. The blotches around Antonia's neck and on the side of her face remained visible. Antonia could poison the mistress with her sullen stares.

Christmas saw a wagon pull up in front of the house. Mr. Thompson, one of Louisville's Quaker overseers, climbed down from the wagon, and Christmas led him into the house.

'Glad thou could make it,' Mr. Preacher said, and shook the man's hands in the sitting room.

'I'm honoured. Guess thou find Louisville interesting,' Mr. Thompson said on sitting.

'It is a beautiful village. Quite a small population full of kind folks,' Mr. Preacher said.

Christmas remained by the door.

'Been five years now since thou indicated interest in freeing thy slaves and rejoining the society. This was discussed in our last quarterly meeting and I was assigned to follow up on thee,' Mr. Thompson began.

'It's a hard decision to make considering the huge work that needs to be done here.'

'Thou stated it will be done.'

'I have freed one slave already, and I still plan to do the same for the others.'

'There's something else.'

Mr. Preacher looked at Christmas and waved at him to leave.

Christmas went out and shut the door but remained in the corridor so he could hear them.

'Some concerns about thy character was raised. Adultery, they say and the committee would like thy response in writing...'

Silence.

'Some believe thou keeping a slave woman because of thy lustful habit,' the visitor added.

'Thou must leave,' Mr. Preacher said abruptly and got up from his chair.

'Thou have made mistakes, and what the Society of Friends can do is bring thee closer to God,' said Thompson on standing.

Christmas led the man back to his wagon and returned to clear the empty teacups. He noticed Mr. Preacher deep in thought. 'Massa, you is a good man.'

Mr. Preacher looked up.

Deep down in his mind, however, Christmas wished him dead. 'I knows what's goin' on between you and Antonia,' Christmas said.

Mr. Preacher laughed, got up in sudden fury and in a raised voice said, 'You listened to my conversation with Mr. Thompson?'

'Massa, I saw you come out of her room on Sunday mornin'...'

'I'm on your side, Mr. Preacher.' Christmas wanted to give him a different impression to that of his thoughts. 'You must have known I be on your side no matter what.'

Mr. Preacher sighed. 'I will be alone now, Christmas.'

In the following week in the coffee room, Mr. Preacher confided in Christmas.

'Christmas,' Mr. Preacher said. 'I have attended the most terrible Quaker meeting of my life.'

The master sat with his legs crossed. Christmas rested his back on the wall.

'A good number of them protested against my presence today, but... Mr. Thompson pleaded on my behalf. I was indeed grateful for that.'

'Massa, they ask you about Antonia?'

'They asked me to stay away from Louisville for a couple of months. Live where I can heal and be delivered from my... weakness.'

'Where at, Mr. Preacher?'

'To live with one Mr. Desmond in Frankfort.'

'Two months too long, Massa,' Christmas said. He imagined life in the residence without Mr. Preacher. It sure gon be a good time.

'They want me to undertake spiritual counsel with Mr. Desmond,' Mr. Preacher said and laughed sadly. 'We never learn enough... I have made mistakes,' Mr. Preacher managed to say.

'Thank goodness thou know that... From a damn adulterer to a liar,' Mrs. Preacher said.

Neither Christmas nor Mr. Preacher knew she stood in the doorway.

Christmas remained quiet and watched Mr. Preacher and his wife argue further.

'You can never change,' she said.

'What have you heard?' Mr. Preacher asked her.

'You are not even ashamed.'

'Speak out and I will explain.'

That night Orinya came to Christmas, an old bald man. In a feeble voice, he said, 'We have something to do.'

Christmas felt his spirit evolving. First his head transmuted to a horse head, and the rest of his body slowly followed. He felt enormously strong. It didn't take long for old man Orinya to mount him. His ancestor, once again, rode him into the realm of Mr. Preacher's dream.

The rider and the horse got busy knocking down furniture, ornaments and photograph frames in the main lounge of Mr. Preacher's big house. Mr. Preacher scrambled to the floor. Orinya, using the horse, chased the master into the darkness. Mr. Preacher got lost in the woods. He found a heap of snow and sat on it, panting hard. He couldn't continue running. Orinya soon caught up with the frightened white man. The forebear came down and patted Christmas.

'Let's kill him,' the ancestor voiced.

Mr. Preacher flared out of his sleep, breathing hard. His wife remained asleep.

Christmas, back in his body in the dwelling, breathed hard too. His joints were sore from the night ride. In the morning, Mr. Preacher called for him and the other slaves. Christmas got to the sitting room. Black John, Moses and Antonia were already there. Mr. Preacher appeared elated, and this confused Christmas.

Mr. Preacher announced his intended visit to Frankfort. 'My brother will come in from Richmond to manage the affairs of my household.'

'What is the use of keeping slaves around if you cannot trust them?' asked his wife, walking down the mahogany stairs with one-year-old Harriet in her arms. 'You keep saying you will free these slaves... A day that will never be.'

Mr. Preacher ignored her and continued speaking. He assigned Christmas fully to the farm.

'Moses may give you a hand, Antonia, in cleaning. And Black John, you will continue to tend to the horses.'

* * *

Master Gill arrived like a dark cloud settling over the Preacher residence. Christmas trembled at the name. He never worked this hard since he set foot in the Preacher residence. Master Gill wanted the hog house clean and tidy, like the big house. He wanted the hogs neat like Marcus and Simons. Christmas spent all day at the farm house but still couldn't meet Master Gill's requirements. Master Gill deprived him of dinner for days because of this. No one spoke freely in the residence anymore. Even Mrs. Preacher didn't trust the man. Black John believed Master Gill possessed many ears, and they were stuck on every wall in the big house and even in the dwelling so no one could speak evil of him. Christmas tried willing Orinya to help in attacking this new overseer but received no answer.

Christmas longed for freedom. He remembered the time Mr. Garble led him and the other slaves through the black forest, from Oli'doma to Ole'gbo. He remembered how a white Christian priest led the people of Oli'gra against Mr. Garble and his fellow slavers in order to set them, the slaves, free. The priest fought for the slaves. Bullets were exchanged. Christmas remembered himself and the other slaves lying flat on the ground. He remembered the full-breasted woman holding onto his arm in fright. Every man in the company of the priest died. Mr. Garble personally hung the priest from a tree, leaving him to perish. Christmas wished Master Gill could die like Mr. Garble. Master Gill, probably twenty-one years old, turned out to be much worse than Massa. The devil himself.

They received a letter from Mr. Preacher. And Mrs. Preacher, indifferent to the content, handed Master Gill the letter which he read out proudly in front of Christmas, Black John, Moses and

Antonia. Mr. Preacher indicated he wouldn't be coming back for another month. Christmas felt bitter. He didn't expect to experience another ugly spring month of 1795 with Master Gill around. Days passed, and the whitened vegetation retained its dark green colour. Louisville smelled fresher. Antonia became bigger. Her stomach started to protrude. Christmas couldn't speak about this to Black John or Moses for Master Gill's many ears were all over the place.

* * *

Mrs. Preacher came out of the boys' room and headed for the stairs to confront Antonia. The slave woman, busy polishing the mahogany handrails, didn't expect the looming attack. Christmas, shining the shoes Master Gill wore, anticipated it. The filth and venom in this man drew all his attention, and he nearly didn't see Mrs. Preacher grab Antonia by the neck. Mrs. Preacher shook her violently on the stairs before pushing her down. Christmas got to his feet. Antonia's weight thundered down. A section of the carpet over the stairs ripped apart revealing a crack. Antonia moaned.

Master Gill's fingers reached for his throat and began to squeeze. Christmas struggled with breathing. Master Gill cursed, 'You supposed to be polishing my shoes, you scumbag nigger?'

Master Gill's fingers were firm and rough against his throat. Christmas felt a tooth bite into his tongue and the taste of blood slowly overwhelmed his mouth.

* * *

Night came and his ancestor appeared. Orinya wanted Mr. Preacher and not Master Gill. Christmas transformed into a horse. The ancestor mounted him and rode into the dream realm of Mr. Preacher. They found Mr. Preacher in a humble state, lost in the woods. Christmas, staring through horse eyes, saw the recent happenings – how the white man spent three hours earlier in the day in front of Quakers admitting his sin of adultery and subjugation. Mr. Preacher longed to reach the final week of his misery in Frankfort.

'Dirty fornicator,' Orinya began in the realm of the white man's nightmare. 'You think they love you? You think they don't laugh at you? Let me tell you something, whoreson, Mr. Desmond just pretends to be comfortable with you in his house.'

Christmas the horse, grunted.

Orinya continued. 'Mr. Desmond thinks you will rape his wife.' Orinya started walking around the white man. Dried leaves crumbled underneath his feet. 'Look at how beautiful Mrs. Desmond looks. You thought about being with her like the many times you continue being with that slave you own.'

Mr. Preacher desired this fine woman. She uttered her impression of him on the very first day he set foot in their household. She claimed the devil hardened his heart, hence making him reluctant in freeing his slaves. She respected his requests to be excused from some meals. She cleaned and cleaned. She didn't own any slave yet the curtains and tiles were of exceptional polish. She maintained the house in the absence of slaves and this, Mr. Preacher found impressive.

Again, Christmas felt sore all over his body at dawn.

* * *

Christmas fed the pigs and tried to wash every dirt away from their dwelling. Master Gill wanted the pigpens spotless. This impossible task weakened his body. Slouched on the floor of his room, his angry spirit returned to the Desmond household in coffee-smelling Frankfort and dwelt in his master's mind.

Mr. Desmond broke the news to Mr. Preacher, 'Thou must address the committee in the next weekly meeting on thy intent to abolish slavery in thy household.'

Anyone could experience God directly and inwardly, and he, Mr. Preacher, felt the need to experience God to meet the requirement.

'What do I say to the committee?' he said to Mr. Desmond.

'Thou speak as thy spirit leads... What thou have learned. Decisions thou would make in regards to the gradual freeing of thy slaves...'

Mr. Preacher sighed. He lay in bed to sleep but couldn't. He began to speak, rehearsing what he might say to the Quaker committee overseeing his case. 'My coming here is to declare my wrongdoings. I am no more a slaveholder nor a fornicator. The cry of slavery has been heard in my household. I go back to Louisville to set my slaves free. A free people. I have an African slave named Christmas. He has been with me since he was sixteen. He is twenty-one now, and he will be the one I will miss most. Very hardworking. I will see to it that he or any of the slaves I free do not become marooned. I handed freedom to a slave woman I used to own after my daughter was born. She is the mother of two other negro boys I will free. She became the first slave I ever freed after she raised a brow over my misconduct in marriage. I freed her instead of selling her because of the good advice of friends like ye. I have this slave called Antonia, whose presence in my household led me into the detestable action unacceptable to our Lord. I do not blame her. I blame myself, and I have asked God for mercy. I thank ye, oh friends!'

* * *

Christmas kept trimming the plants by the side of the fence. Master Gill, seated in front of the big house, watched closely. Christmas noticed a few words coming out of his lips to Mrs. Preacher. She looked up and continued knitting. Black John and Moses were transporting water from the well to the garden beside the big house. Marcus, now five, ran around playfully. His three-year-old brother tried to follow. Christmas felt tired and needed a quick break but couldn't stop lest Master Gill vomit venom on him. Somehow relief sprouted out from the sky. Christmas sensed Mr. Preacher approaching from a distance. In a vision, he saw his master clearly avoiding several potholes on driving toward the residence. Mr. Preacher, guiding his horse, noticed the construction of a new building. He stopped and said some words to the builders. One of them laughed and pointed at various spots in the site in response. He drove past the Baptist and Methodist churches.

On sighting Mr. Preacher, Mrs. Preacher stood up, turned heel and entered the house. She did not want to see him, Christmas observed. Young masters Marcus and Simons and even little Harriet raised their voices in elation on seeing their father. Mr. Preacher smiled at them and gathered up Harriet in his arms. He glanced at Black John and Moses. They started to unload the wagon. Mr. Preacher rubbed his hand through Christmas's hair and shook hands with Master Gill.

'I have kept your affairs running well,' Master Gill said.

'Thank you,' Mr. Preacher said.

Christmas opened the door to the big house for Mr. Preacher. He followed his master through the hallway. They met Mrs. Preacher in the sitting room, seated with her back toward them. She didn't turn around. Mr. Preacher walked toward her. The bones on the back of her shoulders recently became visible.

'Have you seen Antonia?' Mrs. Preacher asked.

'I am a new person now, Fiona.'

Christmas thought of excusing them.

'Did you see her?' Mrs. Preacher repeated.

Mr. Preacher glanced at Christmas before he answered her. 'Yes. I saw her doing some chores in the hallway.'

'You lie,' Mrs. Preacher said.

Christmas wondered if he really saw her. If Mr. Preacher saw her, he didn't look closely enough to notice the protrusion.

'I come home a changed man.' Mr. Preacher almost raised his voice.

'A changed man.' She sighed. 'Those that keep using words "thee" and "thou" are the worst of humans on earth. You are much worse than evil, Mr. William Preacher.'

'To undo all my evil is not possible. I do not deserve you, my love, but I have asked God for mercy, which He has given me. I do ask for your forgiveness too.'

'A changed man, you say.'

'Yes, a changed man.'

'God may forgive you, but not I,' Mrs. Preacher said. 'You come home a changed man to meet an unchangeable circumstance that will forever change our lives. I advise you to have a closer look at Antonia. If I claim to forgive you, I lie.'

'Christmas,' Mr. Preacher called. 'What happened to Antonia? Did I not see her when I arrived?'

'You should look at her close, Massa,' Christmas said. He enjoyed the spectacle and couldn't wait to see Mr. Preacher's reaction.

Mr. Preacher made his way out to the hallway and Christmas followed. Antonia emerged from the dining room. Mr. Preacher's eyes widened.

'She pregnant,' Christmas whispered.

Antonia looked up at them. She turned around and left without saying anything.

Mr. Preacher sighed, faced Christmas and asked, 'Anything else I should know?'

'Massa, Massa Gill been bad to us.'

Mr. Preacher didn't seem to care. 'Did he strike you?'

Christmas nodded. 'He squeezed my neck so bad one time, I thought I gon die.'

Mr. Preacher walked briskly outside. Christmas followed. Master Gill, smoking a corn pipe, looked up.

'Thank you, brother. I'm grateful for your time here. Our deal remains unchanged,' Mr. Preacher said.

'The negro behind you was slothful, William.' Master Gill puffed out some smoke. 'It was hard managing him, and I think it is in good judgements to demand far more than we agreed. Five hundred dollars more, brother William. Remember I stayed longer than we agreed.'

'You sick and greedy man.' Mr. Preacher sounded mad.

'No matter the skills you have, you will not see half of that which I offer over in Richmond. Why should I pay you more? For hitting or trying to kill my slaves?'

'I see you are no different from your slaves. Lazy.'

Mr. Preacher walked up to his brother. 'Say that again.'

'Lazy. Slothful. You no different from them.'

Mr. Preacher knocked Master Gill to the ground in front of the house. Christmas didn't see Mr. Preacher hit Master Gill. It happened too fast. Before the younger man struggled to find his feet, Mr. Preacher pounced on him, and released more blows onto his face.

'Never call me slothful,' Mr. Preacher yelled.

* * *

They were having a conversation. Christmas and his forebear. They spoke about Abutu Eje. They spoke of the silence of the leopard man. A silence too long for Ayi'doma to keep remembering him. During this conversation, a full light beamed in. Oda'nyaa appeared and gave Christmas her hand.

Orinya shielded his eyes with his wrinkly fingers. 'What do you want, water being?'

'He's mine and not yours,' she replied.

'I will make sure you see death, if you ever say that again,' the ancestor said to the mermaid.

'Orinya, my ancestor,' Christmas said. 'She means no harm.'

'His words are empty,' Oda'nyaa said. 'He is after your life, Ochigbo. He doesn't want you in Kentucky, a place that will treat you well.'

A bang came on Christmas's door. Black John ambled in panting. 'Christmas,' he called.

Christmas looked at Oda'nyaa and Orinya.

'He can neither hear nor see us,' Oda'nyaa said.

'What you want?' Christmas answered.

'We got to kill a hog. Antonia says we runnin' out on meat.'

'We can do it early tomorrow.'

Black John left, and Orinya vanished.

'Orinya want you to suffer which is the reason he wants Mr. Preacher dead,' Oda'nyaa said. 'Stay far away from all his schemes lest you get in trouble and be accused of killing your own master.' She led him out of the residence and they walked a long distance, going past the Beargrass Creek, on which several Indians canoed. They arrived at the bank of the black river and sat on the sand. A fisherman, a free negro, stopped by.

'Get rid of him,' Oda'nyaa warned.

'Hey fella. You at the Preacher's residence?'

'Why you want to know?'

'Don't be rude negro, just want to know if the fat woman still there.'

Christmas replied, 'I don't know where she at.'

'Tell her Handsome Paul inquirin' about her,' he said walking away. 'Last time I sees her, she ain't lookin' no good. That massa of hers ain't no good man either. I hear he into some Quaker and witchcraft business.'

'Don't listen to him,' Oda'nyaa said. They watched the man walk away

'Why have you been staying away?' Christmas asked Oda'nyaa.

'That man Gill has a foul spirit with a smell so strong I couldn't set foot near you,' she replied.

'A mere man got powers to make you stay away?'

'Everyone has got *ofu*,' Oda'nyaa replied. 'Even you.'

'You say that I got powers...'

'You think I don't know you went into the future? You think I don't know you sneak into people's minds.'

'True!' A smile settled on his face.

'You have the power to become any animal but you must not be any animal just because of the excitement of it. The crocodile is your safest abode.'

'I'm naturally a crocodile man.'

'You must listen to me.'

'I am listening.'

'Other safe abodes are the dog and the owl.' She took his arm and caressed it gently. She pulled him toward herself and sang:

> *Into the black river ano nyo*
> *Into the black river ano jeje*
>
> *Through the black river we see the unknown*
> *Through the black river we ride unseen horses...*

Christmas saw the snow underneath them loosen. Louisville melted away. He saw the leaves and branches of the oak trees dry up to nothing. He saw the black river darken. History resurrected. It became four years before his birth. Christmas's spirit roamed about Opialu with Oda'nyaa. He could see his father and other men working on a building under the direction of a white man.

'Let us become the *ewo*,' Oda'nyaa said.

Christmas, excited, wondered what it felt like being in the skin of a dog. It didn't take long before they continued roaming Opialu's past in the bodies of two black dogs. Oda'nyaa roamed in the body of the Azawakh – a tall and slim breed. Christmas roamed in the body of the Africanis. He could feel the dust in the air. It filtered through his wet nose, and this made him cough. He felt different in the new body. It felt more exciting compared to the horse Orinya often morphed him to be. The past felt real in contrast to what his spirit experienced. He got back to his body wrapped in a quilt on the heap of snow on the bank of the black river.

* * *

Christmas wanted to see his mother in his second existence, a time wagons used wheels of great brass and moved without horses. He emerged in front of a bungalow too foreign for Louisville and Oli'doma. He shrunk in size into the body of an owl, developing bulgy little eyes and tiny wings. He enjoyed the lightness he felt even more. His eyes and neck were imbued with magic, and from the tree he settled on, he saw everything. In his new roundish eyes, he could read minds easily. He saw the mother of his reincarnation. He watched her perform some rituals over a steaming pot. She used a big spoon to fetch food from it. In the process of tasting the food, her eyes caught his. A tremor went down her spine. She truly hated owls. She began to curse the witches in Opialu. She began calling the names Joseph, Mary and Jesus. Christmas didn't fly away. He stayed there. Legs affixed firmly on a tree branch. His reincarnated form, only four years old, rushed to peer through the kitchen window. Christmas saw the smile. Olofu recognised him. Christmas saw him follow his mother. They emerged out of the house. The mother held a bowl of water and a broom. She came in his direction. His owl eyes watched closely. Christmas saw her dip the broom into the bowl and sprinkle water at him.

'Receive holy water,' the woman shouted, and she repeated the same ritual over and over.

Christmas saw the four-year-old dragging his mother by the edge of her wrapper, protesting against her actions. Christmas noticed the boy's gift in hand gestures. He passed on his message. The bird brought no harm. The woman, being stubborn, continued in her actions. She believed in her water. The confidence in Christmas meant nothing to her.

Each drop of water stretched in its might to reach up to him. One drop stretched so hard in the process and became a tiny glaze of fire. Christmas, in his owl body, trembled. He flew high into the night sky of the future. The owl, a great creature, reached the stars.

* * *

Summer came again. A busy time. A slave could mistakenly sleep in and face the wrath of it. Someone banged on the door. Christmas jumped up from his straw bed, put on his pantaloons and opened the door. Antonia cleared her throat.

'I need me some help in the big house. Mrs. Preacher got visitors,' she said.

'Who be visitin' at this time? Not yet dawn!' Christmas said.

'Massa fightin' his wife again and these Quaker women here to calm the mistress.' Antonia sighed and looked away trying to hold her tears.

'Antonia, I knows how you feel but don't do nothin' stupid.'

'If I got the chance I sure gon kill her with my hands.'

'Antonia!'

He could see the scar on her chin even in the dark. She turned out to be reasonably tolerable toward him over the past five years. She no longer said he stank. She no more strained her eyes to look into his room. Or even moan about him sleeping with some spirit.

She asked Christmas to remain in the big house's sitting room and attend to Mrs. Preacher or her visitors' needs. She left for the kitchen house to fetch some hot water for tea. Christmas stood with his hands behind him, right beside the tray of jugs resting on the low shelf. The visitors, all women, were dressed in plain dresses.

Mrs. Preacher hardly looked up from her seated posture. They all took turns to speak.

'Mrs. Preacher, I understand all thou have been through,' one of the women said.

'Ye know nothing,' Mrs. Preacher replied bluntly.

'We know of the infidelity that occurred. In Christ, Mrs. Preacher, there're no irreconcilable differences.'

'He may be back attending meetings, but I'm not him. I wish to remain as I am. I beg ye, please leave me in peace. I'm presently being delivered from this marriage by the same God ye serve.'

'Mrs. Preacher,' Mrs. Gregory began, 'Mrs. Donovan here has a husband who had six babies from different negro women. Mr. Donovan is now a transformed gentleman who God is using greatly. He fought for the freedom of eighty slaves and wants to do more, as I talk to thee.'

'Mrs. Donovan, I am sorry to say thou art a fool to think men change. My husband, whom I know better than thee, has for years and years spoken about freeing his slaves and changing. I bet thee he would rather sell than free them. Let thy husbands deal with him in the first place before ye come here to me. I sure know my husband still visits the room of his pregnant slave.'

Both women dusted their feet, waved off the tea Antonia brought, and followed Christmas outside to their wagon.

Christmas thought over his master's crumbling marriage. In his dream later in the night he turned into a wounded dog, and Mr. Preacher found him in the dark woods. The master carried Christmas's dog body over his shoulder, and walked a long distance. Christmas woke in the morning and went to the farm, he met Mr. Preacher gathering a heap of hay.

'Had a good night, Christmas?'

'No, Mr. Preacher.'

'Neither did I. I keep seeing one old negro ghost in my dreams.'

* * *

Massa scheduled meetings on the third floor of the dwelling every Sunday and Tuesday, and free blacks from his Louisville neighbourhood attended along with Christmas, Black John and Moses. 'Black Quaker' became the designation of every negro that attended the meeting. Benches were arranged in a way that people sat opposite each other. In the second meeting, one negro called Tallie raised an issue.

'Why they ask negroes to come to thy house, Mr. Preacher?' Tallie began. 'Quakers say all men equal in the eyes of God, and now they tell negroes to come here.'

'Tallie, there's a committee that has been set up to see to that. For now all negroes around this neighbourhood will keep converging here,' Mr. Preacher advised.

'Who made thee minister?' Asked a free negro.

Mr. Preacher didn't answer the question.

'If we ain't allowed in white meetins' no more, we ought to have our own minister,' the man continued.

'Mr. Preacher, we see thou still own them slaves?' Another added.

'A plan is in place. What I can say now is that their emancipation is imminent.'

The meeting went on, with Mr. Preacher narrating a story about Cain and Abel. He said Abel's sacrifice got accepted because of his disposition. 'He was a good man. Abel had the heart of that man called Jesus.'

The meetings continued to be held. Weeks passed. Members got more acquainted with each other. During one of the meetings, Mr. Preacher said his spirit led him to let one negro share a word with the rest of them. They waited in silence. Tallie stood up briskly, headed straight to Mr. Preacher and took Mr. Preacher's bible. He walked toward the fireplace in his tall frame and put the bible in the fire.

At the back seat, Moses got up to his feet crying, 'That ain't right.'

'Take a seat, Moses. I ain't the first Quaker to do this.'

Mr. Preacher sighed.

'Moses, why it ain't right?' Tallie asked.

Moses looked at the fireplace and glanced at Black John before speaking. The seventeen-year-old, quite bulky in appearance, kept a beard which gave him the look of a man older than his years. 'How this right?' he replied and sat.

'I am led by the spirit to teach us about the word today,' Tallie began. 'I will also answer back with a question. What is the word of God?'

'You just throwed it in the fire,' a negro man said and someone laughed.

Tallie ignored the answer and repeated the question.

'The bible,' Black John replied.

'You wrong,' Tallie said.

'I knows what you mean now. The bible is the writin' of white people,' Moses said.

'Thou wrong. The word of God is Jesus Christ hisself. I ain't the first Quaker man to do this for the essence of teachin' what is right. The word of God came upon the folks who wrote the bible many years ago as the spirit and life of Christ, and this same word of God, Jesus Christ, still come upon we, children of God this day. We is encouraged to hear more of God, and write more epistles.'

Christmas enjoyed the single act of the bible being thrown into the fireplace, although the meetings often brought him to boredom. He suffered from distraction and couldn't follow all the teachings.

* * *

He missed Opialu. In his dwelling, he meditated with eyes closed:

> *I see the* owu *coming*
> *I see the* ewo *coming*
>
> *Take me oh* owu *to Opialu*
> *Take me into the* ewo

His spirit walked out of his body and, like a handful of dust, he emerged in Opialu. He landed quietly and roamed through the village in a dog's body. He came across his present-day mother. He watched her fetch some water from one of Opialu's black rivers. He followed his father hunting and watched the man kill an eagle to take home. He came across his brother Abah seated on the bank of the black river with many dead chickens around him which he kept flinging into the river one after the other, meditating and calling out the name, Orinya.

'*Adam* – my father, Orinya. You mustn't remain dormant in my life. The farm isn't yielding good crops. Our family members are dying every day. Orinya, resurrect again and bring joy to our family,' Christmas heard his brother say.

Christmas barked to distract his brother. Abah glanced at him and perhaps saw only a dog. He continued tossing the slaughtered fowls into the water. Christmas left the bank, heading toward the market square. His front legs stepped on a cobra. He felt a sharp pain and fell. Startled, he wriggled over the sand. Dust climbed into the air. He didn't see the snake in his path on time. The venom insinuated its way through his limbs and sent him wheeling into blackness. Christmas, trapped in a dog's body, could only sense some young village girls with earthen pots of water over their heads travel past. The snake, satisfied with its action, discharged itself into the bush. Christmas wished he could cry out. He wished he could leap out of the animal body. He felt strange – drowning in heat and sweat. Christmas couldn't bear the smell around him.

An old man, walking by, shovelled the dog's body into the ditch. And this place became his dungeon. His spirit indeed went missing in the Preacher residence. Louisville soon opened its door to autumn.

* * *

He felt so much pain. Christmas's spirit suffered being stuck in the body of the dog. His body, sentenced to his straw bed in his room, possessed no hope of life. But his mind wandered around Louisville, now colourful with the deluge of little dry and green leaves in the air. His mind became the convulsing air within the big house in the Preacher residence. He witnessed another fight between Black John and Moses. Black John punched Moses in the face. Moses brought his brother down to the ground, crouched over him and started to punch. Christmas's mind kept communicating to his lifeless human body and his spirit tucked in between layers of the dog's brain.

His mind, drenched in sadness and hopelessness, wandered around the big house. Antonia placed Harriet in a copper tub upstairs. She poured a bowl of water over the fast-growing one-year old. The little girl screamed loudly. She stiffened her body in the wondrous copper tub in the master bedroom just in front of the colourfully designed master bed. The child's yells of excitement stopped. She began a wail without reason and tears poured out of her small eyes.

The child cried so loud, and Mrs. Preacher, on her sewing machine in the lobby upstairs, walked down to check on them. 'Gentle with my child,' Mrs. Preacher said on entering the room.

Mrs. Preacher soon left. Antonia rubbed some soap over Harriet's head. The child started to cry again. Antonia felt knifed by the cry of this child. She felt the child's voice squeezing its way into her head. Antonia felt herself bleed on the inside. All the pain Mrs. Preacher caused her started to surface in her thoughts. Christmas, drenched in the tears flooding Antonia's heart, knew Antonia could kill Mrs. Preacher at this moment. Antonia's breath began to cease. She stopped bathing the child. Using her trembling fingers, Antonia grabbed Harriet by the neck, and dunked her head into the water. Christmas's mind stiffened. Antonia squeezed every ounce of hatred for Mrs. Preacher into the innocent life and gradually, the little life of the child breezed away. The trotting sound of the sewing machine ceased. The dead dog in the ditch in Opialu shook. And Christmas's lifeless body in the dwelling started to sweat.

Silence.

'What have you done, Antonia?'

Antonia turned around. Mrs. Preacher stood in the doorway.

The white woman screamed and rushed toward her dead child. A sound of someone running in the house echoed. Mr. Preacher arrived. Mrs. Preacher carried the body, knelt and looked up at Antonia. 'See what you have done to Harriet.'

'Someone get the patrollers! Black John!' Mr. Preacher called out, and covered his face with his hands. He sank in guilt. The white man fell on his knees beside his wife and took hold of his lifeless daughter.

'Why?' Mrs. Preacher's raged. She looked at Antonia, leapt up and lurched herself forward clawing the black woman's face with one hand until she saw the ire in Antonia's eyes. She moved back.

Mr. Preacher stood up and guided his wife out of the room with the dead child still in his hands. 'The fault is mine,' he struggled to say. 'It is my goddamn fault for contemplating over the years on letting these slaves go,' he said kicking a bench out of the way. 'Why should God punish me like this?'

Moses, standing outside the door, looked too scared to enter the room. The door of the bedroom closed on its own, and Moses froze.

'No one should go in there. Let Antonia dwell in her deeds,' Mr. Preacher warned from the lobby.

Mrs. Preacher began to kick. She started by kicking the air before kicking at him. She pushed Mr. Preacher. Horses grunted outside. Black John led the patrollers in and they separated Mrs. Preacher away from Mr. Preacher. Mr. Preacher shook his head in remorse and led the patrollers to the room door. Antonia wailed. A wail too frightening for anyone to want to push the door open. The taller of the patrollers opened the door. The black woman, unclothed from her waist downward and lying on the floor, tried to get up but couldn't. They sighted the gory head of a baby between her legs. The stench of a young soul struggling into life poured out at them.

'She is birthing,' Mr. Preacher said. He walked disconcertedly toward Antonia and squatted. He took hold of the baby's body awkwardly and pulled. Moses, Black John and the patrollers watched.

'Someone get me a knife,' Mr. Preacher said in between heaves.

Black John rushed out to the kitchen house.

The baby began to cry. Mrs. Preacher clutched onto her dead baby and stared at Antonia from the doorway.

Black John returned with a knife, and Mr. Preacher took his time in cutting the connecting cord between the new born and his mother. He gave the knife back to Black John and carried the crying baby away toward his wife.

Antonia seemed to flare like a mad lion saying, 'Give me back my child!' She lifted herself up. Blood dribbled across her lap. She staggered toward them. The patrollers, though reluctant, acted fast in restraining her. She tried to bite one of them but received a slap across the face. She struggled between their holds until they took her away.

Christmas's mind swayed about. He truly felt dead. Everything in the world smelt of corpses. In a faint vision, he saw Mrs. Preacher holding a knife and dashing for Antonia's child in the arms of Black John. In a fainter vision, Christmas saw Moses and Mr. Preacher restraining the white woman.

* * *

Christmas's mind, disarrayed, became thick heavy clouds gathered in the sky above the Preacher residence. Mr. Preacher cried. He cried silently all through the burial of his baby girl. Mrs. Preacher on her part tossed herself onto the floor and rolled over the earth wailing. Her husband, now tired of seeing her restrained, wouldn't let Moses lift her up. She sat up. And with her fists, she hit the sides of her head. They buried Harriet's body in a space between the slave dwelling and the farm. Later the same day, Mr. Preacher inquired about his very own slave, Christmas.

Moses ran toward the slave dwelling. Mrs. Preacher now cried quietly in the company of Marcus and Simons. Mr. Preacher, in front of his daughter's grave, squatted and gently picked some petals from the violet flowers almost covered in snow.

'Massa, Christmas ain't wakin',' Moses said on his return.

Mr. Preacher looked up. He remained still and quiet for some time before heading toward the dwelling. He entered Christmas's room. Nothing spoke of life in it. He shook the body. 'Christmas,' he called. Mr. Preacher sent for Doctor Fruitvale on a second thought.

Christmas's mind swayed about and waited.

The doctor came before dusk on his horse. Carrying his medical box, with his hat in hand, he entered the dwelling.

'His temperature is very high,' Doctor Fruitvale said. 'Has he been working too hard?'

'He has an everyday routine, and doesn't complain,' Mr. Preacher said.

'How is your wife?' The doctor stared deeply at Mr. Preacher. 'I am sorry, William.'

'It is indeed a sad time,' Mr. Preacher said.

'It's vital to keep an eye on the young negro man, but you must also rest. If by tomorrow morning, nothing happens, we might have to take him to my practice,' the doctor said.

Christmas, still stuck in the dog's body, could feel the dog move. The weakness felt like death and nothing could be done. Flies began to settle around.

Three times he saw Massa dive into the black river trying to help him. The visions were blurry. Christmas got more confused. He now saw himself trapped in a river and not in a dog's form. He couldn't lift himself up to the water surface. He saw the old man, Orinya, still in his misery, struggling to stand to his feet on the bank of the black river. The dead chickens being thrown at him from the sky were just vanishing, being swallowed by groundwater. In another blurry vision, Christmas saw Mrs. Preacher with a knife searching for Antonia's child.

* * *

Christmas could see nothing. He could feel his spirit still drowning in the decomposing body of the dog. Morning came, and his mind settled in the air within the big house. Mrs. Preacher and her children were dressed up in their outing clothes. She wore a squirrely fur cloak and fur-lined shoes to match a riding hat with veils.

'I will be going to New York to live with my brother,' she announced to her husband.

Silence.

'I see you are going with Marcus and Simons,' Mr. Preacher said. He seemed to have been expecting this.

'I want to grieve comfortably, William. It's something I owe my daughter and must do.'

'Please take Antonia's boy with you.'

'I have been trying to kill that child and you know it.'

'Black John! Moses!' he called.

Black John, carrying the baby, came into the lounge before Moses did.

'Fetch me a knife, Moses.'

'What do you intend to do, William?' Mrs. Preacher asked.

'You are a good woman. Please raise the child slave or kill him at this very instant before you leave. You must agree to an option for me to allow you to go with Marcus and Simons.'

Mrs. Preacher remained quiet. Moses brought a knife but she refused to take it.

'You are a good woman, Fiona, and I am a terrible man. The children will be raised well with you.'

'What makes you think I wouldn't kill the infant?' she asked.

'Because you are now healing,' Mr. Preacher said. 'I know who I married.'

'I will not raise him a slave. New York is a different place.'

'You right. I should never think of this negro baby as my slave,' he replied.

'Well, my brother hired someone to fetch us. He should be here now. We are taking the noon ferry.'

'I am sorry Fiona for all I caused you. Even if we never be together, you must forgive me.'

'If the time ever comes…'

'I never for once anticipated a broken marriage for myself. I'm only thirty-years-old.'

Christmas's mind swayed out of the sitting room, roamed about restlessly before settling in a corner in the hallway.

* * *

He sank in a great black ocean. Bubbles slid out his mouth. He could not breathe. Massa emerged from his right, seized his body and swam upwards until they burst out to the ocean's surface. Christmas breathed in life and felt relieved. His spirit emerged out of the dog's body and his body regained consciousness in the doctor's room. He got his mind back there with Massa seated beside him, wiping sweat off his body.

'Christmas, can you hear me?' Mr. Preacher asked, pulling his body against his. 'Doctor, he is awake. I just saw him flip his eyes.'

Massa's words faded away and he, Christmas, fell deep into slumber.

Again, he saw Mr. Preacher helping him out of the water. Out of the water, Christmas fell to his knees and held onto his master's feet. He kissed the feet repeatedly. Tears ran down his cheeks.

'Thank you, Massa! Thank you, Massa,' Christmas cried.

They were wet. They headed for the cold mountains. Christmas felt weak. The mountains were still far ahead and he needed to eat.

Christmas watched the man. He walked differently. Remained quiet most of the time. Mr. Preacher? No, it couldn't be. The white man transformed to the old black man wearing a loin cloth. Orinya.

Christmas woke and found himself back in the dwelling and no more at the doctor's. He felt a great urge to see Oli'doma. Black John placed a meal by his bed side – a slice of bacon, two eggs and a jar of water. The changes he encountered hit him like a blizzard. They were still in the sad year of 1795. Harriet really died. Antonia remained in jail. The mistress, her children and Antonia's infant were gone. The Preacher residence turned out a different place.

'Christmas, what happened to you?' Moses asked.

'I got trapped in a dog.'

'How?'

'You ain't gon understand,' Christmas replied.

Moses smiled and nodded his head before saying, 'Sure you ain't trapped in the head of the white man, Preacher?'

This made Christmas wonder. In the head of Mr. Preacher? Could this be possible?

Days went by. Mr. Preacher gradually became a different person. He hardly checked on the farm. On the days he checked, he showed up unkempt and stank. Christmas didn't know Mr. Preacher to be like this.

The month ended on this day. Mr. Preacher went out in his wagon, and came back with three crates of liquor. Christmas and Moses helped in carrying them into the big house. The house stank like Mr. Preacher did. The same smell. Massa permitted no cleaning. Two cockroaches feasted on some crumbs of bread on the floor.

'Massa sick,' Christmas said to Moses on their way back to the dwelling.

'Yes. He sick in the head,' Moses replied. 'I wish he dead.'

Christmas sighed.

'You know what he did to Antonia's infant?'

Christmas remained quiet.

'He gave the poor child to his wife to kill,' Moses said. 'If the infant gon live, it be a miracle.'

Tallie and the other black Quaker men arrived in the evening.

'No meetin' today,' Christmas said to them. Earlier on, he saw Mr. Preacher lock himself up in the house.

'Why that is?' one of them asked.

'Massa ain't well.'

'We heard he drinkin'.'

'Why come if you hear that?' Moses asked.

'Why he been drinkin'?' another one of them asked.

Christmas sighed and said, 'Because Mrs. Preacher gone away with the children.'

The men left quietly, not looking surprised.

Christmas admired their freedom. He felt the need to own his own life and build a family.

* * *

In the difficult year of 1795 Antonia got sentenced by the judge, and for a moment the clouds were pure grey. They marched her around the courthouse so negro men and women could learn a lesson. The day came. The authorities paraded her. Louisville residents threw rocks at her. Black slaves stoned her too. Christmas, Black John, Moses and Mr. Preacher hung together, and followed at a distance. Each step she took seemed difficult. The clouds gathered. She took her most difficult step, and the clouds gave way for rain. A few onlookers left. Most remained determined to see her end. Moses couldn't hold on anymore, and ran in tears to Antonia.

A rock aimed at Antonia landed on his head. The yelling increased. A woman shouted, 'The fat negro woman deserve no son's love.' The sound of the rain made it impossible for anyone to hear what Antonia said to Moses. A patroller forced them apart. Moses wept. Christmas understood the bond Moses shared with Antonia. Since his mother became free and left, no one cared for him like Antonia did. This same woman brought him and Black John food from the kitchen house. The same woman washed their clothes and tightened the ropes underneath their straw beds without them even thinking on it. Some men led her to the platform, her final destination in life. Christmas held his tears. Mr. Preacher tried hard to do the same. Black John walked away.

A patroller placed a rope around her neck. They suspended her body, and with a sickening snap, death came knocking. She struggled against death. Her entire body trembled. Her neck twitched between her right and left sides repeatedly. The downpour subsided. It began to snow. The crowd became silent and Antonia died.

Everyone left, including Christmas, but his spirit remained on watch. The body swayed at times. Vultures hovered around. Moses came back deep into the night with Mr. Preacher's ladder and one of the knives often used to slay hogs. Christmas's spirit got restless and wheeled about like the vultures in the air. Moses wedged the ladder against the platform and into the snow and climbed up to reach Antonia's heart. He took his time and dug it out. Blood dribbled down the body and got sopped up by her dress. He held the whole heart. The knife slipped off and fell to the ground. The ladder shook. Moses fell but he didn't let the gory heart touch the ground. He groaned and looked around, suspicious of sombody's presence. Christmas's spirit followed Moses back to the Preacher's residence. He watched Moses dig the cold ground in front of the master bedroom window with a spade. Moses planted the heart. Lightning hit the ground. The roar of thunder failed to follow.

* * *

Christmas noticed the changes. Mr. Preacher acted indifferently toward the changes in his own life. He became a little forgetful and at times made incomplete sentences. On this day in December of 1795, Mr. Preacher called Christmas, Black John and Moses to his sitting room, and handed each of them pieces of paper.

'Christmas, you are a free man now. Moses and Black John, you all free.'

'I got nowhere to go…' Christmas stammered.

Black John pinched Christmas, trying to silence him.

'Massa, Christmas gon come with us,' Moses said. 'We gon look for our mama. I heard she works for this white folk in Lexington milkin' them cows.'

Christmas, in tears, embraced Mr. Preacher. Black John did the same.

'You all are always welcome back. I will offer twenty-five dollars each on a monthly basis if you find it hard to get work outside these gates and want to come back to live here and work for me. Go and see the world, boys.'

'Thank you, Massa,' Moses said.

At night, Christmas's heart pounded so hard he couldn't sleep. He got out of the dwelling and thought of doing something in gratitude for liberty. Perhaps just kill the white man. No. He headed straight to the big house, lit the candles and began to sweep. Mr. Preacher came downstairs.

'You ain't stoppin' me, Mr. Preacher, from cleanin' your house. It is one last service to you.'

'It's night time.' Mr. Preacher sighed. 'I have been indeed grubby. I will wash myself,' he said and headed back upstairs.

Christmas, Black John and Moses headed out of the Preacher residence a week later with their sacs, embarking on a long walk. On passing by the Beargrass Creek, they saw white boys skating around. At the end of the road they turned left and walked along the waterfront. They travelled a whole day walking and resting in places they were welcomed.

A black slave family welcomed them for a meal by noon the next day. They were mostly field hands on day's work. On their first evening in Lexington they were chased by white men and barking dogs for trespassing. At midnight, they found the farm Esther lived and milked cows. Christmas could hardly move his legs anymore. His joints were sore. Esther opened her cabin door. She squeezed her face in surprise. Christmas still found her attractive. The now forty-year old looked around her neighbourhood before she led them in. She lit a candle and whispered, 'You negroes want me losin' my work?'

'Mama, we free now,' Black John said.

'Massa Preacher free y'all?'

'He did,' Moses confirmed.

'And Antonia?' Esther asked.

The brothers looked at each other.

'She dead. Done murdered and the...' Christmas began.

'Who she kill?'

'Massa's daughter,' Moses replied.

'God have mercy on them souls. I warned Antonia. I done told her bein' with Massa Preacher ain't gon end no good.'

'Massa Preacher never likes her,' Moses said and sighed. 'He just use her for hisself.'

"Mr. Preacher like nobody. You right, Moses. He just care for hisself. He free us because he was about to lose his mind,' Christmas added.

'Mr. Preacher truly a snake.' Esther sighed. 'What done happened to Mrs. Preacher?' she asked.

'She left too, for New York,' Black John said.

'And she took Antonia's child with her,' Christmas added.

'What child?' she asked.

'She born a child for massa,' Black John replied.

That child ain't gon survive. She try to kill the infant many times before she left. In New York, no one gon stop her,' Moses said.

'Massa let her take the infant?' Esther asked, shocked. She sighed and went on, 'Why y'all come here?'

'We want us some place to stay, Mama,' Moses said.

'Don't think y'all gon stay here. My boss don't like no niggers. I done seen him chase a whole lot of them.'

'But you here,' Moses said.

'Because I'm a woman.'

'Where we gon go, Mama?' Black John asked.

'Y'all gon wander around. Maybe a white man gon give y'all some job.' She offered them wheat and milk and, before morning, they were gone.

* * *

For days they went around Lexington begging every white man they came across for a job. They slept anywhere – in the cold, in front of butcher shops, the market place, by the walls of the courthouse, in stables. They went without food on some days. On one particular day, Moses convinced them to follow him into a cotton farm to find work. They got in, and some white men, ten or more, confronted them.

'What you negroes think you doing trespassing here?' one of them asked.

The white men didn't wait for answers. They pounced on Christmas, Black John and Moses, punching and kicking them hard. They fell to the ground. The white men continued kicking them. Christmas, Black John and Moses groaned in pain. One of the Lexington men lifted Christmas high and let him drop on the hard earth. Christmas bled from his mouth.

PART THREE

NEDI

THE ANCESTOR, ONCE A LEOPARD MAN, watched Christmas become dust from his world above the earth. Christmas climbed into the air from the Opialu soil. The crier went all over the village announcing the coming of masquerades and mermaids. The crier said men alone were to have the privilege of watching the masquerades and mermaids compete in the ogrinya dance. Women and children were to stay in their huts. Only the eyes of men could see this sacred day in Oli'doma. It didn't take long for the most talented of flute players to assume his position in the village square. He played a rhythm which invited the ordinary gods and goddesses of the land. The rhythm, quite soothing, spoke of a season awaited by the land. The flute sent shivers into the bones of the gathering men, and of the hut-bound women and children. The flute attracted men from neighbouring villages, all around Oli'doma country. The music of the flute first got the council of Opialu chiefs dancing, and in the rising dust Christmas's vision got clearer. The dust rose higher, and the great one arrived – the chief priest of Opialu, the one whose feet never touched the ground in times of war. The chief priest sensed the presence of spirits; he sensed the watchful eyes of Abutu Eje, and nodded at the dust before he danced ogrinya.

During the ogrinya dance, arms were spread out in front of the body. Shoulders were ostentatiously raised with waists slightly bent forward. Feet freely hammered the ground in quick pulsations. Drummers took their place beside the flutist and more men were driven to dance. Through the eyes of the dust, Christmas saw his father in his colourful wrapper.

The moment the village waited for came. The masquerades approached, and men screamed. Some in panic. Some in euphoria. These resurrected ancestors finally reached the square. They were seven in number, and Orinya could easily be identified being the tallest among them. His eyes appeared frail. His movements were quick. He danced like a cat on baked earth. Invisible ancestors with no living children to offer them food and libations announced their presence by causing a whirlwind.

The ancestors danced. The black river vomited its mermaids onto the land. Oda'nyaa and all her special maids marched in their womanish forms into Opialu, dancing to the rhythms of the flute. The crowd noise shook the village. Most men prayed for the mermaids to win the contest against the ancestors. In the culture if the mermaids were declared victorious, the masqueraded ancestors were to leave for their world and let the men impregnate the mermaids. If the ancestors won, they must chase these mermaids back into the black river with whips before they left for their world. These mermaids didn't fail. They shook their waists and wiggled their behinds. People whose resurrected ancestors frequented the village on occasions like this desired victory for the masquerades. To them, nothing could be more important than the honour rightly deserved by the ancestors.

The men, captivated by the strong spells released by the dancing mermaids, marvelled in lust. The time arrived for the chief priest to announce the conqueror of the night.

'No winner,' he declared.

The ancestors held on tight to Opialu. The mermaids' spells worked well. Opialu men drank and celebrated.

* * *

Christmas's spirit returned and settled back in its twenty-six-year-old lanky body sprawled on the straw bed. His entire being sank into a dream, and in this dream he found himself in a ship sailing from Africa. His face, so grimy with shit he could hardly talk. He turned to his side to catch a man's glare.

'Who there?' Christmas asked the man.

'Rogers.'

'You ain't from Africa?'

'My ancestors was.'
'What you doin' on this ship?'
'Don't know.'
'Where you come from?'
'Georgia.'
Christmas awoke. He repeated the name, Rogers, got out of the bed and opened his little window. The morning light streamed in. He yawned, changed his clothes and headed to the farm.

The hogs grunted, shoving their bodies against each other. Mr. Preacher truly freed Christmas, Black John and Moses. But they all needed the return since Kentucky, outside the Preacher residence, treated them badly. Their heads ached in their wandering under the sun. They hungered for days. Christmas got the hogs to look after again in the Preacher residence, and he did this for a living being a free man. Christmas spread the milled grain over the floor in the hog house and put water in place for the hogs. A big problem lingered in his heart. Mr. Preacher failed to pay them, going against his own words. Christmas accepted this bitterness. The days of 1800 appeared sweet but they weren't.

* * *

A boar squealed. Christmas ensured enough food and water were in place for the excited hogs. On his way out, he heard someone whistle from a pen. Christmas gazed further and spotted a man, in dirty rumpled clothing, squatting and obviously in hiding.

'Come on out, negro, whoever you be,' Christmas said.

Startled, the man stood and leapt out of the boar's pen. Christmas rushed over and wrestled him to the floor. 'What you doin' here? Stealin' from this farm?'

'Get off me nigger. I'm a runaway from Georgia.'

Christmas got off the slave and started to wipe the grubby stain off his shirt. 'From Georgia?'

'My name is Rogers Phillip, and a Quaker in Georgia done asked me to find one Mr. Preacher.'

'Rogers?' Christmas nodded and thought for a moment. He indeed dreamt of the moment. 'Wait here,' he said and went to fetch Mr. Preacher.

Christmas opened the door to the coffee room and saw Massa counting some money. A huge sum. For a moment, he wondered why the white man wouldn't pay him, Black John and Moses the wages he'd promised them.

Mr. Preacher, obviously angered to be interrupted, said, 'Where's your manners? This is my house, Christmas.'

'My apologies. Some trouble, Massa. There's a runaway slave in the farm.'

They met fugitive squatted and looking down.

'I'm Mr. Preacher.'

The man couldn't speak. He shed tears into his hands.

Mr. Preacher went closer to him, squatted and placed a hand on the man's shoulder. The white man recently gained some weight.

'You are in a safe station. Christmas will take you to a shelter in the house,' Mr. Preacher said.

Christmas led the runaway to the back of the big house, and spent some time scrubbing the man's weak body with soda. The man sustained several cuts from his last master. The cuts, some healed into scars, were darker in contrast to the rest of his mutilated skin, and they were linked. Christmas couldn't bear looking at it for long. The man, however, looked calm in his new clothes. He ate the roasted chunk of pork Christmas thought might be enough for two. Christmas began telling him a tale of Oli'doma – how his great forefather saved the Idoma people from the torturous kingship of the Hausa tribe. The man couldn't listen to the end. He drifted off to sleep. The night got windy and Christmas decided to sleep in the attic along with the new arrival. His tale ended in his own dream. Orinya embarked on a journey into paradise above the sky. In his wise words, he convinced *Owoicho* to have mercy on his people.

* * *

Christmas posted the mail given to him by Mr. Preacher. He didn't want an early return from such an errand. He sat on the bank of the black river and listened to the breath of breeze. The noise of the Ohio falls echoed about the vicinity. Mr. Preacher recently announced the coming of more fugitives, the dubious route he chose since fully committing to new Quaker doctrines and practices to appear acceptable to his Quaker society. Christmas knew Mr. Preacher meant no negro any good. He failed in paying wages on time. Moses recently stopped helping Black John do the cleaning inside the main house. He wouldn't cook on his set day either.

A young negro girl of about eleven years old ran past, behind Christmas. He turned around to stare. A quadroon boy seem to be chasing her.

'Hey, why chasin' her, boy!' Christmas shouted, now standing and facing the road.

'They only playin',' came a woman's voice from a distance.

The negro woman, about twenty years old, sauntered in the direction of the children. He looked away, and thought for a moment. The beautiful woman might be a new slave in the neighbourhood. She looked at him and smiled. His heart skipped.

'You livin' around here?'

'Not far from here. At the Peterson plantation.'

'You belong to the horrible white man, Mr. Peterson,' Christmas said.

'He ain't stupid like Mr. Preacher,' she replied.

'My massa ain't stupid,' Christmas said. 'But he sure be as horrible as your massa, I can say.'

'My massa ain't a sorcerer like your massa, you knows.'

'Bein' a Quaker got nothin' to do with sorcery.' Christmas sighed.

'You talkin' strange,' she said.

'You beautiful.'

She laughed.

'The children runnin' and playin' around is yours?'

'Yes. They mine... I got to get goin'.'

'Gon see you again?' Christmas asked. The children were running back now.

'Why?'

Christmas looked away.

'I go by here most of the afternoon to post letters for Mr. Peterson. You gon see me if you like,' she said.

Christmas watched her go. He couldn't get her off his mind. He walked excitedly past the large rectangular building next to Richardson Store. A regular member of the meetings held in the Preacher residence came by in a buggy. Christmas smiled at his invitation and hopped on. He alighted close to the Beargrass Creek and waved at the man. On reaching the Preacher residence, he sighted a patroller on a white horse.

'Hey, you one of Mr. William Preacher's negroes?' the officer asked.

'I free now... But I live here.'

'Tell Mr. Preacher I would like to talk to him, boy.'

Christmas found Mr. Preacher in his study. The white man left to see the patroller. Christmas watched Mr. Preacher converse with the officer from a distance. Mr. Preacher laughed briefly. Christmas watched the officer look around. Massa pointed in several directions. Soon the officer left.

Mr. Preacher headed toward his house. He reached the entrance door, turned around and beckoned to Christmas.

'Yes, Massa,' Christmas said on reaching him.

'Make sure Rogers doesn't come out of the attic. You must warn him.'

'Yes, Mr. Preacher,' Christmas said. He headed up to the attic and found Rogers seated on the pallet. He passed on the message.

The man began to shake in fear.

'You don't have to be afraid, Rogers.'

Rogers remained quiet.

Christmas got back to the dwelling and found Moses seated in the sitting room. He smiled at Moses. Moses frowned at him.

'What the white man say to you? I sees you two talkin',' Moses said.

'Just speakin' to Massa Preacher about Rogers,' Christmas replied.

'Don't lie to me, Christmas,' Moses said raising his voice. 'I knows he askin' you about me.'

Christmas sighed. He shook his head in displeasure and said, 'Mr. Preacher only thinks about hisself and he ain't got no time talkin' about you. You think I don't hate him? Why should I lie?'

* * *

In the spring of 1800 Louisville residents became very cautious of strange weeds around their regions. No one knew how one strange weed in particular came into Kentucky. If not controlled, Jamestown weeds grew so rank like trees. They took over most of the ways and open fields, and negro slaves were brought in great numbers to remove and burn them. Christmas and Black John got rid of every weed in the Preacher residence. Late in the evening Christmas knocked on Moses's door and pushed it open. Moses, asleep with the quilt over his body, snored. He did nothing other than eat and sleep. He wouldn't speak a word to Mr. Preacher either. Mr. Preacher could only pay three months out of the four he owed Christmas and Black John. Moses got nothing despite working for a month.

'You still lyin' in bed,' Christmas said.

'What a free negro gon do with hisself on a beautiful day?'

'You know Mr. Preacher gon kick your behind out.'

'The white man comes here the other day and ask for rent upfront, sayin' my first month of work covers the rent until now. I done told him I gon keep stayin' here and gon pay nothin'.'

'What he say?'

'Nothin'. Black John stupid tellin' the white man that he gon pay my rent,' Twenty-year-old Moses said.

'You ought to work to save Black John the burden,' Christmas replied.

'Stop that, Christmas. That don't make no sense. Negroes right in the head should work for no white man after all they keep doin' to us.'

'Be sorry for Black John.'

'Ain't gon feel sorry for a brother actin' a fool. I ain't gon think that way. Look what the white man made them do to Antonia. Mr. Preacher took Antonia's child and gave to his own wife. I bet the child gon be dead before long. How that different from what they did the baby mama? Because of the white man, Antonia got hung like she a hog.'

Christmas pulled a stool toward Moses's straw bed and sat.

'Ain't here to listen to no preachin' about them white people bein' wrong. Just here to tell you that I be meetin' a negro woman, Moses. I just wonder if you might be able to tell me some woman tricks... If you got any.'

Moses giggled and sat up. 'Sound good. You sure got yourself a woman?'

'She livin' in the Peterson plantation.'

'You talkin' of Nedi?'

Christmas's heart skipped. 'I suppose that her name.'

'She got children – a daughter for Eric and a son for Mr. Peterson.'

'Eric?'

'Yes, I heard Mr. Peterson done sold him. Some folks say he dead. That Mr. Peterson could have killed him as soon as Nedi bore that girl. Christmas, you gon be careful there. He lash them slaves until he sees blood. All but Nedi. He never gon lash Nedi.'

Christmas sighed. 'Why?'

'He might be her real father, some folks say. She fine. You never gon get her until you get rid of Ole Mr. Peterson, I tell you.'

Christmas didn't like what he heard.

'I can help you kill him,' Moses said smiling. 'And no white folk gon know.'

'If I got to do that, I gon do that alone,' Christmas said. He stepped out of Moses's room, headed out of the dwelling and stood in the terrace. He saw the tree beside the big house tilted clumsily. Christmas sighed again. Moses soon joined him in front of the dwelling.

'You thinkin'?'

'Yes. Just thinkin',' Christmas replied.

'Of Nedi?'

'Guess so.'

'Hahaha... Good luck, Christmas. I got to find me a woman too. Headin' off to woods to relieve myself,' Moses said and walked away. Christmas sensed something awkward. Moses hid something from him. His spirit saw how Moses once waited for his luck in front of the Peterson plantation built in the section of the neighbourhood rich folks lived. Tall poles with oil lamps provided light on streetways of this neighbourhood during night time aiding the passage of wagons and carriages travelling by. On this fateful day, Moses waited around this place in the company of some men repairing a few broken streetlights. Sixteen-year-old Nedi ran out of the plantation and he called to her.

'You stay out of my way. I done seen plenty niggers all better than you is.'

The oil men laughed and teasingly asked Moses to become a white man before trying his luck again.

* * *

Christmas collected Mr. Preacher's letters from the post office and headed to the bank of the black river to wait for Nedi. The waters appeared to rumble. The tide rose before the wind came, and this caused the low grasses and leaves on the trees to stir. The wind soon became words.

> *Orinya once dormant*
> *And lifeless*
> *Now lives*
> *Greatest of Masquerades*
> *The flyer*

The words showed him Opialu. The village showed him his brother, Abah Ogah. Abah lacked the spirit of Orinya. To Abah, Orinya's burial shroud appeared colourless and torn in several places. This powerlessness drowned the Ogah name. But not too long ago, Christmas saw a jubilant Orinya dancing amongst other alekwuafias in Opialu through the eyes of dust.

The wind showed him how his brother, Abah, kept killing chickens and goats in sacrifice to a dormant state of the alekwuafia in his own life. Abah Ogah in his early twenties looked energetic and fast in movement. His strides spoke of determination and strength. His eyes spoke of focus and profound wisdom. The mounting sacrifices soon became a great flame roaring toward the sky, jubilant over nature. Orinya resurrected in the destiny of Abah Ogah. The true alekwuafia appeared in the form of a masquerade. The horse-like face looked around. The burial shroud came to life, displaying flying colours of red, yellow and green. His attire consisted of two vertical panels of red and yellow appliqued triangles which shone brighter than all the elements around.

In this resurrection, Orinya catapulted himself into the sky. A sudden transformation from misery to greatness. The same sense of pride which lighted up Abah Ogah's face came upon Christmas.

The wind died. Christmas's vision blurred. A strong desire to see Opialu in person revisited him. The figure of Nedi approaching him from afar caused him to gather his senses together. She walked alone this time. There were puddles before her. She managed to walk over the trunks of trees serving as paths. She reached him, and Christmas smiled. She sat beside him. They stared at the black river. Many fine passenger steamboats arrived to ply the river recently.

'You knows my name?' she asked.

'Everybody got to know the name of a beautiful woman like you in the neighbourhood.'

'I ain't free.'

'That ain't stoppin' me from marryin' somebody,' he said.

She laughed. 'Waggish negro.'

'Ain't jokin'.'

'What it like to be free?'

'Ain't nothin' much except for bein' free to go nowhere. You black, and them white folks do you no good.' He told her of his plight, the experience in Lexington. He told her of Mr. Preacher's habit in delaying wages.

Nedi began to play with her braids.

He stopped and looked at her hair. 'Your mama born you this way?' he asked.

'Yes. She got locks. Her mama too. My grandma's mama from Africa had it too.'

'Can I touch?' he asked.

'No,' she laughed.

'Why?' he asked.

'Look at this, nigger.' Her voice, firmer. But her smile remained. '...because it mine.'

'What I gon do to just feel them strands. How much you want?'

'Ain't no nigger whore,' she replied and sighed. 'Gon let you just this one time. And don't hurt me.'

He touched them. He caressed them. He desired to fly like an eagle in merriment. He picked strand by strand, and people, passing by, glanced at them, until she shooed his hands away.

* * *

In one of those rainy months of 1800, Rogers got ready to leave for his final stop – Philadelphia. He wore a white cotton shirt and a brown pair of pantaloons. Christmas led the man into the gathering of the Society of Friends and everyone present stood up.

The fugitive expressed his appreciation. 'There be more comin'. I've three brothers who gon be headin' this way. Please help them as you all done did to me.'

'It be our pleasure to do everythin' we knowed to break the foul system of slavery,' Tallie said.

Mr. Preacher and Christmas led the man to the cargo box in the lobby.

'You enter this box, lie comfortably and we will seal and post it to our good friends in Philadelphia,' Mr. Preacher said to Rogers. 'You need not panic. Adjust thy posture when need be and be wary not to draw attention.'

Christmas raised his brow reassuring the man. Rogers removed his shoes.

Mr. Preacher took a nail from Christmas, held it to the lid and hammered it a couple of times. He got another nail, and another, and soon sealed the box.

Christmas complained about the hole on the box. 'Too small, Massa.'

'Our friends in Virginia have been doing this and it works, Christmas,' Mr. Preacher advised.

Mr. Preacher's only concern seemed to be his reputation amongst Quakers. Christmas harnessed one of the horses to the buggy, and Mr. Preacher left for the harbour carrying the cargo box. Before dusk the ship left Kentucky, and freedom awaited the man.

* * *

Christmas couldn't hide it anymore and revealed his mind. 'Massa, I knows you help the fugitive because it gon to make you look good in front of them Quakers.'

Massa Preacher pushed him so bad he fell and struck the back of his head on the pantry. A couple of tumblers fell and shattered on the floor. Christmas got up. The white man looked at him and said, 'Never say such things to me again.'

Midnight came. Orinya appeared and placed his wrinkly old hands over Christmas's sore head. The moon's ray dimmed. Christmas metamorphosed into the usual able horse which the ancestor mounted and rode toward the big house. The wind became noisy. The door to the big house sprang open on its own. They halted. Christmas climbed up the staircase with ease and found Mr. Preacher's room. The giant clock stuck to the wall fell and shattered. They peered over Mr. Preacher, alone in bed. The white man snored quietly. There came a force sealing the lips of the night, and the sound of the wind died. The master's bedroom became laden with doom. Mr. Preacher woke straining for breath. He fell off his bed to the floor and struggled to his feet. He tried to light the candle. The fire flickered. The white man's eyes met Orinya's. The ancestor, still on the horse, stared back. Mr. Preacher shuddered. The candle light went out. By the corner of the room Antonia appeared. She stared at the white man reprovingly. She clung to the ceiling using several tentacles. Mr. Preacher began to shout. Black John entered the room in the dark. The ancestor faded away. And Antonia vanished. Christmas touched himself and felt his human body. Black John lit the candle.

* * *

Christmas and Black John returned. Moses opened his door slightly.

'He alright now?' he asked.

'You ought to come help if you was truly concerned,' Black John yelled back.

Christmas sighed, entered his room and slammed the door. He stood in the dark room, with his back against the door and thought about Antonia. Christmas closed his eyes. He remembered her hanging body. He didn't notice his quick transformation back into human form. The scared white man did not even ask how he, Christmas, got into the room since he didn't come in with Black John. Christmas kept thinking of Antonia's spirit. He recalled how Moses dug out her heart with a knife. Thinking about it now, he understood she asked Moses to take her heart out to plant in the residence. Antonia indeed wanted a chance to get revenge against Mr. Preacher.

* * *

Mr. Preacher joined Christmas on the farm in the morning. They fed the hogs and washed the pens. He didn't say a word about the happenings of the night.

'Rogers reached our friends in Philadelphia safely.'

'Good to hear, Massa.'

'He's free now. Quaker friends in Philadelphia are saying good things about me. And trust me, my motives are unselfish. Negroes benefit more.'

Christmas touched the back of his swollen head. He welcomed the good news, but felt sickened about Mr. Preacher's interest in acquiring a positive reputation. The white man overcame last night's shock to Christmas's surprise. He joined Black John at the stable and Christmas headed for the kitchen house. He met Moses looking for some food.

'In search of food so early?' Christmas said.

'Ain't too dumb to know I'm hungry. I was sick last night because of the dinner Black John done cook. You cookin' tonight?'

Christmas nodded.

'I trust you. When you cook it's real good and we get much. That how life supposed to be,' Moses said and found himself a corn. 'Gon cook this for breakfast... Any luck with Nedi?'

'I be marryin' her soon,' Christmas said. 'Please, cook me one too?'

'Will do. Mr. Peterson ain't...'

'Mr. Peterson ain't gon stop me,' Christmas interrupted Moses.

Moses smiled. 'Tell me somethin'. What you gon do?'

'Can't say now,' Christmas replied.

'Another one you got to look out for if you really mean what you sayin' is the Preacher white man. He a dog.'

* * *

Christmas met Nedi and her children at the post office. He came to collect Mr. Preacher's letters. Nedi came to post several letters written by her master. They took the longer route different from the one along the bank of the black river on their way back. Nedi's children walked ahead of Christmas and Nedi.

'I been thinkin' about you since the last time,' Christmas said to her.

'You got to keep dreamin',' she said laughing.

'You sure don't like me?' Christmas asked.

'I do not hate you.'

'That don't mean nothin'.'

'You should get to know my children, Christmas Preacher. Sally! Ark!' she called. 'You two come say good evenin' to Christmas.'

The children ran toward them.

'Come on. Say good evenin',' Nedi said looking first at her son.

He appeared shy.

'Say good evenin', Ark?'

'Good evenin',' he said and squatted looking away.

'What your mama call you Christmas for?' Sally asked.

'That is what white folks call me,' Christmas replied.

'I love Christmas,' Ark said still looking away.

'He mean Christmas Day,' Nedi said.

'Good evenin', Christmas,' Sally said in response to her mother's nod.

This one, Christmas thought, would grow up to be a fine woman, just like her mother. 'Your children so fine,' Christmas said.

Sally and Ark soon ran ahead of them again.

'Tell me Christmas. What you really want from me?'

'I wants me everythin'.'

She swallowed.

'I wants you to marry me,' Christmas said. He stopped and held her hands. He looked into her eyes. 'I wants to be able to hold you like this forever. I wants to see that smile for the rest of my life.'

She couldn't look back. She searched for her children, and saw them building something on sand.

'Mr. Peterson ain't gon accept you.'

'How about you, Nedi?'

She looked away again. 'He a hard man. Mr. Peterson.'

Silence.

'I be marryin' you,' he said to her. 'I knows you like me. I sees it in your eyes.'

In the evening, Christmas's spirit remained with the young woman back in the Peterson plantation. Tears filled her eyes. She got rid of each teardrop so Ark could see nothing. But she couldn't hide it from Sally. Poor Sally took her father's looks. On the night of Sally's birth, slave traders entered the plantation and bundled Eric away, down south.

She thought of men once interested in her. Black men, white men, enslaved, free – all wanted to worsen her miserable life. She thought of Christmas. She liked him, and Christmas felt glad.

'Hey, Nedi,' Mr. Peterson called on seeing her and the children. 'Why did it take you so long?'

'Sorry, Massa, we done walked the long road because of them puddles,' Nedi replied.

'Sure you only posting and getting me my letters and not meeting no damn negro putting trash in your head?'

'I swear, Massa. That ain't true.'

The master walked away. He first forced her to his bed before she turned twelve. Many were sold and yet she remained. A few were suspected to have been killed by Mr. Peterson's own hands yet she remained. Mr. Peterson, obviously her father, also fathered her son.

Christmas's spirit sank further into the young woman's dreams deep into the night, and her spirit got awoken by a force which lifted her out of bed and through the roof of her cabin. Christmas felt helpless for he could see everything but couldn't help. She couldn't understand how she landed on a floor made of gold. She needed to understand the developing circumstances. Multitudes of women surrounded her. A number of them approached and wrestled her to the floor. She cried. They were strange fair women all dressed in strange glittering gowns. They finally forced her to stand between two rods. Her legs and hands were tied to these rods, and she stood with legs and hands spread wide apart.

A woman in a crown appeared in front of her with a whip. Oda'nyaa. Christmas couldn't stop her. He couldn't announce his presence. The woman's stare bore into Nedi painfully before the whip struck. The whip took away flesh from her body in the Peterson plantation. Blood gathered around the spot the whip struck. It stung her and she screamed. She closed her eyes and shook her head weakly. She opened her eyes in anticipation of another lash, but her spirit sank back in her weakened body on her straw bed. The candlelight wavered. Her children were awake. Some of the other slaves came into her cabin and all stared in awe.

Mr. Peterson stood in the doorway. 'What's going on, Nedi?'

She kept bleeding. She looked at herself. Touched her own blood.

'Oh dear Lord!' Mr. Peterson said. 'What happened, Nedi? Somebody help her.'

Two slaves helped her lie back on the bed, and tore the upper portion of her dress to expose the injury.

'Who did this to her?

'No one, Massa. I woke to find me this way.'

'There should be a wild animal in here?' Mr. Peterson asked.

The slaves behind Mr. Peterson took to their heels on hearing this. The ones in Nedi's room looked around and trembled.

Nedi began to cry. 'No animal here, Massa. In a dream, I see a woman who whip me real bad.'

No one could sleep anymore at the Peterson plantation. Some spoke of the ghosts of dead slaves. Some spoke of deaths at the hands of Mr. Peterson. Christmas's spirit roamed about helplessly between Nedi's mind and the Peterson plantation. He couldn't save Nedi.

* * *

Christmas hung around the bank of the black river each time he passed by. He waited endlessly for hours expecting Nedi to show up. Her injury seemed more serious than he thought. He desired to hurt Oda'nyaa for this.

Steamboats arrived at the shore in numbers. Somewhere a man rang a bell. Christmas joined the people gathering around the man. This man announced the sad collision between a boat headed to Cincinnati and another coming to Louisville. The barrels of oil laden in one of the boats ignited, and the resulting fire took lives. The news worried Christmas more. *Ikwu* could define mystery. He headed away from the black river and toward the Peterson plantation. He walked around the neighbourhood. He peered into the plantation but there weren't any signs of her. He saw two negro men loading grains into a bag. He saw several children – mulattos, quadroons and octoroons, running around. He didn't see her children. He found his way back to the Preacher residence. Three fugitives arrived a moment later. They were ushered into the attic. Mark, Winston and Toby. He headed to the kitchen house to bake some sausages. Moses came in.

'I hear we've got them new arrivals.'

'Yes. Cookin' for them.'

'What is in the kitchen house for us?'

'You can have them sausages.'

Moses took a bite of a sausage. 'Too hot,' he struggled to say. 'How is the girl, Nedi?'

'I see her no more. I done did everythin'.'

'You should sneak into that plantation tonight. I go with you.'

'That be no good. I gon see Mr. Peterson, myself.'

'He gon shoot you, nigger.'

Silence.

Christmas took the food to the attic on a tray. The new arrivals ate in silence and drank their water. Their faces and bodies were scarred.

'We owe great gratitude to you and your massa. When we free, we gon mention the good deeds of this household,' the one called Mark said.

Christmas struggled to remain quiet. He wanted to tell them not to trust Mr. Preacher. He wanted to reveal Mr. Preacher's lies and carnality.

Toby spoke about their journey from Indiana. Winston laughed sadly at the memory Toby recounted. They were nine in number that set out of Indiana. Slave catchers and dogs hunted them for days. Right on the river border between New Albany and Louisville, they hid in trees and sometimes tried to hide under water. They saw the unimaginable. They hung on to tree branches, shielded by green leaves. They saw six of their friends heaped on each other and set ablaze. The slave catchers laughed and enjoyed their appalling acts. They used sharpened and smoky sticks to dig into the marred bodies. The white men took delight in dumping more hay on the burning bodies. They delighted in hearing the fire crackle.

* * *

There were three boxes, and the three fugitives hopped into them. Massa hammered respective sets of nails into each box, sealing them. Christmas and Black John helped lift the boxes into the carriage, and they watched Mr. Preacher and Tallie head away with them.

'Unkind white man,' Christmas muttered.

Black John giggled. 'You mean white man Preacher? He becomin' good...'

'Good to Quakers, I agree,' Christmas said sarcastically, and found his way to the bank of the black river again. He walked along the waterfront. Carts clattered past. A horse neighed and a white woman in one of the carts gave him a mean stare. People walked by. None looked like Nedi. He walked around the Peterson plantation neighbourhood and hid behind a pine tree hoping to see her. Nothing spoke of death. He wanted her. He wished he could see her. He went back to the Preacher residence more troubled. His spirit left him twice in search of her but couldn't locate her. He couldn't locate her face amongst the many slave faces on the Peterson plantation.

* * *

Christmas entered the house. Mr. Preacher closed *The Kentucky Observer* in his hands. The white man cleared his throat and said, 'Mark and his friends should be on free land in a couple of days.'

Christmas didn't say a word.

Mr. Preacher sat on a chair.

'I wants you to talk to Mr. Peterson.'

'In what respect?'

'I wants to marry one of Mr. Peterson's slaves.'

Mr. Preacher sighed. He stood up and walked up to Christmas. 'I see you want a wife.'

'I wants only Nedi.'

Mr. Preacher nodded. He placed a hand on Christmas's shoulder. 'You consider yourself a Quaker?'

'Yes,' he lied. He could never be a Quaker. Mr. Preacher wasn't a Quaker either, Christmas thought. Christmas believed in no religion other than the existence of his ancestors.

'It is against the doctrine to marry a non-Quaker. I can talk to Tallie. He's got a beautiful young daughter, or I can take you to see the overseer who has a lot of knowledge on issues of marriage amongst black Quakers.'

Christmas shook his head in disagreement. 'I wants Nedi and no one else.'

'You wouldn't just listen, Christmas. Just go.' Mr. Preacher waved him away.

Christmas walked out of the big house and left the residence. Mr. Preacher should never be trusted.

Christmas arrived at the Peterson plantation and banged at the gate. A negro man came running.

'You don't hit the gate like Mr. Preacher got this plantation.'

'I'm here to see Mr. Peterson,' Christmas said.

'Why that is?'

'I ain't here to see you. I'm here to see Mr. Peterson.'

'If you don't say why that is, I ain't lettin' you in.'

Christmas pushed the gate with all the force he could build within himself. The man fell. Christmas headed toward the big house, walking in between farmlands of cotton.

'Stop there. This ain't your massa's plantation. Ain't no place here for Quakers and witches!' the negro man yelled and followed.

Christmas ignored the man and advanced toward the master's mansion. He got to the front of the house and his high shoulders shrunk. He lost his courage. He placed a foot on the stairs leading up to the massive mahogany door and a voice stopped him from proceeding.

'Whose nigger are you?' Mr. Peterson appeared to stare at him through a big window.

'I free.'

Mr. Peterson's negro caught up with Christmas and shouted, 'Massa, he livin' at the Preacher residence.'

'Enough, Thomas,' Mr. Peterson said and came out to the balcony, scratching his crotch. This made Christmas more uncomfortable. 'What brings you here?' Mr. Peterson asked Christmas.

'I comes here with high respect for you, Mr. Peterson. You should know that I have deep affection for one of your slaves.' He wanted to say he came to see her. Just to see her. '...I comes to propose marriage,' he ended up saying.

'Which of my slave girls do you propose to marry?'

'Nedi, Mr. Peterson.'

Thomas laughed.

The white man glanced. 'What do they call you?'

'They call him Christmas,' Thomas said.

'Thomas, I did not ask you to speak,' Mr. Peterson said.

'Sorry, Massa.'

'You got courage. You know what happened to Nedi?' Mr. Peterson asked, now standing in front of Christmas.

'No... Mr. Peterson,' Christmas stammered.

Mr. Peterson spat at him.

The spit hit the white of one of Christmas's eyes. Anger and fear consumed him. He flinched. He tried to bend over and rub his eyes, but Thomas grabbed him roughly from behind, forcing him to remain straight on his feet.

'You want to put your filthy manhood in the same black hole as me?' Mr. Peterson asked.

Christmas remained quiet.

Mr. Peterson slapped him on the side of his face. A punch followed. Christmas tried to scuffle off his body away from Thomas's hold but couldn't.

Thomas's hold around Christmas tightened.

Another punch blinded him briefly. He opened his eyes and saw Nedi.

'Please, Massa!' she said. Her arms rested on the shoulders of two older negro women. Her face, pale.

'Nedi?' Mr. Peterson called.

Her lazy eyes were fixed on Christmas. Thomas lost grip and Christmas managed to free himself. Thomas fell, and Christmas staggered toward her.

'I... I... done dreamed a bad dream,' Nedi said to him. 'In the dream a woman whip me real bad.'

There were blood stains on the back of her dress above the waistline.

'Stay away from her, nigger!' Mr. Peterson raised his voice.

Christmas held her hand. 'You gon be better.'

'Stay away from Nedi,' Mr. Peterson repeated.

'I gon give myself to the black river, Massa, if you don't let him see me,' Nedi threatened. 'I sure gon kill myself.'

'I will go in now,' Mr. Peterson said and sighed. 'By the time I come back and he is still here, he will be taken back to the Preacher residence a dead nigger.' The slaveholder started for the big house.

Christmas decided to leave immediately. He couldn't tell her about Oda'nyaa. He wanted to embrace her but feared what Oda'nyaa or Mr. Peterson might do further.

His strides back to the Preacher residence were quick, and he failed to recognise familiar faces walking past him. His thoughts, hazy. In his room, he called for the mermaid:

> *The most beautiful of mermaids*
> *Egaa la hou – where are you?*

Oda'nyaa appeared and he wrestled her to the floor. He dug his fingers into her neck.

'The queen never dies,' she whispered with no attempt to fight back.

He tried to strangle her but she felt no pain and laughed at his act. He noticed the presence of a strange breeze. A resounding voice followed:

> *I have come to free my own eyi.*
> *He is me and I am him*

He turned around and became aware of Orinya's presence. Oda'nyaa's laughter ceased. The masquerade's colourful regalia almost blinded her. He danced a slow dance and Christmas watched Oda'nyaa rise to her knees.

'Only a command, and her existence ends now,' the masquerade announced in his chanting.

Christmas felt Oda'nyaa trembling. 'Have her stay away from me.'

'She will never. She is very deceptive. But I can warn her. If she fails to listen, her end will come.'

'Warn her,' Christmas pleaded.

'You must leave us, Ochigbo,' the masquerade said. 'You cannot be here when we negotiate.'

Christmas vanished into the future and wandered about in the reincarnated years of his childhood. He didn't intend to vanish. He didn't want to leave beings of the spirit alone in his room to negotiate. Now he wanted to go into his future life with Nedi but couldn't. Despite having a glimpse of their future together, he just couldn't visit the point in time.

He saw himself, a seven-year-old Olofu, being spanked by his mother. She urged him to talk like his contemporaries. But he couldn't. Christmas refused to accept the muteness in the boy. He could never be dumb. The mother spanked his innocence. Why? She birthed him this way.

Christmas's spirit launched into the air, this time in a vulture's body, and flew to the past, to a time of festivity in Opialu. Every woman must stay home, but men could stay out to see Opialu masquerades roam around. Through the eyes of the vulture, he saw his real mother. Why did she come out? Women weren't allowed out?

Attired in colourful, bushy straws of green, black and red, Orinya emerged. His yellowish horse-like face glittered. Bangles were around black clothed arms and ankles. Orinya caught his mother. His left hand held Mother hard. The right hand held a whip. He whipped the woman and she danced to every sting. Orinya could be in several places at the same time. In Opialu. In Louisville.

Christmas wanted to grab Orinya's neck and scream at him and ask him why he lashed his mother. He saw through the eyes of the masquerade. Orinya didn't mean evil. He taught the woman a lesson. If he, Orinya, came from another family, the woman would certainly be stripped and raped. She only got whipped. She leant to stay in her hut whenever any masquerade came into the village.

Christmas tried to return to his room in the Preacher residence but the meeting spirits resisted him by using the force of the wind and he got transported back to an earlier Louisville, on the second day after Antonia's death. From the far corner he again saw Moses up on the ladder digging a knife into Antonia's body. Soon Christmas found his body in real time with Oda'nyaa and his ancestor gone, and he vomited on the floor of his room.

* * *

He woke and saw Massa standing in his doorway. The room stank of his vomit. Mr. Preacher came in and sat on the straw bed.

'You love that girl?' Massa asked.

Christmas nodded his head.

'Our friends say you can go ahead but you will worship with Quakers no more.'

Christmas sighed and sat up.

Mr. Preacher got up. 'Black John cleaned up your mess. Make up your mind. Think on the outcome of your action. You can take the day to regain your strength. Black John will tend to the hogs,' Mr. Preacher said and headed toward the door.

'Massa, you never gon believe this.' Black John almost bumped into Mr. Preacher in the doorway. 'A pregnant woman here. A runaway!'

Christmas followed Mr. Preacher and Black John toward the big house and from a distance, Christmas saw her. The heavily pregnant woman started toward them. Her face spoke of fear. She fell on her knees, directly in front of Mr. Preacher.

'You gon save my infant. Please you gon save my infant,' the woman cried.

Mr. Preacher squatted. 'God will save you and your infant.'

'You never gon understand, sir. I walk from far. North Carolina. Ain't no way my infant gon be born a slave.'

'I once owned slaves. On realisation of this evil, I made a vow – to fight for the enslaved. So I understand you,' Mr. Preacher said and turned around to Christmas and Black John. 'Get her some food and water. I will take her to the attic.' Mr. Preacher helped the woman up.

* * *

Christmas's heart pounded hard. His spirit longed to leave in search of his beloved woman. Nedi must be in trouble and he felt it strongly. He entered his room and bolted the door behind him. His spirit soared out of the Preacher residence. He hovered over the Peterson plantation. He couldn't see Nedi. He couldn't see Mr. Peterson either. Christmas's spirit found her running toward the black river. Behind her were Mr. Peterson and four of his negro men in pursuit. She entered the water and dragged her body further to the deeper area. Mr. Peterson and his men reached the bank. Her entire body disappeared. Christmas's spirit groaned. Two of the negroes dived into the river. They brought Nedi's lifeless body up the water surface. On the bank they made her to cough and bring out the water in her belly.

'I should just let her marry that negro,' Mr. Peterson said. 'She's worth six hundred bucks.'

Christmas, being the thin air, sighed.

Right up to the winter of 1800, Mr. Peterson kept going against his words, failing to permit the marriage. Christmas found it difficult to see Nedi in person. But his spirit kept watch. His worried spirit, being the night, witnessed Nedi leaving the plantation again. Someone rang the alarm bell. Mr. Peterson along with seven of his male slaves followed. She started to run. Thomas along with three other negroes chased her. Her injury began to hurt and slowed her down. Christmas could feel the pain her movements brought her. Thomas truly wanted to impress Mr. Peterson. He caught up with her. Thomas wrapped his hands around her body and they fell over the hard earth. The clotting over her wound tore. She cried. She fought Thomas.

'I can't live without Christmas,' she yelled repeatedly. 'I gon drown myself.'

'Christmas ain't the only negro man in Louisville,' one of the negroes said.

'He better than you is,' she said to the negro.

'I will let you marry in the negro way to whoever, but know this: I still own you,' Mr. Peterson finally said.

She stared at him in the eyes.

'I mean it this time,' Mr. Peterson added.

In the evening of the next day it occurred. No slave in the Peterson plantation believed their eyes. The slaves clapped and clapped. Even Thomas, the smallish negro with profound dislike for Christmas, jollied along. Moses and Black John were there. Tallie came but isolated himself from the crowd.

'Massa say I'm allowed to spend two days and two nights – Thursdays and Fridays – at the Preacher residence if Mr. Preacher agrees,' Nedi whispered into Christmas's ears before they walked toward the broom.

Christmas smiled at her. He admired her fortitude. 'Today is Thursday.'

They danced on their way to the cheer of the other negroes. They jumped over the broom. Negroes shouted and jumped in delight. Christmas and Nedi jumped over the broom again. And again. The other negroes sang deep into the night.

Black John and Moses walked ahead of them on their way back. Under the reflection of the bright full moon, Christmas stopped and held Nedi's hands.

'We be comin' soon,' he yelled after the brothers. He smiled at Nedi. 'I think I'm dreamin'.'

She smiled. 'Because you dreamin''

'Your wound healin'?

'Ain't that bad no more.'

'Ain't gon stop me from bein' with my Nedi. Nothin' ever gon pull us apart.' He longed for her body. He looked at her soft jaw. Her locks. Her bright eyes. He felt proud. It felt like he waited a long time for her. He drew her closer and held her face close to his. They looked deep into each other's eyes. And searched each other's bodies with their fingers. He brought his lips to touch hers. She longed for his body in passion but wouldn't open her mouth. He buried his face gently into her uninjured shoulder, and she opened her lips and faced the sky with her eyes closed.

They laughed like children running to the Preacher residence. She held her left arm with her right hand and ran with care. Nedi's locks now hung loosely. Inside the slave dwelling they kissed. She wanted him quick but he needed to be slow because of her injury. He rubbed his fingers gently over the clot. Her faded pink dress fell to the bricked floor. He lifted her on to the straw bed. She rubbed her fingers over the grey quilt with black stripes. Cold wind blew into the room. The faint sounds of mermaids disrupted them but only briefly. He thought of the woman in the attic. With his eyes closed and his hands around Nedi, he encountered a vision. The pregnant runaway's body shook and moved in rhythm along with a man's. Mr. Preacher! Christmas stopped breathing in deeply and sat up. He felt the great need to squeeze the white man by the throat.

Christmas's spirit became fully alive in the attic. The woman, now alone, cried. He sank into her. She slept off. He sank further into her dream. She saw the thick and dense cloud coming. A purple form, like the wind, seemed to come over the clouds, darkening the earth. Black people fled in mass. They ran for their lives. The escaped woman, not pregnant here, carried her infant and ran. The screaming and crying of people were deafening. She fell but got up and looked back. A negro man bumped into her and she fell again and her eyes caught a moving fire in the sky. The fire seemed to lighten the earth, and moved through the purple clouds. It left sketches of horsemen in the sky, and these sketches became real riders thundering down to earth.

The woman awoke. Christmas rose out of the woman's dream. She trembled and struggled to get up. Her unborn child seemed to nudge against the front wall of her belly. She found her feet and struggled to the door leading out of the attic. She tried to open it but couldn't. She squatted and started to cry.

Christmas's spirit came back to his body. Morning came. He yawned. Nedi started to snore lightly. His crotch became itchy. He quietly put on his pantaloons and properly covered her before heading for the big house. On opening the wooden door of the attic, he saw the pregnant woman squatting in fright. He reached out and embraced her.

'You gon be fine.'

'I never gon make it if I don't leave now, Christmas.'

'Massa Preacher still plannin'.'

'I dream, Christmas. In the dream I see them white folks comin' to fetch me. I see them comin' from North Carolina, I tell you, Christmas. I got to go fetch me my freedom.'

'I go have a word with Massa,' Christmas said and gently pushed her away from his body. He gave a reassuring look and left her pacing between the walls of the attic.

He knocked on Mr. Preacher's bedroom door.

'Who's there?'

'Christmas, Mr. Preacher.'

Mr. Preacher opened the door and asked, 'What is it?'

'It's Naomi. She done had a bad dream and now wants to leave.'

Both of them left for the attic.

'Naomi, Christmas said you had a dream,' Mr. Preacher said on entering the attic.

'I gon leave,' the woman said.

'Give me until noon to talk to friends.'

'I gon leave, Massa.'

'We could send her off in a box, Massa,' Christmas said.

'Not in her state,' Mr. Preacher replied. 'She is pregnant.'

She began to advance toward the doorway.

'Wait.' Mr. Preacher stopped her.

'We can take you to Covington and, by the grace of God, the river is still frozen. Christmas can go with you, across to Cincinnati.'

She gave Mr. Preacher a hostile look.

'Get the carriage ready, Christmas.'

Christmas ran to his dwelling and found Nedi awake.

'You been in the hog house?'

'In the big house. Got to be goin' away with Mr. Preacher and the runaway woman.'

'Where?'

'Covington.'

'Wait,' she said.

He stopped.

'You see Moses?'

'No. Why that is?'

'He came lookin' for you. He wants to know if we heard of one Gabriel Prosser,' she said.

'Who that?'

'Moses say the man got hung for plannin' to kill them white folks... Now white people killin' black folks all over. Be careful where you go, Christmas.'

'I gon do that, my love,' Christmas said. 'Can you let Black John know I am off to Covington with Massa so he could tend to them hogs?'

'Come back to your love alive,' She said.

*   *   *

The carriage ambled out of Louisville with the sun still too shy to emerge. Horse legs and carriage wheels sunk in and out of different puddles littering streetways. Christmas could sense the woman's fears. She clutched her fingers to her elbows and breathed audibly. Her eyes were reddened. She kept looking backwards in great anxiety.

'Tell me about North Carolina,' Christmas said.

'Slave life there was work, work and work,' she replied. 'If it was just about work, I be the happiest negro woman alive. But them white mens gets you pregnant, and take away your child and still make you work. They done take my first three. No way I gon let them this time.'

'You come the right way.'

'You free and still stay on the farm with Massa Preacher?'

Mr. Preacher, still controlling the horses, cleared his throat.

Christmas felt the breeze rush against his groin leaving a tiny explosive itch. He wanted to scratch it. He struggled to look into the woman's eyes. 'Could find me no work. White people out there do black people bad,' he replied.

'I see why you here,' she said. In whispers, she continued, 'Your massa ain't good as he look. Seen no Quaker like him.'

'You right,' Christmas replied thinking about the vision he saw during the night.

'Christmas,' Mr. Preacher called out. 'If we come across patrols, you say Naomi is your wife.'

'Yes, Massa.'

'You ain't from here, I believe?' the woman asked Christmas.

'I born in Africa.'

Mr. Preacher brought the carriage to a stop in front of the Covington black river. Naomi hopped down, and Christmas did the same. Mr. Preacher shook his head in displeasure. The river wasn't stone frozen. A good number of broken cakes of ice floated on the river.

The woman smiled and said, 'Goin' to Cincinnati.'

Mr. Preacher gently hopped down. He placed a hand on his waist, and took off his hat. 'How can you make it?'

'Be watchin' me,' she said and started toward the river.

'Stop her,' Mr. Preacher said to Christmas, alarmed.

Christmas sighed. The floating cakes over the freezing waters were like waiting blades. He followed her. She leapt upon a cake and floated awkwardly on it, trembling and stepping onto another. And another again. The more she advanced, the louder Christmas and Mr. Preacher called out in panic. Her confidence increased, her stature straightened.

Christmas wanted to close his eyes. There were ripples and bubbles on every step she took toward liberty. Christmas took his first step in pursuit. And another. He saw Naomi's pace increase. He marvelled so much that he lost his footing and fell into the freezing water. She came upon a section that appeared to be sailing smoothly.

Christmas swam back to the bank. Mr. Preacher stared. Christmas's hands were almost stiffened by the freezing water. He looked at the frozen cake transporting the woman. It didn't look like an ordinary cake of ice. Mr. Preacher's telescope lying underneath the seat in the carriage came in handy. They continued to watch. Christmas got convinced Orinya's back transported her. The woman leapt off on the other side. Christmas saw his great alekwuafia leap into the air and sprout out his wings.

'Did you see that? What is that?' Mr. Preacher asked, alarmed.

Christmas couldn't move. Deep in thought, he wanted those wings. The cold water seemed to have frozen the blood flow in him. His clothes were all wet, and his entire body felt cold and weak. He started to cough and couldn't stop until he fell. Mr. Preacher bent over to check him. Christmas felt darkness come upon him. His spirit slipped into Oli'doma in a time of war. He saw his brother, Abah, on horseback slaying the Hausa raiders in attack. He put a sword in one attacker's stomach, got it out and took off the head of another. By the time the war ended, smoke filled the entire Oli'doma. Father and Mother survived. Father's other wives too. Oli'doma won in war. Huts were burnt down. The dead were littered around. Few people mourned. The chiefs gathered for a meeting. Night came before Christmas woke on the bank of the river. He saw Mr. Preacher seated before a fire.

PART FOUR

EMILY MARGARET

THE ANCESTOR, ONCE A LEOPARD MAN, WATCHED with folded arms from his realm. Christmas, more confident and matured in spiritual insight, made the bold journey into the world of the mermaids. Christmas walked with shoulders high between the walls of the kingdom, and flinched in response to the gazes of the many strange women he came across. He stood before Oda'nyaa's throne and pointed. The strange women under Oda'nyaa's reign despised this but Oda'nyaa smiled. Christmas recognised her smile of control, a smile of ridicule for him.

'You come to me yet you requested that I stay away from you?' she asked. 'That is a very costly request to make.'

'You left but failed to take with you the evil you brought upon me and Nedi – you know how much I want her pregnant. I know you have bound her womb.'

She laughed. 'Orinya Ogah only made one request – that I leave you alone and I have been away over the last four years.' She stood up in her splendour and walked slowly around him.

'The moon is my witness. I didn't summon you here. You came yourself, and I have the right to ask you to reopen your heart to me and treat me like the queen that I am.'

'That will not happen!' Christmas, in fury, leapt up. Wonder built up among the mermaids and they began to murmur amongst themselves. He remained suspended in the air. He got absorbed in this ability. He felt like he could levitate anywhere, with or without his body lying in the Preacher residence.

Oda'nyaa stood, impressed. 'You are becoming your true self. A flying crocodile from Oli'doma.'

Lightning struck. The sound of thunder followed and the whole place shook. Rain burst from above. Orinya appeared, kneeling on one leg and holding onto a stick. His face, downward. The mermaids all bowed.

'Orinya, *N'ya* as we agreed. I have stayed away for the past four years. It was he...' Oda'nyaa pointed at Christmas. '...who came here on his own.'

'*N'je,*' Orinya said quietly.

Still suspended, Christmas dropped gently onto the golden platform. 'I couldn't find you, Orinya, and the evil she left is consuming me,' Christmas tried to explain. 'I, a crocodile, should have impregnated Nedi by now but Oda'nyaa seems to...'

'Let us get away from here,' the masquerade interrupted him. 'You must never come back here.' The tall ghost raised a hand and powerful lightning struck the platform again. Christmas and Orinya vanished. No longer were they under the blue reflection of the moon in the waters. They were in Georgia, along the coastline of the black ocean. And not far away came the chants of the breeze. Chants of warriors. Chants which Christmas recognised. Chants from Ole'gbo. Orinya pointed, and Christmas saw them coming.

> *The black ocean brought us here*
> *The black ocean will take us back*

They were black men. Big men. Some fairer skinned. Some darker. There were nearly one hundred. All marching into the black ocean. Christmas watched the black ocean embrace the men. Christmas, surprised, opened his lips to speak, but his very own alekwuafia raised a hand to stop the words.

'Watch! Differentiate your kinsmen from the ones from Ole'gbo.'

The last of these men walked on deep into the waters until he could be seen no more. There came the sound of the flapping wings of buzzards. Some of these men in the form of vultures leapt up wet from the waters, journeying high into the sky. Their black feathers gradually darkened the clouds. A few others leapt in their human forms into the clouds. Their noise shook the ground on which Christmas stood.

'Look well and identify your kinsmen,' Orinya repeated.

Christmas peered further into the blackened sky and he longed to become like the few levitating men among the buzzards. 'I see them,' he whispered.

The flying men and buzzards headed west and soon disappeared.

'I brought you here to show you the worth of your ability. You are a flying man,' Orinya said. 'The slaves are going back home. Some to Oli'gra. Some to Oli'doma as you know. A good number of them to Ole'gbo.'

'I go home one day?'

'You will. You will at the right time.'

'Will I go with Nedi?'

'That I cannot say.'

'When is the right time?' Christmas asked.

'You are special. You know how you feel flying in the clouds? That burning energy that makes you feel omniscient, that you could go anywhere in body, spirit and mind all at once and see anything… You will experience that feeling in the future at the appointed times destiny has in place. *Aah gei je*,' Orinya said and looked upwards. 'Let's go somewhere else.'

This time, they vanished into the deep future, in the world of his seven-year-old reincarnated body. Olofu suspended his body in the air. Christmas and Orinya became the breeze in this surrounding area. The haunting eyes of the reincarnated boy's mother saw this and raised an alarm. She couldn't comprehend how her mute son acquired the ability to remain suspended in the air. She pulled his ears and pushed him. She called him a wizard, spat on him and called her new husband. She called the neighbours. She told them the son she bore out of wedlock seemed to be a wizard. People gathered. They encircled him. They wanted him to fly. But he wouldn't. They pushed him. They lifted him high and let him fall.

'This is not good,' Christmas said to Orinya.

'What appears bad isn't always bad,' Orinya replied, and the breeze gently quietened and the people of the future began to look around.

* * *

Thomas Jefferson became the president of the United States three years ago. And he established the state of Ohio a year ago. Christmas wondered if the *Achadu* of Oli'doma, Abakpa II, still lived. He didn't understand why the white man's president didn't have to die before being replaced.

Nedi still spent two days of the week in the Preacher residence. He saw how Moses whispered something to Nedi. If it hurt her, she didn't show it. She, in return, urged Moses to hire himself out to Mr. Peterson. Moses laughed it off. From a distance Christmas saw Mr. Preacher stare at her formidably without consideration over what she, Christmas or anyone else thought. She acted in the same manner to everyone in the Preacher residence including Mr. Preacher. She maintained her bright smile and avoided long conversations with the men of the residence. Conception in women may be a secret but not for long. Christmas felt overly excited; his journey into the world of mermaids yielded a fulfilled dream. He thanked his alekwuafia and made a new request. He wanted the ancestor to create a way for him, Nedi and the coming infant to Opialu. Christmas barked at Oda'nyaa to see if she could hear him and hurried toward the big house. He found Mr. Preacher coming down the stairs to the lobby.

'Massa, Nedi pregnant! Pregnant with my child.'

'I'm delighted to know that, Christmas,' Mr. Preacher said taking off his spectacles. 'I suspected all along. Come to the study.'

In the study, Christmas sat on one of the wooden chairs with red chaise. He thought for a moment. He shouldn't expect the white man to rejoice with him.

'You know that child, your child, will be born a slave?'

In a depressing realisation, Christmas nodded his head.

'I will speak to Mr. Peterson on the possibility of buying Nedi her freedom. I hate to tell you that I am unstable financially so you may have to save up as much as you can. I fear Mr. Peterson will offer a high price.'

Christmas's jubilation watered down. Afterwards, he walked Nedi down the road. He felt glad she didn't notice his grief.

'I can't wait longer to hold our infant, Nedi.'

'Me too,' she replied.

'I only got to work harder to purchase you, our infant, Ark and Sally from the horrible Massa Peterson.'

Back in his room, seated on his bed with his elbows against his lap and palms over his eyes, his spirit travelled. He walked through the corridor of his reincarnated future. He went gently into the sleeping place his future self. The dark room lacked life.

'You looking for yourself?' a voice said from behind him.

Christmas turned around and saw Oda'nyaa. He looked away. 'Stay away from my life. Orinya warned you.'

'How can I? It is hard.'

Silence.

'I can show you where he is.' Oda'nyaa walked toward him and took his hand.

'You mean Olofu?' Christmas said.

'Yes.'

Wise or not, he let her lead him, and they walked through the concrete wall into the thin air. They floated high into the sky, and above the sky Christmas saw a massive but gorgeous vulture crocodile. Its smooth body glided through the sky, roaring with a deafening voice. This strange creature carried lights by its sides. Beautiful yellow lights.

'Olofu is in the belly of that vulture crocodile. He is in it seated next to his mother. Both are among other people.'

Oda'nyaa led Christmas into the vulture crocodile's body. Their spirits penetrated the walls of the animal with ease. In their invisible forms they saw arranged seats all filled with people of different colours. White, brown and black. His reincarnated self, seated amongst them, smiled. Olofu seemed older now. Perhaps around twenty years old.

'How could a vulture crocodile have people living in it? Where are they going?' Christmas asked.

'It is the strength of the future. They are travelling.'

'To?'

'Ask him,' Oda'nyaa said.

Christmas looked at Olofu.

Something occurred. Christmas heard a shout from within him. He felt an urgent need to leave. The smile on Olofu's face became an oblivious stare. Christmas's spirit snapped back into his body in Louisville. He could hear Moses shouting. Christmas got on his feet, unbolted his door and headed toward Moses's room. The shouting increased. Mr. Preacher and Black John arrived. Black John kicked the door open. Moses, still shouting in bed and covered in sweat, kicked into the air repeatedly.

Christmas made an attempt to approach Moses, but Mr. Preacher waved him away and approached Moses himself. On reaching the bed, he took hold of Moses's body. What happened afterwards scared Christmas. Moses's eyes, which were closed, opened.

'Get your white filthy hands off,' Moses quietly said before launching out in madness. He jumped off his bed and continued to scream. 'You never should touch me. Don't try that no more. I swear, you be the first white man I kill.'

'Massa, we got to go,' Black John pleaded.

Mr. Preacher became infuriated. Christmas saw fear grip the white man. The combination of fear and infuriation made him look stupid.

Black John led Mr. Preacher out. The latter seemed to overcome his weakness, and he turned around and rushed back with a raised fist. Moses didn't expect it. He fell flat on his back, and blood spilled down the side of his chin.

'I should turn you out of my residence but that will only make me look bad. It is only because of Black John I let you stay. Try anything with me, the patrol men would come for you,' Mr. Preacher said and walked out.

Christmas asked Moses, 'What you do that for?'

'He never should touch me,' Moses replied and raised himself to sit up.

Black John sighed and went out.

'You be dyin' in your sleep if Massa never touched you.'

'How you know that?'

'You never gon know if no one done told you. You was screamin' in your sleep.'

* * *

Moses covered his face with his palm, stood up and walked toward the little window in his room. 'I dreamed of a man, and he done told me he gon save all them black folks. But he got captured by them white folks. They drag him and hang him. Hanged like Antonia. I sees him hanged, Christmas. Hanged like Antonia till his eyes bulged out. That's why I yell.'

'You ever see this man around?'

'I never saw no man like that fella in my wakin' life.'

Christmas sighed. 'I got to go,' he said.

'Wait.'

Christmas looked at him.

'You don't know that man, Preacher,' Moses began. 'You sees how he look at your woman. I fear he gon pounce on her any chance he got.'

This disturbed Christmas.

'You got nothin' to say?'

'If I got some I be tellin' you,' Christmas replied, thought and continued, 'Problem is this – I can't do nothin'. She ain't free like we is...'

'You think any negro in America free?' Moses asked. 'You ain't free, Christmas. Look at you. No black fella in the Preacher residence or even all of America free.'

* * *

Christmas, on the straw bed, kept scratching his crotch. He thought of Massa. The thought of Mr. Preacher trying to be with Nedi tormented him. His spirit found Mr. Preacher on the staircase of the big house. Christmas's spirit slunk into Mr. Preacher's mind. The man wondered why Moses hated him. It started after the emancipation. He came across Harriet's wooden infant walker in the lobby. Christmas kept it clean all through the passing years. It indeed symbolised and signified the importance of Harriet's existence. For some reason he found himself staring at it. Mr. Preacher thought he saw Harriet on it for a moment. The seat in the middle of the walker dangled. Mr. Preacher launched himself forward toward it. He felt a sudden hold on his collar from behind. He scrambled over the floor, turned around and saw Antonia hanging down from the ceiling holding on to a gory knife. What scared Mr. Preacher more were her insect-like legs and how they clung to the ceiling. The white man screamed, turned around and raced down the stairs and toward the door leading outside.

Christmas wasn't satisfied with the extent of her punishment. The man deserved more than this. For purchasing him at sixteen, for lusting after his woman, for messing with Antonia and – God only knew which – other slave women. Christmas prayed to his alekwuafia. His spirit drifted back into his body, and he headed into the dark for the big house. He saw Mr. Preacher approaching.

'Please take me to your dwelling,' Mr. Preacher pleaded holding onto Christmas's arm.

Mr. Preacher slept on Christmas's bed. Christmas found a space on the brick floor. Morning came. Mr. Preacher remained asleep. Christmas left to tend to the hogs. The hogs ate more than they usually do.

The white man woke on Christmas's return.

'Mornin', Mr. Preacher.'

'Morning, Christmas,' he murmured.

Mr. Preacher avoided looking at him in the eye. The master went back to the big house. He came back shortly and announced his intent to see Mr. Peterson in regards to the acquisition of Nedi. Christmas became anxious and his spirit trailed Mr. Preacher.

Thomas led Mr. Preacher into the Peterson mansion. It didn't take long for Mr. Preacher to notice how much this man, Thomas, disliked one negro in his household.

'I tell you that negro, Christmas, got no brain. So much goin' wrong in his life, Mr. Preacher.'

'Did you two fight over Nedi?'

'Trust me, Mr. Preacher, I got better taste. I would plead with you to come for my marriage ceremony, and I gon let you compare... I done told her before that she makin' a hell of a mistake marryin' that negro. But she stubborn. I pay no mind to her business since.'

Mr. Preacher followed the man through the lobby into Mr. Peterson's office.

Mr. Peterson pulled out a chair for Mr. Preacher. 'I see you have come for business.'

'I came to discuss Christmas.'

Mr. Peterson sighed. 'Would you like to avail yourself of a drink... bourbon?'

'No thank you. It has been in my recent manners to stay away from the bottle.'

'I wish I could claim to do the same, Mr. Preacher. I call any meeting of this sort business, especially if it has a connection to any of my properties.'

'In fact it does. We would like to purchase Nedi.'

'I presume the "we" in this context includes the negro, Christmas. Nedi's worth has doubled in price. Much appreciation to the good job your boy is doing.'

'It is not in my values anymore to refer to negroes as property, however I would like to hear the price.'

Silence.

'Presumably, I understand that your reason is to do this and hand her freedom?'

'You are absolutely right. I do this for the sake of Christmas.'

'You truly want to hear my response?'

Mr. Preacher nodded.

'No price.'

'You changed your mind?' Mr. Preacher asked.

'Don't put words in my mouth, Mr. Preacher. I need her to bear me that child, and if it's a girl, it gon fetch me thrice of what Nedi can fetch me any day. Come see me after the infant is born, Mr. Preacher.'

Mr. Preacher stood up to leave.

'I will walk you to the gate,' Mr. Peterson said. 'How come you don't use words, 'thee' and 'thy', when talking to non-Quakers like myself? I really enjoy hearing that style of speaking, you know...'

Christmas's spirit returned to the Preacher residence long before Mr. Preacher did. Christmas felt weak. Night soon came. Mr. Preacher walked into Christmas's room and sat on the bed with an arm on Christmas's shoulder.

'He said no. He asked me to come back only after she births the child.'

Christmas began to weep even before Mr. Preacher finished speaking. This Preacher white man wasn't even trying to be kind. He only desired to look good in the eyes of society. Mr. Preacher left. Christmas's spirit stepped into Olofu's world and saw Olofu crying too. This reincarnated soul held what looked like a banana across the side of his face. One end of the fruit-like material rested on an ear. The other end rested around his lower lip. Olofu seemed to be listening to this banana talk. Christmas paid closer attention and heard the voice of Olofu's mother.

'You are a wizard. You are the devil. Please leave my husband alone. Stop hurting him. Let me enjoy my life you evil being!' she lamented. Olofu's mother truly metamorphosed into a banana.

The sight pushed Christmas back into his own world, and in the middle of the night on his straw bed he kept thinking about it.

* * *

He woke up in the night, surprised to see himself floating in the clouds. Looking around him, he saw Oda'nyaa floating before him with her head cast downward. He could see Orinya in chains at a further distance. His tied hands were suspended from an unseen pole. The ancestor possessed no sign of life in him. Two mermaids floated around his supreme body. The colourful burial shroud appeared faded and torn in several places.

'What've you done to him?' Christmas asked Oda'nyaa.

Oda'nyaa didn't respond.

Strong winds approached. Moving clouds trembled. Christmas began to shudder.

'Oda'nyaa, answer me. What've you done to my ancestor?'

She lifted her head up.

He never saw her face this wrinkled.

He began to fall toward land and she let him. His clamouring voice resounded. She caught him moments later and levitated east with him. They soon landed. This place didn't look like Opialu. It looked familiar. The natives spoke Idoma, but this wasn't Oli'doma.

'This used to be the country of your ancestors. This is fifteenth century Kwararafa country!' she stated.

He could feel the hunger in the land. People ate dust to survive. People cried. Breastfeeding mothers lacked breastmilk. Children died.

'This,' Oda'nyaa said, 'was in the time of Orinya Ogah. He was a weak warrior and couldn't save his people. Look what the Hausas did to your people. The *Achadu* was captured along with seventeen thousand people who would become slaves in Hausa-land. Your own people, Ochigbo, became refugees in Orinya's time. The ones left prayed to me, and I rescued them. I let rain fall after years of drought. They worshipped me like never before. I took them out of that land as crocodiles, as red and black monkeys, as civet cats, as the owuna birds. And now you neglect me. Orinya ridicules me. You! You disappoint me. I am not a fool. Let me show you how it all began.'

She opened her arms and a violent wind left her aiming at him. Christmas's spirit became the gust. He moved at speed raising dust and dismantling huts. Christmas saw his people in the form of crocodiles journeying along with mermaids through the black river. True; they were led by Oda'nyaa, her younger self. There were red beads around her wrists. Her tail reflected intensely, brightly lighting the underwater. A shiny red and black clothing hung loosely around her chest and around her waist.

'They know me. They worship me. I give myself to you and you turn me down for a wretched woman. Orinya worshipped me. Who is he now to warn me?'

The wind died and Christmas desired to pray to the first one of all his ancestors to intervene. Oda'nyaa gently tossed his spirit into another realm by placing a finger on his shoulder. In this scanty and massive place, Christmas discovered a flowing stream. Beside the flowing waters, a leopard mated a beautiful woman. Christmas opened his eyes and found himself back in his physical body on the straw bed. He wouldn't pray.

* * *

In the summer of 1804, a hired carriage pulled up in front of the house. A gentleman got down and let two agile boys hop down. The boys ran toward the big house. The gentleman helped down a woman on a bath-chair with a little boy of about four on her lap. Christmas recognised them. He dried his washed clothes on the line in front of the dwelling, washed his hands and called out to Black John.

'Mrs. Preacher and them boys is back.'

'You lie!' Black John replied.

'You come see for yourself,' Christmas said.

They entered the lobby of the big house and saw the boys all seated around their father on the floor.

'Good afternoon, Mrs. Preacher,' Christmas said bowing. The gentleman beside her, moved away.

'Goodness, you have become a man in a short time. Is that you, Black John?' Mrs. Preacher asked.

'Yes Mrs. Preacher,' Black John said.

'Come embrace me folks,' she raised an arm.

She embraced them and said, 'I heard you all are free now. Why are you folks still here?'

'No place better than the Preacher residence, Mrs. Preacher,' Black John said.

'Come to my home in New York, you will find it better. There's work in the printing press close to where we dwell.'

'Ma'am, we happy here in Louisville,' Christmas said. 'What happen to you?' Christmas asked looking at her legs.

'Mrs. Preacher finds it difficult talking about it,' the man with her said. 'If you must know, she developed an ailment of the heart six months ago.'

'My brother, Gerald, is sounding too formal again,' Mrs. Preacher said, amused. 'It's a sign that I am not getting younger even though I'm just about to turn forty. The doctor says it is angina. Where is Moses?'

'I'm sorry, Fiona. I never learned about your ill health. Moses is one roguish fellow now and I entreat you earnestly not to see him. He has become a delinquent over the years,' Mr. Preacher said on getting up. The boys carried their luggage upstairs. Marcus, only fourteen now, looked more mature, quiet and composed. Eleven-year-old Simons chatted nonstop.

'I will see him. I don't believe that. Tell me it isn't true, Christmas,' Mrs. Preacher said.

Christmas didn't say a word.

She looked at Black John and got the same reaction. 'Gerald, can you take me to the quarters?' She looked at Mr. Preacher. 'You may have the boys for the summer. You may want to get a tutor for their schooling.'

The gentleman led Mrs. Preacher away. Christmas noticed the unusual complexion of the youngest of the boys. 'Look at Antonia's boy,' he whispered to Black John.

'I been wonderin'. So white that fellas may think he got no negro blood. But look at his hair. As dark as mine.'

They heard a shattering sound. Mrs. Preacher yelled. They all rushed outside.

'Hey, stop that before you hurt someone,' Gerald shouted.

'White man! You don't tell me what to do!' Moses replied.

'Come on, Moses. It's me. Don't you recognise me, Mrs. Preacher?'

'Ain't no slave no more,' Moses shouted back and they saw him pick up another beer bottle to throw.

The bottle thrown this time shattered on the wall of the big house. Gerald and Mrs. Preacher were behind the oak tree. Christmas and Mr. Preacher kept a safe distance watching.

Moses started to throw broken pieces of plank.

'How in God's name did he come upon beer bottles?' Mrs. Preacher asked.

'He has been stealing from me, no doubt,' Mr. Preacher replied.

'When did you start drinking,' she asked.

'I took to drinking for a period – after you left. It's been two years since I fell into those ways.' Mr. Preacher looked away.

Everyone soon retired to bed. In the middle of the night, Christmas woke to a sound. Someone entered the dwelling. He heard Moses shout. Christmas sneaked out of his bed. It got darker outside his room, but he could identify the man's figure in Moses's room. Standing by his door, he could see Mr. Preacher strangling Moses. The negro kicked into the air repeatedly until the white man left him. Moses, breathless and shocked, shifted away in fright toward the wall.

'I kill you next time you try harming any of my loved ones,' Mr. Preacher said.

Black John came out of his room confused, and Mr. Preacher headed out of the dwelling.

* * *

Christmas stood behind the door leading to Moses's room listening to Moses snore. He went back to his room but his spirit went further into Moses's room. The spirit peered over Moses's body and immersed into his dream. Moses's snoring stopped and he woke. He smacked himself hard on the head and struggled to turn onto his other side in bed due to the fat accumulation on his waist. In the dream, Moses lit the candle by his bedside and walked toward the door. He unbolted it and saw Christmas.

'What you doin' here at this time of the night?' he asked letting Christmas in.

Christmas took only two steps in, but the rest of the movement appeared to be in the air, a few feet above the ground.

'You floatin', Christmas? Damn!'

Christmas turned around to Moses and opened his eyes wide. The eyes were pure white with no pupils.

'You dead?' Moses asked quietly. 'You some ghost now?'

'I comes to talk about your misconducts.'

'It ain't by doin' some magic that you gon scare me like the white man did.'

'Why you do that, Moses? No doubt you a warrior. But you must choose the right road. I see for you a road where all negroes be warriors...'

The slave dwelling seemed to transform into a field with green lawns. There were infantry regiments of negroes in uniform marching to the admiration of their families.

'You ain't in the future. You long dead. This is the future you ought to be in. If you must live to join slaves that gon be warriors, you must change. You must change to be able to win against the white man,' Christmas said.

'Why show me?' Moses asked.

'To warn you. You ain't supposed to fights all fights. The time gon come when the real fight gon be won and when this happens some white and black folks gon die. But it a fight that ain't never gon be regretted. Negroes gon win.'

Moses woke. 'Hell. White man Preacher ought to change hisself first,' he muttered.

Christmas spirit swayed out of him. Morning came.

* * *

On the Monday of the following week, The boys were too noisy at their play for Christmas's liking. Their mother went back to New York and they wouldn't be seeing her for three months. Mr. Preacher went downtown with little Hugh in the buggy to pick up Miss Emily Margaret Thatch, a skilled teacher and daughter of a Quaker member in Lexington.

Mr. Preacher slowly guided the horse onto the premises. The woman, in a colourful dress, smiled before Black John helped her down.

Mr. Preacher introduced her to his household, firstly to his bigger sons. 'Emily Margaret will be living with us henceforth until it's time for you boys to return to your mother. She will ensure you all improve your geography, English language and arithmetic.' He turned to Emily Margaret and continued, 'The eldest is Marcus, the second is Simons and thou have of course met the little one, Hugh. Thou will add to thy commitment to educate the free negroes in this residence on reading and writing – that is Christmas and that, Black John.' He pointed.

The horse, still latched to the buggy that brought Emily Margaret in, lowered his head and sniffed at the lawn.

'It is my pleasure, Mr. Preacher,' she said.

Christmas watched her walk up to Marcus and Simons, shaking their hands. Simons appeared shy, rubbing his fingers through his hair. Moses watched from the front of the dwelling.

'Thou may want to do it this way, Miss Emily Margaret. Arrange for the boys' classes in the morning, and in the afternoon for Christmas and Black John... and Moses, if he is interested,' Mr. Preacher said.

'That would be Moses?' she pointed toward the dwelling.

Moses stood there with hands folded across his chest.

* * *

Mr. Preacher and Christmas spoke privately in the study.

'He is likely to agree to sell the child and his mother in the near future if it's a boy.'

'If it be a girl?' Christmas asked sounding worried.

'It would be hard, I must confess, Christmas,' Mr. Preacher said. 'You and I know that girls or women are worth more. He may sell if persuaded, I presume.'

'I talk to the butcher, Mr. Cooper, and he gon give me work.'

'How come you have such skill and I never knew?' Mr. Preacher asked.

'All I done learned, was from you, Mr. Preacher. How you butchered them hogs when I first come to you,' Christmas replied.

'Is that enough for Mr. Cooper to hire you?'

'He say he gon teach me more.'

'That's good Christmas. Wise decision. I will give you an increase too. Save as much as you can. I will see how I can help once Mr. Peterson confirms he will sell, and keep praying for a son.'

Christmas smiled.

Nedi, now heavier, arrived in the evening. Christmas led her to his room. She raised her blouse up, and he felt his child move.

'We've this white woman livin' in the big house now. She be teachin' us to read,' he said.

'Massa Peterson say that ain't right.'

'Because he want no negro better than hisself.'

'Why should any negro be better?' She turned around and he pulled her body close to his.

He couldn't answer. He left her and took a shirt hanging on a nail. 'I be back after the learnin'. It is somethin' you should be happy about. I gon read stories for my son one day.'

Black John, already there seated, held on to a nicely cleaned slate.

'Christmas, please take a seat and we can start,' Miss Emily Margaret said.

Christmas could hear the boys arguing upstairs.

'We will start by learning the alphabet, and I...' she stopped.

Christmas looked up, and traced her stare to the entrance of the sitting room. There stood Moses.

'You... are Moses?' she said counting her words.

Moses looked away but walked in and took a seat.

* * *

He started work right in front of the large factory by the corner of the market street. Christmas skinned a hog hanging from the tree in front of the butchery store of his new employer.

'You learning how to read and write, they say,' the butcher started the conversation.

'Yes,' Christmas said and thought about their first class. He wondered why Moses got interested in learning to read and write the white man's words. No one saw it coming. Not even Massa.

'You could teach me to read, to acquire the knowledge,' Mr. Cooper said.

'Ain't seen no white man who can't read and write,' Christmas said.

'You seen one today,' Mr. Cooper replied, and laughed. 'You got your infant yet?'

'Not yet.' Christmas carved off the head of the hog with a long blade.

'You got a name yet?'

'If a boy I gon call him Ijeyi. Means wise in my language, but I guess Mr. Peterson ain't gon let me,' Christmas said.

Mr. Cooper sharpened the two knives he held against each other. 'Ahh... That's true. Slavery, the evilest thing in Kentucky...'

Christmas arrived at the Preacher residence on time for the learning. Black John and Moses were already in the sitting room of the big house holding on to their slates. Miss Emily Margaret wrote the letters A to Z on the big board beside her. They all recited the letters. Later on Moses pulled out a sheet of a newspaper, stood up and handed it to Miss Emily Margaret.

'Read,' he said. 'Read it to us.' He sat back.

'Is this right...?' She looked at it briefly before scrutinising it momentarily. 'We are in September of 1804 and this... is dated about several months back. Never mind. Learning to read is acquiring full liberty,' she said displaying to them the page of the *Kentucky Gazette*.

Christmas knew Moses acquired the article from the same place he stole Massa's beers.

'The article Moses wants me to read is about New Jersey which is the last state in the north to abolish slavery,' Miss Emily Margaret said.

* * *

The very first month of winter arrived. He came back from the butchery early. It took some time before the learning began. He saw Marcus, Simons and Hugh running into the woods. Their father encouraged them to hunt possums on days like this. Christmas heard Simons shout. He heard them running. Silence. Christmas ran into the woods. He sighted them and stopped. Hugh and Marcus were confronted by a cobra with a raised head. Hugh clung on to Marcus's leg in profound fright. Christmas couldn't make any more noise. The cobra, a rare kind, looked dangerous. He could do nothing. A single bite meant death. Christmas saw Simons descending from the oak tree he took refuge in. He landed beside the cobra, lifted its tail and swung it away. Christmas couldn't contain his breath. They ran out of the woods. He too began to run. He stopped briefly and panted.

During class, they were taught to write some words like box, jug, run, rat, hog and hen. Christmas couldn't focus. He imagined becoming a snake in his next spiritual expedition. Miss Emily Margaret avoided looking at anything Moses wrote. She seemed forgetful too. Dusk came. Christmas went to sleep. His mind transcended through the roof bound for the dark sky. The ancestor, still in chains, appeared sallow and impassive. The air troops of mermaids with dangling cobras on their necks confronted him. They mocked him and laughed out loud. Orinya remained unresponsive. His burial shroud appeared much more worn. Oda'nyaa emerged beside Orinya, inviting more mockery from her maids. Christmas woke up. He wondered if he slept for too long. He heard the sudden sound of a duck and some movements. He lit his lantern and opened the little window. Under the moon rays, he saw a woman with a quilt wrapped around her running toward the big house from the dwelling and in the process, she kicked a tin bucket which released a wrangling sound. What did he see? His heart skipped. Miss Emily Margaret truly visited the dwelling. Christmas found it hard getting back to sleep.

She visited Moses. He once heard a tale of a black man having sexual relations with a white woman. He feared for Moses. He could get himself killed.

He worried about something else. Oda'nyaa still held Orinya in captivity. She may be back in his life. She could summon him anytime. She could even come to his room any moment. She could hurt Nedi again. He wandered desperately into the future. Into Olofu's dark bedroom.

'Why are you sad?' Olofu, seated on the bed, asked.

'I thought you are dumb and couldn't talk,' Christmas asked.

'My spirit speaks and it is very much alive in me now.'

Christmas felt the soft bed with his palms. 'What this bed made of?'

'Foam,' Olofu replied.

'You mean feathers or straw?'

'I said foam,' Olofu repeated.

Christmas sighed and sat down. 'I'm worried.'

'Why worry over things that are dead to my world? They don't exist to me...' Olofu dug out a beautifully designed black box and pressed a button on the top of it. The music which exuded jolted Christmas.

'What sort of magic do you practice in your world?' Christmas asked.

'You have seen nothing,' Olofu replied.

'I have seen a lot. Last time I came, your mother was a banana,' Christmas argued.

'Stop insulting my mother.'

'Why should I lie?' Christmas replied. The music coming out of the black box distracted him. 'Take that box away.'

Olofu turned off the music and placed the box back underneath his bed. He stood to his feet, found a button on the wall and pressed it, igniting a candle light in the middle of the ceiling. This got Christmas sprinting around the room before leaving for his room in Kentucky. In this room he could hear Olofu's laughter.

Christmas tended to the hogs in the morning. On his way to the big house he found Black John carrying a load of clean dishes. 'You been busy, I see,' Christmas said.

'Need to work to earn me money, Christmas.'

'You still go about catchin' chickens?'

Black John put down the load of dishes. 'Christmas, please don't say nothin' to Massa.'

'Who say I gon say a thin' to Massa,' Christmas asked. 'I heard the sound of one last night. Must belong to those white church folks across the road. I gon go with you the next time.'

Black John placed a hand in his pocket. 'You knows how I love chickens, Christmas. And you knows we hardly eat it here. To spend my hard earned money buyin' one is foolish.'

Christmas thought. A sacrifice of chickens could save his alekwuafia. His father used to do it. And even Abah, his brother.

Black John lifted the load of dishes and headed toward the dining room.

Christmas found Mr. Preacher in his study writing.

'How can I help you today?' Mr. Preacher asked.

'I need to talk to you, Massa.' He wanted to raise his concern about Moses's affair with Miss Emily Margaret.

'And what is it?' Mr. Preacher fixed his stare on him.

Miss Emily Margaret came to stand in the doorway. Christmas couldn't look her in the face.

'I... I... don't know how to say this but... but...' He rubbed the back of his head and thought of the sight of Miss Emily Margaret during the night. 'The boys was in the woods yesterday,' he began. 'They came across a snake.'

'You sure about that, Christmas? Why has no one reported this to me until now?'

'I thought they was goin' to tell you.'

'How did it happen?'

'The cobra, Massa, raised its head to attack young Massas, Marcus and Hugh, but young Massa Simons take the tail and flung it away.'

'Morning, Christmas.'

'Good mornin', Miss Emily Margaret... Massa, you must excuse me,' Christmas said and headed out of the room. He stopped just outside the door to keep listening them.

'What?' Christmas heard Emily Margaret ask.

Mr. Preacher laughed. 'What do thee mean?'

'I hope it is not a bad decision that I stay under thy roof. I'm not comfortable with the way thou stare at me.'

'Don't disregard my integrity, Miss Thatch.'

Christmas sighed quietly and walked on. He felt glad he said nothing about Moses.

* * *

Christmas put three hog bladders in his bag and closed the butcher store. He intended to give them to Mr. Preacher's sons – hence they might be kind toward him and not hold any grudge against him for reporting the incident of the previous day. Back in the residence, he brought out the bladders and blew some air into them. They became a bit hardened and round enough to be played with. He knotted their opening with some strings and headed toward the big house. Hugh grabbed one of the balls.

Miss Emily Margaret, more focused and enthusiastic, taught well during the learning session. They learnt to write a couple of phrases. The lady held her shoulders high, walking mostly toward Moses to see his progress. Toward the end of the class, Christmas glanced through the window. He noticed a negro boy, about six years old, in the compound kicking one of the hog bladders around. Christmas recognised him from the Peterson plantation. Miss Emily Margaret soon finished for the day and Christmas walked out to meet the boy.

'What you doin' here?' Christmas asked the boy.

'To look out for you,' the boy said. 'My grandma wants you. Aunty Nedi done born. It a boy.'

Christmas got lost at first. His mind instantly lit in elation. He looked up.

Moses embraced him from the side. 'Good news, Christmas. You ought to go see them now.'

The news made him giddy. The world felt strange. Black John held his hand out. He looked into Black John's face but didn't make out what Black John's gesture meant. On his way to the Peterson plantation, all the children followed him excitedly. Mr. Peterson, in front of Nedi's cabin, held the new born. Around the bare-chested slaveholder were a few slave children trying to touch the newborn. Nedi, seated by the corner, held a pale look. The elderly midwife stood by her side.

'Christmas, come see the child you bore me.' Mr. Peterson chuckled.

Christmas took the child and looked into its wary eyes. Crocodile eyes already. He placed the child on his chest and walked toward Nedi. 'You fine?'

'Course I am… I suffered all mornin',' Nedi replied.

'Christmas, I can give you the chance of naming the child,' Mr. Peterson said.

Christmas's heart leapt in great delight. He named the child born to him in December of 1804 Ijeyi – he who is wise.

* * *

Night came. Christmas's spirit left the dwelling, saw Mr. Preacher asleep in the big house and settled upon his body. Christmas took over his mind and eventually, his dream. The sleeping white man, taken back to his boyhood days in Virginia by the massive wings of the slumbering night, shifted his body restlessly in bed. The howling sound of flying Indians filled his ears. The clouds couldn't even be seen. No place to run to. His father warned them about Indians. The hogs squealed noisily. The flying Indians landed. One of them approached with a raised sword. Little William passed out. He didn't know if the sword struck him. He didn't know if he died. He woke and realised his clothes, his entire body, drenched in blood. The gory bodies around him were lifeless. His father lay over the wooden table, his tongue hanging out. Three negro slaves owned by his father lay upon each other, all dead. This included George, his father's closest and most notable slave.

William Preacher passed out again. He opened his eyes hours later and found himself surrounded by his father's friends – all Quakers. They told him George carried him and fled away from the Indians. They told him George ran with two arrows stuck to his back. 'He picked thee up and ran like a warrior to safety. Let his soul rest well.'

'But I woke after the Indians killed everyone and I saw everyone dead. I saw father dead, I saw George dead,' William Preacher exclaimed.

In his Kentucky house, Mr. Preacher woke up breathless from revisiting the scene. Christmas still clung to his mind. It rained heavily, and the rain tapping on the roof wouldn't let him go back to sleep. He heard a sound downstairs. Mr. Preacher walked out of his room and looked. Miss Emily Margaret. Her dress seemed profoundly wet.

'Where have thou been?' He startled her.

'Oh, Mr. Preacher.' She breathed in. 'I went out to catch some air.'

'In the rain?'

'I... I... went before the rain. I was sitting on the front steps and nodded off...'

'Hmm...'

'I must change my clothing, Mr. Preacher,' she said heading toward the guest room.

Mr. Preacher knew the truth. He saw her talk to Moses during the day and saw the affection they showed each other.

For the next fortnight, Christmas anticipated more dramatic reprisals, and his spirit kept hovering within the big house and searching the thoughts of vigilant Mr. Preacher. The white man started to drink again. He sat in the study by the burning candle and emptied several bottles. He dozed off briefly. On waking he saw Emily Margaret staring at him.

In the mornings he drove the wagon downtown to fetch more crates of beer. In one of the Quaker meetings he fell asleep and the others in attendance waited in silence. On waking he claimed the spirit instructed him to sleep. He further claimed he dreamt and in his dream he saw rain drizzle upon America for days. Everywhere became flooded. Houses and children were taken. And the Quakers all prayed for this not to occur. Only Christmas, in absence, knew the words were lies. One Sunday night, Christmas again seeped into his mind. The white man, drunk and excited, sang until he fell asleep on the cushion in the sitting room. Emily Margaret's shadow moved over him. He opened his eyes and saw her in the doorway. He got to his feet and staggered toward her.

'Thou going to Moses again?'

'Dare not question my character, Mr. Preacher,' she replied.

'I know. Everyone knows. What do thee find attractive in a negro that thou would prefer one to... one of thine own race?'

'I don't believe the words thou have just spoken,' the woman said.

Christmas felt mortified.

Mr. Preacher launched himself at her and grabbed her shoulders. Christmas hated this.

'Please don't,' the woman pleaded.

'I am the man thou should desire.' He grappled her against the wall and forced his lip on hers. 'Not that negro.'

'Mr. Preacher, please let me go,' she said and managed to push him away before running out of the house.

Christmas, relieved, separated himself from Mr. Preacher. Christmas's spirit watched the white man move about in frustration.

'Don't come back here, whore.' Mr. Preacher looked around before he staggered upstairs. He fell onto his bed leaving the door ajar.

* * *

Christmas wondered if Mr. Preacher ever tried to have Nedi. Perhaps the latter just sealed her lips about it. He could kill the white man if he got to know. Christmas didn't see Emily Margaret the next morning. But he saw her with Black John later in the evening fetching her belongings from the big house. A lot changed in a few days. Mr. Preacher's boys were sent back to their mother in New York. Miss Emily Margaret rented an apartment near the courthouse but still came in the evenings to teach Christmas, Black John and Moses. They used the dwelling for the learning now and not the big house anymore. Neither Christmas nor Black John asked why. Sometimes Moses chose to attend.

On one quiet weekend Miss Emily Margaret led an elderly man in a grey plain suit to the residence.

'This is my father, Christmas,' she said. 'He has just come from Lexington.'

The man nodded at him.

'Good to meet you, sir.' Christmas led them to the big house. Mr. Preacher didn't expect to see them. Christmas could see the shame in Mr. Preacher's eyes. Mr. Preacher led Miss Emily Margaret and her father into the sitting room and closed the door. Christmas, left in the hallway, wondered. He heard the sound of glass tumblers and placed his ears over the knob of the door.

'Thou letter reached me in Lexington, and I was extremely concerned by the manner in which thou vacated this premises, my dear Emily Margaret,' the old man began.

Christmas heard the sound of a chair slowly dragged over the floor.

'Mr. Preacher, I cannot wait to hear thou side of the story so that I, in my aging wisdom, can repair the wrongdoing.'

'Papa, there's nothing to fix,' Miss Emily Margaret responded. 'I feel betrayed in the first place. How can thee let thy own daughter come live with this wretched man?'

'Stop it, daughter,' the man pleaded.

'She is right, Mr. Thatch. I'm a worthless man. But... Miss Emily Margaret, I would like to apologise for my wrongdoing. It was the liquor.'

'To be frank with ye,' Miss Emily Margaret's father began again, 'I do admit that it wasn't right in the first place to ask Emily Margaret to come live here. I am disappointed in thee, Mr. Preacher. A Quaker should detest liquor.'

Silence.

'I entrusted her in thy care,' Mr. Thatch continued. 'She is only twenty years old.'

Christmas could hear the man's voice break. A sudden scrambling of furniture followed. Mr. Preacher yelled.

'How dare thee,' Miss Emily Margaret said raising her voice.

Christmas waited, exhaled twice and opened the door.

He found Mr. Preacher on the floor beside a broken side chair. Miss Emily Margaret and her father were on their feet. The woman held a stern look.

Christmas squatted beside Mr. Preacher. He saw a cut above Mr. Preacher's left eye. 'Who done did this, Massa?' Christmas asked.

'It doesn't matter,' Mr. Preacher whispered, and held onto Christmas's hand.

PART FIVE

IJEYI

CHRISTMAS JOURNEYED THROUGH the sophisticated roads of the future. He saw and felt the places his reincarnated being went to. The scattered dust settled, and Christmas became the road.

Olofu carried with him a set of cards. He stopped the commercial cart with magnificent wheels. The cart drove on its own with the driver controlling the wheels using a round rusted tool. Christmas enjoyed the gliding effect of the wheels over the black hardened ground.

The twenty-something year old Olofu got in. He showed the young mulatto driver one of the cards with the address of his destination.

The man drove through the summertime future of Louisville.

For a moment the passenger enjoyed looking at the other carts without horses. The carts sped past like lightning.

'You from around here?' the driver asked.

Olofu selected one of his cards, scribbled on it and showed it to the man.

'You from Africa?'

Olofu nodded.

He got dropped off at the Preacher residence. He looked around and followed the direction leading to the big house. Christmas felt proud his reincarnation found this place. The future got to remember Christmas's days in America. However, the house looked different. The walls which used to be milk white and not so new were now pure white and new. The flowers around the house never used to be there. And what happened to the little puddles all around? The grounds which were once covered in patches of carpet grass were now covered with bricks.

Two middle-aged women were in the lobby. They welcomed Olofu with smiles. He wrote 'tour' on one blank card and showed it to them.

'You are here for a tour. I am Maggie and this is Sarah,' the bigger of the two women said. 'I will be showing you around.'

He showed her another card which said: My name is Olofu and I have a disability. Not able to talk.

'I noticed. Alright, we can start.'

She led him through the lobby pointing out the candles and explained how they were made by the slave residents. She showed him a room with a reading desk made of mahogany. The chair in front of it appeared to have been woven using bamboo threads. The tour guide said the owner of the resident, Mr. William Preacher, bought the house in 1790.

'Mr. Preacher used to be a Quaker but wasn't consistent with their practices. The gentleman held slaves until early in the nineteenth century. He freed them after a lot of pressure from his Quaker friends. It might surprise you that Mr. Preacher left the Society before his death. The truth is that his beliefs were unknown. Let's go to the sitting room.'

Christmas sighed. All the furniture of his time were no more. Deceit. The woman showed Olofu the sitting room and said, 'The red cushions are all made of horse hair.' The woman showed him the room William Preacher's sons stayed in whenever they came for the holidays. 'Records had it that Mr. Preacher separated from his wife in 1795, and she spent the rest of her life in New York.'

She showed him the kitchen house.

'The slave woman once in charge here committed a terrible crime. This happened prior to the period Mr. Preacher freed his slaves. She murdered Mr. Preacher's little daughter, Harriet. She was only a child.'

The woman proceeded to the meat house and described how pork used to be salted and preserved. She showed him the spring house, and explained how milk and other food were preserved in the days. They walked further behind the big house. She showed him a tomb. The inscription read:

Christmas
1774 – 1840

Olofu shook his head in disagreement. He selected one of his cards displaying the word, 'ancestor'. And the road which brought him here frowned.

'I do not believe this. You don't mean it. Christmas was your ancestor?'

He got out a pen, found a blank card and wrote on it: He didn't die in Kentucky. He went back to Africa.

'Really?' the woman said quizzically. She didn't believe him.

Some child laughed. Somebody ran across the corridor. The woman turned around in fright but saw nothing. The seat of the wooden walker next to the children's room entrance dangled.

* * *

Emily Margaret stopped showing up during the winter of 1804. Moses, now thirty-four, isolated himself to his room for months on hearing of her departure. In this first month of 1812, the smell of war got stronger in Kentucky. Stories were heard. Horrific stories. Christmas could read almost anything now although he still struggled with spelling. He appreciated Miss Emily Margaret. Now thirty-eight, he could read simple sentences. It felt like magic.

One evening Christmas took some milk into the spring house, and returned to the dwelling to meet Black John and Moses consuming a roasted chicken, a product of Black John's theft. He felt bad they didn't invite him to partake in the theft, but still joined them in devouring the pieces on the plate. He thought of Orinya. Oda'nyaa still held him. Eight years since she shut the ancestor's door to the physical world. This chicken, he thought, could be offered in sacrifice to break the chains. It may work. It may not work. The chances of Orinya being free for him again were uncertain. He could try buying some chickens, but he needed to keep saving money to buy his wife and son.

'How much y'all think a chicken gon cost me?' he asked, licking his fingers.

Moses and Black John looked at each other and started laughing irrepressibly.

Christmas nodded his head. 'Only ask a question. I knows I could find me four or five chickens but...'

'Why do you ever think of buyin' a chicken? We gon go out there, Christmas, and catch us some chickens some other time,' Moses said.

Christmas sighed. 'Ain't feelin' right about it.'

'Let me tell you somethin', Christmas,' Moses began. 'White people feel right about nothin'. These folks gone Africa and stole them negroes. Black people. They done stole my ancestors. They done stole you. Don't waste no money. White folks all same. Forget all the Christian or Quaker thins' they comes up with. Negroes got to start waitin' for their own messiah.'

'Moses. Not all white mens is same,' Black John interrupted.

'Black John, I knows you sayin' this cause Mr. Preacher freed us, but we ain't supposed to be slaves in the first place. We is royal folks...' Moses replied. 'Look at how he done separate Mama from us. Look at how he got Antonia killed.'

* * *

Orinya's captivity troubled Christmas. The rumoured war expected in Louisville troubled him too. Nedi and his son were too precious to him. They were always on his mind. They shouldn't experience war. The Indians, people said, were going to join forces with the British in kicking President James Madison out of the White House and take over all of the United States. His spirit swayed out of the building through the roof. The blurry vision of Orinya in chains came back. The blur soon cleared, and he saw Oda'nyaa in the clouds lift up a blinding sword, and with great might she swung it in front of Orinya's lifeless body aiming for the neck. The sword struck the neck, and Christmas's spirit felt the pain. A detonation deep down in the throat. Christmas's body lying in the Preacher plantation flinched. Christmas's spirit saw Orinya jerk forward and become lifeless. Christmas fled his own, his alekwuafia, and headed in search of his wife and child.

He found Nedi sitting in front of her cabin, sieving some flour. Her mind, like the morning rainbow, embraced him. Through her eyes he saw her master head out with Ijeyi through the gate in the buggy. Nedi, now thirty-two years old, dropped the pan aside and followed discreetly at a distance. Ijeyi's locks were now visible. The seven-year-old looked too tall for his age. He behaved like a fifteen year old. The boy, strong and zealous, carried out Christmas's tasks in the hog house of the Preacher residence without help on the days of visit. He spoke few words. Hardly shy. Christmas hated the tavern Mr. Peterson often took Ijeyi to. Christmas really hated it. Mr. Peterson, a drunk, sang all night long each time he came home from the tavern, and slept all through the following day. She saw Mr. Peterson lash her son several times in the past. Once for refusing to drink more liquor even after taking half a jar to the entertaining display of the tavern audience. The owner of the tavern, no doubt, loved this. People loved to see a small negro boy drink hell. Other negroes weren't allowed in there. The white men in the tavern were jollier each time Mr. Peterson showed up with his negro boy. They enjoyed the boy's presence. They enjoyed seeing his drunkenness. They loved his strange tales. The small negro boy always told this never changing tale of the first man ever to exist in the world. How the man, parented by a leopard and a beautiful woman, walked on earth for the first time. They interrogated him on how he thought animals made babies? How humans made babies? They laughed into the night.

She walked for half an hour to the tavern. Nedi could see and hear Mr. Peterson already singing in merriment. Through her eyes, Christmas could see the other men in the tavern singing and hollering in delight. Ijeyi awaited Mr. Peterson's instructions. Nedi wiped her watered eyes, turned around and headed for the Preacher residence. She planned to spend the night in the residence without Ijeyi. Christmas's spirit left her to return to his room. It took a little time before he heard her voice out in the dwelling's sitting room.

'Howdy, Moses,' she said.

'How is the young man, Ijeyi, doin'? Your damn Massa ought to let you bring him with you,' Moses said.

Christmas came out of the room. Black John, seated on the old wooden stool, smiled.

'Ain't allowed to bring him along on Thursdays,' she replied.

'That ain't fair,' Black John said.

'We got to spend time together as man and woman,' Christmas said.

'Where he at now?' Black John asked. 'Ijeyi?'

'With Massa,' she replied.

'A white Massa so fond of a black boy. Christmas, be keepin' a close watch,' Moses said sarcastically.

Christmas forced a smile. 'I'm just the father of the slave boy owned by Mr. Peterson.' He led Nedi to his room and bolted the door.

'You ought to learn to keep your mouth shut about some thins',' he said to Nedi.

'Ain't my fault we slaves,' she said.

'Ain't sayin' that.' Christmas sighed.

'Eight years now since you say you was goin' to convince Mr. Peterson to sell us.'

'Right now, I got just half of the money to buy you. I need to save some more.'

'I would like to do some extra work outside the Peterson plantation to help out,' she said. 'Not sure Massa Peterson gon let me.'

'I got to keep savin', Nedi. The day gon come that we all be free. You, me and Ijeyi. After the time come we gon start savin' to help buy Ark and Sally their freedom.'

* * *

President Madison officially declared war on the Indians and the British. Louisville still possessed an aura of calm but people worried about the future.

Christmas threw the well-bucket into the well. A Shawnee with a luxuriant silver colour ponytail hanging down his back entered the premises and smiled broadly on sighting Christmas. It appeared unusual for an Indian to come into the Preacher residence. Christmas's heart froze for an instant, but the man's pose and demeanour conveyed no threat. The declaration of war, on the other hand, made this man an enemy. The Indian looked different from others Christmas saw in the clapboard houses on the outskirts of town, perhaps because of his attire. It wasn't the usual Shawnee breechclout and leggings. No poncho either. It wasn't usual for an Indian to adopt the white man's dress style and mannerisms. He wore a long black suit jacket over a grey shirt and a white hat on his head. He bowed before he began speaking.

'My name is Edward, and I would like to see Mr. Preacher.'

Christmas finished pouring the water into a bigger bucket and said, 'Wait here.' He went to the big house, and found Massa in the study.

'Mr. Preacher, there's this Indian fella here to talk to you,' Christmas said. 'Says his name is Edward.'

Mr. Preacher, now forty-seven with patches of grey hair, took off a reading glass and stared at Christmas. 'Does he bring trouble?'

'Doesn't look so, Massa.'

Mr. Preacher closed his book and followed Christmas to meet the man.

'Good day Mr. Preacher,' the man said.

'Good morning,' Mr. Preacher replied.

'Is this a good time to talk to you?' the Indian asked.

Mr. Preacher nodded his head and gestured at Christmas to leave. Christmas headed to the farm house with the bucket full of water. The Indian soon left. Christmas returned to see Mr. Preacher.

'He came to seek help for some fugitive slaves who arrived at his place last night. The only information they brought with them was my name.'

'You trust the man, Massa?

'Do I have a choice?' Mr. Preacher replied.

'How many they is?'

'Four, he said.' Mr. Preacher placed a foot on the raised platform of the well. 'We must be careful. Louisville has become dangerous. War is coming but slave catchers are everywhere. We will go to his place tonight.'

'Ain't he livin' in the woods, Massa?'

Mr. Preacher stared at Christmas and thought for moment. 'Christmas, this one is different from his savage brethren. He is civilised and perhaps lives in a descent cottage.'

The sky turned dark. Christmas and Mr. Preacher left quietly in a wagon into the very first night of spring. They were welcomed by Edward and some of his relatives. A white woman among them smiled but said nothing. Four negro men climbed into the wagon. The fugitives were all in thick coats. They looked anxious. One of them spoke of his shock on seeing Edward and the white woman living together as man and wife.

* * *

On his way back from work, he met some Igbo-speaking black men and women. He started up a conversation with one of them – a stout man with tribal marks on his face. These people were returning from a long day in a rice plantation.

'My village was no far from your people back in Africa,' Christmas said.

On hearing this, all of them took interest in him. They wanted to know the name of his village. Some of them knew the people of Oli'doma but never heard of Opialu. One even mentioned his stepmother originated from Oli'doma.

'What it gon be like on the rice plantation?' Christmas asked.

'Money good but very dangerous,' the stout man said. 'People say war is comin' to Kentucky. I think now is a good time to save as much as a nigger can before it comes.'

Christmas wanted to know what good money meant. He learnt work on the rice plantation could fetch him thrice of his current earnings. Christmas desired such work and asked the stout man how he could hire himself to the rice farmer.

The stout man called Fred said, 'Can you wait for us early tomorrow mornin' at the butchery side of the market?'

Christmas got back to the Preacher residence and saw Black John and Moses hopping and diving over the lawn. He got closer and realised they were catching grasshoppers and storing them in a little wooden box.

'What that for?' Christmas asked.

'To lure them chickens,' Moses replied laughing. 'You comin' with us, Christmas.'

'You gon join us?' Black John added with a sheepish grin. 'There some fat hen in bakery down the road.'

He must partake this time. He changed clothes to a worn red shirt and a milk coloured pair of pantaloons and headed to the kitchen to chop up the salted pork kept aside. Black John joined him afterwards to help, and later took Massa's dinner to the big house.

They headed down the bakery. The moon shone in the dark. Moses shoved his hands into the chicken house. A chicken squawked in protest. Moses got out the body of a white chicken with his fingers wrapped around the beak to prevent more noise. The grasshoppers in their possession were useless.

'More in there,' Moses whispered.

Black John knelt and grabbed two without the slightest sound. His palms covered both chickens' heads to shut their beaks.

Christmas seized two but held them by the feathers. Both birds shook in fright and shrilled loudly to frighten the rest of the chickens in the cage. Black John and Moses started to run. Christmas followed.

They got back to the Preacher residence. Moses severed the heads of each chicken and placed them on the lawn. Christmas fetched a basin from the terrace and thrust it before Black John to drop the birds into.

'Christmas, you make the fire,' Moses said.

'Ain't roastin' mine,' Christmas replied.

Moses looked up, met his brother's eyes and they laughed.

'Ain't banterin',' Christmas added. 'I got to sacrifice them.'

'What damn sacrifice?' Moses asked, hands on his waist.

'Makin' a sacrifice to my ancestor.'

Black John sighed and said, 'Where was your ancestor when them white folks put you in the boat in Africa?'

'You don't say that.' Christmas stood up to confront Black John. Their foreheads were almost against each other. He stared angrily into Black John's eyes.

'Christmas,' Moses spat. 'Do what you got to do.'

Black John turned away.

Black John and Moses started to set up the fire by the side of the dwelling to roast their fowls. Christmas put on his shoes and headed down to the black river with the two dead fowls in a sack. The quiet night air smelt of dust. Some shouting could be heard from a small house, a known residence of a free negro couple. He got to the bank of the black river. The wind rushed out at him. He chanted:

> *Alekwuafia be free*
> *Let the chains of the mermaid fall*
> *Be free again*
> *Abutu Eje, hear this*

He flung the dead chickens into the river and darkness clouded his vision. He felt his body lose every ounce of energy, falling to the ground like a piece of cloth. His soul sped around the earth, and he saw many things. He saw Opialu, his father's constant sacrifice to the ancestors, his brother's constant casting of chickens into the black river. Orinya remained in chains. Christmas saw himself flinging a headless chicken on the waters. He saw the torn and worn-out clothes of the chained ancestor come back together. He watched the clothes glow. The colours of his burial shroud transformed slowly from its faded colour of death to red, yellow and blue. Orinya, still in the midst of guarding mermaids, shook off the chains which held his palms together for eight whole years.

All the mermaids began to panic. Oda'nyaa saw this and she screamed. Orinya cried out. Their voices met in the form of lightning. Orinya became free. Christmas, in his bodily form, felt himself staggering. He felt like a headless chicken falling into the river. Someone caught him from behind. Orinya held him and allowed rays to run out of his eyes deep into the sockets of Christmas's.

'Never sacrifice stolen chickens to me again,' the masquerade said.

'…but my father and my brother, both have been sacrificing their own chickens and still…'

Orinya interrupted in a thunderous voice which shook the ground. 'Because they are not me, and I cannot be present in their lives as I'm with you!' He let Christmas fall. Christmas could see only darkness. Overwhelmed by weakness, his eyes opened to a vision. He saw Nedi in a place like Opialu. She placed a large black earthen pot on her heat. He approached her to look in it but she wouldn't let him.

Christmas soon found himself alone with his ancestor on the bank of the black river. 'What was in the pot? Was he really an incarnation of his ancestor?

'You didn't realise it? We are indeed three persons,' the masquerade said. His wings sprouted out his back. 'I need to go and deal with Oda'nyaa. For now you must find a way to look into that black pot.' Orinya leapt into the air.

Christmas watched the masquerade ascend toward the sky. He got on his knees and wept. His spiritual eyes opened and he glimpsed everything from the birth of Orinya to his death in the sixteenth century. He experienced all the bruises and injuries of Orinya's war. He saw the faces of every wife his ancestor married. He, Christmas, once existed as Orinya. He felt like flying away from Louisville. He longed for Opialu. But even if he could, he wouldn't, since Nedi and Ijeyi were now part and parcel of his soul.

* * *

Louisville became very noisy on this day. Streets were being named. Christmas didn't understand how streets could be named like humans. Moses and Black John seemed excited about it. Mr. Preacher called the process ungodly. Before Christmas left to lie on his straw bed, he inquired about street name assigned to the Preacher residence.

'River Road,' Mr. Preacher said. 'They can't even find proper names.' He crossed his legs and continued reading the newspaper on his lap.

Christmas liked the name but didn't say. He thought of the Peterson plantation imagining a suitable street name for its area. He thought about Nedi and Ijeyi. Sleep crept in and his spirit leapt into the future. He saw Oda'nyaa in bed with Olofu. Her hands were around Olofu's body. Christmas saw Oda'nyaa bury her head below Olofu's chest. A boy younger than fifteen. Christmas couldn't move in his spiritual form. He became the moans exiting Oda'nyaa's and Olofu's lips. The latter yearned, and the mermaid moved. Christmas, lost in wonder, desired to have Oda'nyaa.

* * *

The next morning Christmas waited for the rice plantation workers along the butchery side of the market. Mr. Cooper's butchery, still shut, would open in three hours. They named the area, 'Market Street'.

The rice plantation workers came by, and he joined them. Stout Fred smiled at him but seemed to be in a fierce argument with one of the women in the group. They walked a long distance toward the river. Along the streetway, people registered their boats to be ferried into New Albany.

'Tell Mr. Clinton you a rice farmer from Africa, and he gon hire you,' one of the women advised.

Christmas remembered going to the rice farm only once or twice in Opialu. His father, a big yam farmer, taught him nothing about rice planting or harvesting.

The master of the hundred-acre-plantation stood in the shed in front of the still flood through which rice plants were rooted. 'Who is the new negro?' Mr. Clinton asked before they reached him.

'A free man born in Africa,' Christmas's stout friend said.

'You looking for work?'

'Yes sir.'

'Where in Africa you from?'

'Opialu, in the country of Oli'doma.'

'Never heard of the country,' the white man said. 'You farm rice?'

'Yes sir. My father had many acres of rice farm,' Christmas lied.

'How do you deal with the predators?'

'Uh?' Christmas grunted involuntarily.

'Snakes, alligators, scorpions.'

'They never come close to me, sir,' Christmas said smiling.

On his first day at work, he watched other negroes use their sickles to harvest rice and emulated them. In little time he became fast like the others. One of the women told him the rice plantation owner never owned slaves. He came to settle in Kentucky from the north.

'The massa got only folks born in Africa to work here. Both enslaved and free,' Stout Fred added.

On his way back to the Preacher residence, he went past the butchery. He saw Mr. Cooper butchering a chunk of beef ribs.

'Where have you been?' Mr. Cooper asked in a raised voice.

Christmas thought of breaking the news to the man.

'Answer me, Christmas. Why didn't you show up?'

'I got me some other work.'

'Damn nigger. You think you can just go away?' Mr. Cooper raised his voice, leaving his butcher table and dashing toward Christmas with a raised axe.

Christmas staggered into a run. Mr. Cooper could only chase for a short time.

* * *

Tilling the ground in the rice plantation appeared easy at first. He slipped and got himself buried in mud. The other hands were quick to come to his rescue. They laughed at him, mimicking his panic – how he shouted, *Adam Orinya, Adam Abutu,* and how his heart almost burst out of his chest. In the same week, one of the female hands suffered a snake bite in the course of relieving herself in the shrubs nearby. Christmas saw her running out to the vicinity waving and calling. She squatted and wrapped her fingers around her ankle. Stout Fred tied a cloth above her ankle to stop the poison from circulating. Mr. Clinton ambled into the fields with his hands in his pockets. Christmas and Stout Fred helped the woman up and carried her to the waiting wagon. The closest doctor owned a store seven miles away.

The rest of the hands worked until sunset. Christmas sighted Mr. Clinton's wagon down the hill but not the woman. Women gathered around the master. One launched into a howl. She wept bitterly. Christmas got to the gathering.

'Tanya ain't no more. Tanya ain't no more,' Stout Fred cried.

Christmas didn't know the woman but for a moment felt the pain of *ikwu*. He remembered her smile. Firm and soothing.

The others used to make fun and laugh over jokes likely to hurt him, but Tanya never joined in. She nodded in displeasure and rebuked them.

At the end of the sad cloudy day, he headed home. Christmas stopped by at the Peterson plantation and his son ran to meet him. The little locks over the young soft head wobbled with each movement. Christmas lifted him up to his chest and waited for Nedi at the gate.

'What they name your street?' she asked on reaching.

'River Road,' he replied. He looked out of the gate searching for the street sign.

'They name ours Main.'

* * *

Christmas, Black John and Moses ate dinner with the new fugitives in the attic. They laughed about the street names in Louisville. First Street. Second Street. Right up to Seventh Street.

'If I knowed they gon need them names, I could have suggested good names,' Christmas said.

'Like?' Moses asked.

'Christmas Street, and Black John Street,' Christmas replied.

Other than Moses, they all laughed over this.

The biggest among the fugitives, named Sam, narrated one of his most mortifying moments. 'I got stripped naked in Tennessee. Every white child, boy and girl, laughed and call me fat. Was tied to a pole and lashed so bad for a crime I didn't commit. Any food go missin' and my mistress done blamed me all because I fat. All her children stole them milk, meat and tobacco. The end of the day it was me they be blamin'.'

The only mulatto among them, named Cletus, spoke of how fortunate he felt at not being pure black – how he and his twin were treated less severely compared to other negroes.

'My brother went missin'. He gone lookin' out for one negro girl and never returned. Two days later was when we find him hangin' from the tree – dead. White folks around said it was suicide. I tell y'all, my brother would never hang hisself. I knowed the reason they hung him. Because of Massa's daughter. Her eyes was on him. She fabricated stories when she heard he was seein' a negro girl. And her brothers killed my brother. I had to flee because I knows my turn gon come someday.'

Their stories tore Christmas's heart. One of the five left a six-year-old son behind. The man, in spite of his flight from slavery, said he planned on going back to Tennessee to steal his son.

Christmas got back to his room. Nedi moved Ijeyi's sleeping body gently. Christmas turned out the lamp light, and lay beside her.

'Mr. Peterson says war comin' to Louisville,' Nedi said. 'I can't sleep.'

'Everybody been talkin' about war. There ain't no war comin'.'

'I knows when Massa Peterson say the truth,' she insisted. 'He so scared he stay up all night holdin' his gun.'

'Who gon fight who?' He knew the truth but didn't want his woman and son to believe it.

'He says Indians goin' about killin' all them white and black folks so they could take all America.'

'That ain't comin' to Kentucky,' Christmas said. 'President Madison ain't sleepin'.' He sensed the fear in her and tried to look at her in the eye but she looked away. 'You knows a thin' about a big black pot?'

'What you talkin' about?' She asked.

He didn't want to tell her of the dream he saw her in carrying a big black pot.

He woke the next day, and the recurring itch around his groin became severe. The sound of his scratching woke Ijeyi.

Ijeyi sat up and yawned.

'What goin' on there?' Nedi asked.

'War in there,' he replied.

'You catch somethin' from the rice plantation?'

Christmas sat on the floor and felt like crying.

'You ought to wash yourself proper at the end of each long day,' Nedi told him.

* * *

He tried hard to cut the rice plants from the root and shove them straight into the basket hanging around his neck. The itch forced his misery out into the open. He became a dancing clown. He kicked to the right and jumped awkwardly, closing and opening his reddened eyes. Some moments the itch faded away, to his relief. It always came back to torture him. He stopped work several times to have a good scratch. This attracted a lot of stares from some of his fellow hands.

Before their first break, he hurried to the back of the shed, knelt and got out his penis. It became red with rashes. He pressed it and saw puss. The sight frightened him.

'Don't be ashamed,' One female hand, prying on him, said.

Christmas, startled, covered himself. The woman, old enough to be his mother, left the shed and approached. He sensed her concern.

'I done watched you since dawn. I ain't seen one who worked harder than you does until today. I knows somethin' wrong. You got to show yourself to a doctor.'

'What're you both doing here? I reckon we have much work to be done?' They didn't see Mr. Clinton on time.

'Massa, Christmas sick and I tryin' to see what wrong with him,' the woman said.

'Ain't well today, Mr. Clinton,' Christmas said.

'I see,' Mr. Clinton quietly said. 'You can go. But never come back here.' He turned around to leave.

The woman looked at Christmas pitifully.

They headed back to his farm. Mr. Clinton stood right there keeping a close eye on him. Christmas could only dance in pain. It got so bad the other negroes, other than the concerned woman, laughed and could work no more.

'Stout Fred, get that clown off my plantation,' Mr. Clinton said quieting everyone. He turned around and left.

Christmas lost hope of getting any other work outside the Preacher residence. There must be a way. How can Nedi and Ijeyi ever be free in America? He headed straight for Doctor Fruitvale's Drug Store on Third Street. Standing in front of the counter he squirmed in displeasure. He could see the doctor seated behind a desk full of papers in the simple store. On the walls were shelves on which bottles, labelled in gilt letters, sat.

Doctor Fruitvale looked up, glanced at him and said, 'How can I help you?'

In anguish, Christmas replied, 'I got this itchin' between my legs.'

The doctor sighed in exasperation. 'You got half a dollar?'

He nodded his head and started to scratch without shame. The expensive bottled medicine looked too small. Too small for what he paid. He didn't wait to get to the Preacher residence before applying it. He found an abandoned cart, jumped in it and applied the liquid. He waited. Somehow it eased the inflammation. But it came back before dusk. He applied the liquid once again in his room.

In the middle of the night his spirit entered Olofu's world. He wanted to wander in a world that he could feel no itch. Olofu held an open book with the image of his mother's head on its page. Christmas hesitated. Olofu's mother, boldly visible, kept cursing and releasing a lot of noxious words from the glaring page. Christmas stepped back into his world in Kentucky. Back into his infuriating body.

Doctor Fruitvale's medicine proved useless. It wasn't a nice morning. The irritation often came and went. On his way to the Peterson plantation later in the day, the itch got so bad he fell and crouched. Two children laughed at him. Christmas waited for the itch to subside before he continued his journey.

Nedi, in the cotton field, saw him coming. She met him under the oak tree.

'What you doin' here? It Friday and you got to be at work,' she said.

'What your massa gon do to me?'

'Somethin' gon wrong?' Nedi asked.

Christmas sighed before speaking, 'Ain't workin' no more. Mr. Clinton ask me to leave.'

Her eyes blinked.

'I got to find me a way to keep savin' more money to buy you and Ijeyi.'

Nedi sighed.

Christmas started to scratch again.

'You still scratchin'?'

'It was the reason Mr. Clinton ask me to leave.'

The sight of Mr. Peterson and Ijeyi emerging out of the big house startled her, and she whispered, 'Follow me, Christmas. He ain't gon be happy seein' you.'

'Ijeyi is with him,' Christmas replied.

'Mr. Peterson gon do whatever he want with the boy because he own him. Till you be able to buy us, we can do nothin'.'

'What Ijeyi with him for?' He said.

'I don't know. Sometime Ijeyi come back here cryin' and says he got whipped. Sometime he come back here happy, sayin' Massa gives him some hard liquor to drink.'

They entered her cabin. Christmas grabbed her and pushed her against the wall. He hit her across the face. 'You sayin' it like it alright to give the boy liquor!'

She moaned. What did he do? He just wanted to blame someone.

'What you hit me for?'

Christmas couldn't answer. The side of her eye bled. He ran in shame out of the cabin and out of the Peterson plantation. He soon got into his room and sat on the straw bed.

She didn't care about their son, he thought. But if she did, what could she do? What could he do? He couldn't answer the questions. He felt stupid, and began to hit, scratch and slap his head. Nearly forty-years in age, he couldn't get freedom for his wife and son. Nedi kept a secret. He hated to reflect on it. His spirit sensed Mr. Peterson being with Ijeyi in a carnal way, and this realisation hurt.

* * *

Someone tapped on the door. Christmas woke and got up to open it. Through his drowsy eyes, he could hardly make out the figure of the person standing before him.

'Who is you?' he asked.

'Christmas, it me, Esther.'

He widened his eyes. Esther. Her hair looked fuller than it used to be. He came out of the room and embraced her.

'I been knockin' on Black John's door. No answer. I tried Moses, and it the same.'

'Them boys sleep like dead wood,' Christmas said leading her toward Black John's room. 'You comin' back for good?'

'Got to talk to Mr. Preacher. Got nowhere else.'

'Should be for good.'

They stood in front of Black John's room and Christmas gestured at her to knock again. She hit it gently.

'That ain't gon wake nobody other than me.' Christmas banged the door so loud, startling her. Black John opened the door in annoyance. He saw his mother and his anger vanished. They embraced.

'How is Moses?' she asked.

'He different now, Mama. You don't want to know,' Black John said. 'What you came back here for?'

'Why you ask that now, Black John?' asked Christmas. 'Don't you want her back?'

'In three years I be sixty, and I need my sons around me if I want to keep livin',' she said. 'Life hard this summer in Lexington. Everyone there scared. They said the Indians is killin' white and black folks. Mr. Edwin done closed his farm and told me no job no more. Got nowhere else to go. Ain't gon die without seein' my children.'

'You comes back right on time,' Christmas said. 'Much work to do here.'

'Jesus! Y'all grown.'

'What was you expectin' to see?' Black John asked.

'What Moses look like?'

'Still fat. Wait till you see,' Black John said. 'He been very bad, I tell you. Ain't afraid of no white man. Even Massa avoids him.'

'Moses like no white man or white woman except for that woman, Emily Margaret,' Christmas added.

'Who that?' she asked.

'A woman Massa done brought to teach us to read and write,' Christmas said.

'Y'all read now?'

'Just a little bit, Mama,' Black John said. 'Christmas, you've my thanks for bringin' her over here. She gon stay on my bed till mornin'.'

'You can come share my bed if the floor too hard for you,' Christmas said to Black John on leaving.

* * *

Christmas woke and headed out of his room. He found Moses sitting on a chair in the dwelling's living room.

'You seen your mama?'

'Why, you been dreamin' about her?' Moses replied.

'She came last night. Knocked on your door but you was sleepin'.'

'Where she at?' Moses asked.

Christmas pointed at Black John's room.

Moses stood up, walked to the door and tapped on it before opening it. He saw her but couldn't say a word.

'You a grown man now, Moses,' Christmas heard Esther say.

'She came in the night,' Black John added.

Christmas saw Esther stand up and open her arms for an embrace. But Moses turned away, and headed back toward Christmas. Esther and Black John followed him.

Moses looked at Christmas. 'She a liar and she just white on the inside. Nobody should believe no story she done brought.'

'Moses,' Black John admonished.

'Don't pretend, Mama. You don't care,' Moses went on.

Esther looked down.

'Moses, this ain't right. She our mother,' Black John said.

'Where has she come from now? Ain't seen how we was doin' until now. We go all the way to Lexington and she done chose the white man over us.'

'I did that because of the problem I cause to Massa Preacher before I leave. Life good for you boys. Lexington ain't no better, I tell you. For a free woman like me it was the only place I find work.'

'You ain't got no sense,' Moses said. He looked at Black John and asked, 'Mr. Preacher know she here?'

'Moses, he don't know yet. You got to purge your mind and talk to Mama real good. She got to be here,' Black John advised.

* * *

Tallie brought in a man called Blotface. The man, with a deep scar beside his nose, wore a long brown coat and a black hat. Christmas led them through the hallway to Mr. Preacher's study.

Despite his appearance, the man's smile remained steady and reassuring. He claimed he once led more than a hundred slave men and women to freedom. He spoke in a whisper most of the time. Christmas liked him.

'You have my respect, Blotface. I have a good reputation amongst Quakers in Louisville,' Mr. Preacher said proudly. 'They will be pleased with the work you do.'

'I understand. Inasmuch as sending off fugitives in cargo boxes works, it can end in a distressing manner. A slave died in a box after being posted from Georgia to Philadelphia,' Blotface said.

'How sad that is. Freedom only in death,' Tallie added.

'I trust we can rely on you,' Mr. Preacher said. 'The present fugitives have been here for too long now.'

At nightfall, one by one, Christmas led the runaways in the attic to Blotface's wagon in front of the big house, and their journey to liberty began. Christmas and Mr. Preacher rode with them in the wagon but were dropped off at Frankfort Avenue. They planned to walk back but Mr. Preacher decided to pass by Edward's residence to break the good news to the Indian. Christmas and his master encountered a gathering of people on reaching. Several lamps held by the people lightened the place. Blood slicked the walls around the house entrance.

A patroller stood in front of the crowd.

'What in heaven's name is going on?' Mr. Preacher asked.

'The war has come to Louisville. It's them Indians,' a man said.

Christmas remembered Mr. Preacher talking to Tallie about a Shawnee leader. He mentioned something about this leader encouraging Indians to take the country back from white people.

Christmas and Mr. Preacher pushed their way through the crowd until they got to the patrolman.

'Good morning officer. Edward is a friend,' Mr. Preacher said.

'That savage, the white prostitute he took for a wife and three of his brothers were murdered this morning.'

'Who committed the crime?'

'Fellow Indians.'

'But why? Thought the war was between the Indians and...'

'In all politeness, I don't have much time to stand around talking, sir. We are trying to remove their remains at this moment. But let me ask you a thing. What do you know about these braves?'

'They were good people, officer. They even dressed like civilised men...' Mr. Preacher began, but got interrupted.

'And that was the problem right there,' a woman at the front of the crowd spoke up. 'The Indians have this chief who thinks every

Indian who dresses like white folks and adopts our civilised manners is a wizard bringing curses upon America.'

Mr. Preacher continued the conversation with the patroller, and Christmas turned to look at the woman.

She went on talking to a younger woman beside her. '...the mad ones from the woods are the reason behind this. Next time they come, it's for us white folks.'

Christmas remained troubled as they walked back home. They gave way to a group of cowboys on horses. Christmas fought the desperate need to scratch himself but couldn't stop himself. He scratched discreetly hoping Mr. Preacher wouldn't notice. He thought of Edward. One could be alive one moment and dead the next. He began to worry about Nedi and Ijeyi.

'Massa, I feel Mr. Peterson ain't gon sell Ijeyi no more,' Christmas said.

'Why do you think so?'

'I done lost my temper and beat on Nedi. She don't care for Ijeyi like I do. She don't do nothin' each time Mr. Peterson give him liquor to drink. He been with Ijeyi the way a man be with a woman.'

'She told you this?'

'I know so.'

'No one is going to believe you, Christmas,' Mr. Preacher said. He thought for a moment. 'Have you heard that Mr. Peterson once killed one of his slaves?'

Christmas nodded.

'Christmas, you should stay on the estate until the tension dies down, and what is happening with work at the rice plantation?'

'What good it gon do if I keep on workin' and Mr. Peterson gon sell Ijeyi to us no more?'

'You are not including Nedi?'

Christmas stayed quiet.

'I never seen you behave this way. You acted stupid and un-Christian, Christmas.'

'I agrees, Massa. I been stupid.'

* * *

Thursday and Friday passed. Nedi didn't show up. Christmas worried over this. Orinya, his alekwuafia in his long indigo shroud, sprang down from the sky, raising dust through the night air. A group of birds scattered from the pine tree close by.

'What have you done?' The masquerade's voice filled his ears causing him a little light-headedness.

'Orinya, help me. This itch killing me.'

'Oda'nyaa put that disease on you,' the masquerade shouted startling Christmas. 'She is jealous of your earthly wife.'

Christmas got up. He felt the itch again. 'Why would you let it happen?'

'Why should I care?' Orinya said. 'I let it happen since it would work to our advantage.'

'How is it going to work for me?'

'You would have to levitate back to Opialu without Nedi.'

'And my son?'

'That I cannot speak of.'

'Oda'nyaa has always been the reason,' Christmas said nodding his head.

'Oda'nyaa was jealous. *Awo 'lila*! Her evil will work for us. You are going back to Oli'doma.'

The masquerade advanced toward Christmas and touched him over the groin. Christmas felt fire emanating from the ghostly hand. Christmas screamed and fell. Orinya seemed to leap back into the air. Christmas felt his penis go cold. He knelt and checked. It wasn't itchy anymore. He rolled upright in the grass and gave thanks to his alekwuafia.

* * *

The negroes were all present in the dwelling. Esther wept. Christmas's heart wept. It wasn't really the same Moses she left behind in Louisville. Christmas thought of his own mother in Opialu. He hoped slavery didn't take her.

Christmas always thought of Nedi. He desired going the Peterson plantation to apologise. But a crocodile is never sorry. He should always be able to defend his actions. Even if he could purchase his son, he still needed her to help look after him. He thought of Mr. Peterson's despicable act on his son.

'Massa let Moses be like this all the time?' Esther asked Black John, bringing back Christmas's attention.

Moses, leaning on the wall, spoke before Black John could reply. 'You don't talk about me like that, woman. Who you think you is?'

'Moses, listen to her. She your mama,' Black John pleaded.

'Why should I? She just too white on the inside. When everythin' fine for her she forget us.'

Silence.

They all could hear some footsteps approaching the entrance. The door got pushed from the outside, and Mr. Preacher entered. Christmas and Black John got on their feet. Moses sauntered into his room, swinging his hand and murmuring something.

'Get that fool back here,' Mr. Preacher said angrily.

Black John followed Moses.

Mr. Preacher looked at Esther. 'How come you are here, and no one has mentioned anything to me?'

'I was goin' to do that, Massa,' Black John began on his way back from Moses's room.

'It was my fault, Mr. Preacher,' Esther added. 'We scared you ain't gon let me stay.'

'Would I let you stay?' Mr. Preacher asked. 'I will need to think on it... And where is Moses?'

Fear settled on Esther's face.

'Massa, he said he ain't comin' out,' Black John said.

Mr. Preacher walked toward Moses's room and kicked the door open. Moses scrambled up from his bed. Mr. Preacher dashed at him and held his throat, forcing him to lie back on the straw bed. Moses, at thirty-four, couldn't throw the older man off his body due to his bulk.

'Massa, Massa! Please forgive him,' Esther started to plead.

'Massa, please,' Christmas added.

'Get those white fingers off my throat,' Moses lamented.

Mr. Preacher decided to let him be and stepped away.

Moses struggled to his feet. In anger, he lifted the bed he just left, and pushed it against the wall. This resulted to a loud sound. Christmas, suspicious he might dash at Mr. Preacher, stood in his way. On second thought, he wanted to see Moses end the white man's life.

'I need to get by. Allow me, Christmas.' Moses breathed hard.

'Let him, and I will have him buried tonight,' Mr. Preacher said.

'Moses, I begs you to stay calm,' Black John said.

'I don't want to see him in my residence after this night,' Mr. Preacher said.

Moses appeared to calm.

'Massa Preacher. Please forgive him,' Esther said.

'Massa, I gon pay more on top his rent. Massa please,' Black John pleaded.

Mr. Preacher appeared undecided looking from one to the other. 'Have him behave well. I want you and Christmas to come with me now,' he said on leaving.

Heading for the big house Mr. Preacher began, 'We have larger concerns this night, hence my clemency for Moses. It is certain that war is coming to Louisville. We have to protect ourselves. We will take turns in guarding the residence during the night. We wouldn't be taking any chance.'

Mr. Preacher looked at Black John. 'You will have to keep an eye on your brother. I presume you would double up his rent in the coming winter?'

'I gon do that, Massa.'

'Your mother can stay as long as she is able to pay the rent. I need her to clean and attend to the big house. It has been untidy for a long time, and you men aren't doing anything good about it. The wage will be modest.'

'Thank you, Massa.'

'Just remember this, Black John and Christmas. You see anything suspicious any night, you must come to wake me. I have got loaded long guns.'

Christmas shook his head. 'Yes, Mr. Preacher.'

'Black John, you can go,' Mr. Preacher said.

Black John left.

Mr. Preacher turned to Christmas. 'How is Nedi and your son?'

'Not seen them, Massa,' Christmas replied. 'I gon say sorry to Nedi.'

'When do you intend to go?'

'Tomorrow, Massa.'

'I hope it brings you felicity.'

He left the Preacher residence in the afternoon of the next day. He passed through Jefferson Street. The last set of the day's mails were being handed out through the window of the post office. Christmas entered the Peterson plantation and every slave including children stopped what they were doing. They all stared at him.

Thomas jeered, 'Go back, no one wants to see your ugly face.'

Even Nedi's other children, Ark and Sally, now sixteen and eighteen, stared at him coldly. No one seemed to be on the cotton farm. No sign of Mr. Peterson either. Christmas ignored Thomas and found Nedi under the oak tree sitting on the ground. Her locks weren't nicely held behind on this day. She looked up. Christmas saw tears in her eyes. He tried to touch her.

'Don't touch me,' she said in a brittle voice.

'Nedi, I'm sorry that I hit you.'

'You never should have done that. Massa Peterson knows. You knows he own me? He own me and our son...'

The truth of this cut Christmas deep. He wanted to know what Mr. Peterson intended to do. He wanted her to stop. 'Where is Ijeyi?' he asked.

'Massa gon sell him,' she said softly.

He wanted to hit her again. 'Where is Ijeyi?' he repeated.

'You gon find them at the tavern.'

He turned around to leave.

'Why ain't you scratchin' no more?' She stopped him.

He thought for a moment before asking, 'You know Mr. Peterson do somethin' bad to our son. Ain't talkin' about the liquor he gives our son.'

'I knows nothin' else.' She shook her head, and he could see the fear making her to lie.

* * *

White folks poured into the tavern on Walnut Street, and from the vicinity Christmas could see Ninth Street. In the radius of two blocks lived some Kentucky bureaucrats. Christmas could make out Ijeyi's standing figure. Some of the men wore hats. They were extraordinarily noisy and Christmas wondered why his son wasn't terrified. He saw Mr. Peterson dancing and walking toward his son with a cup of liquor. Ijeyi collected the cup. He drank what they offered in a gulp, and the men in the tavern were lost in wonder. Mr. Peterson proudly walked back to his seat.

Christmas approached a white man at the door.

'Get your cotton-picking negro ass out of here,' the man said.

'I need to talk to Mr. Peterson,' Christmas said.

'You hear what he said?' another white man said on coming out. This man pushed Christmas so bad that he fell.

The other man laughed and said, 'Only nigger allowed in here is the Peterson nigger boy.'

Christmas touched his right elbow, bruised. He looked up. Most of the men in the tavern were out. They gathered around him.

'What's all the trouble?' Mr. Peterson showed up.

Christmas managed to get to his feet. He saw his eight-year-old, naked to the waist, come toward him from the crowd to hug him. The strands of the boy's locks shone.

'Let's allow Mr. Peterson deal with this nigger buck,' the assailant said. All the men went back inside leaving Mr. Peterson out the front of the tavern. Mr. Peterson walked up to Christmas and his son.

'What do you want?'

'I need to talk to you, Mr. Peterson.'

'About what? Or do you think you can take a swing at me this time, like you did to the boy's mother?' Mr. Peterson said. 'You like to take your luck with the noose?"

'No sir, I comes to beg. Please don't sell Ijeyi.'

'Who says I'm going to sell him?'

'Nedi says you gon…'

Mr. Peterson grabbed Christmas by the collar. 'I sell my slaves when I want to, and to whoever I want to,' Mr. Peterson said. He forced Christmas to his knees and turned around to Ijeyi.

'Boy, this is the buck that hit your mama. You want to pay back?'

Ijeyi shook his head. He didn't want to hit his father.

Mr. Peterson struck Christmas hard across the face with the back of his palm.

Christmas groaned. He thought of hitting back but couldn't. He looked at Ijeyi.

'When you got the money, come see me and we can talk.' Mr. Peterson took Ijeyi's hand and walked back to the tavern.

* * *

Christmas, on watch, patrolled around several times through the dark. He saw no sign of any trouble. He needed to wake Black John to do his part. He tapped on Black John's door and didn't get an answer. He went in and shook him. Black John sat up and rubbed his eyes.

'Your turn,' Christmas said.

'I knows.' Black John yawned and climbed out of bed.

Black John headed out of the dwelling and Christmas went to his room. He took off the coat he wore and lay on his bed. He reflected on the happenings of the day. He felt relieved with all Mr. Peterson said. He thought of the assault. He recollected how Mr. Peterson spoke and his long beard wavered; how he stank of liquor. Christmas thought of apologising to Mr. Cooper. He could ask for butcher work again. He needed to keep saving. Christmas's spirit wandered to the Peterson plantation. He shouldn't witness it but he did. His presence became air in Mr. Peterson's room. He saw Nedi beside the slaveholder in bed. The white man's hand appeared to cup Nedi's bare breast.

* * *

Christmas's spirit searched her mind. He felt her hunger. She refused to eat or do anything since morning. She watched her master swagger out of the wagon with Ijeyi following. She watched her fellow slaves end their day in the cotton field, packing up and singing a hymn. The moon stood in the middle of the sky. The night got cold. She stood up and headed for her cabin. She untied her locks before lying on the bed. She closed her eyes and found herself on the same gold platform the mermaid-queen once whipped her.

Christmas sank into her dream. In the dream she knelt and placed her palms resting on the platform. In front of her were numerous black women. Their queen frowned at her. Nedi didn't want to be whipped and began to shiver. Oda'nyaa laughed. The sound echoed repeatedly and the other mermaids joined her in laughter. Nedi covered her ears with her palms. The women laughed at her marriage, and at Christmas. Her bed, in the Peterson plantation, got wet with her tears. Christmas, hurt all over again, remembered how he hit his wife. He recalled how his own father in Opialu beat his mother. His own mother suffered many slaps and blows but she never fled. She stayed and continued being a mother.

* * *

Christmas's spirit hovered over Nedi's sleeping body. He sank into her mind. The old woman, Sus, entered the cabin. Nedi woke and heard some horrible words.

'Massa takin' Ijeyi to the slave market,' the older woman said.

Nedi sprang out of her bed like a cat. She felt mad and she ran through the dark morning to the front of the Peterson mansion. Mr. Peterson, with Ijeyi in his arms, headed for the buggy harnessed to a horse. Two other slave men stopped her from reaching the white man. She lamented, calling for her son. She called for Christmas and tried to swing herself forward. The negro men held her firmly. Christmas's spirit felt like bursting out of her mind but couldn't.

The men dragged Nedi over the lawn. Christmas's spirit leapt out of Nedi's mind back to the Preacher residence. He snapped back into his body, and in his full being he started toward Main Street. He didn't care if the Indians were killing people on the streets. He didn't care if the British were doing the same.

On his way, he came across gatherings of people watching two houses crumble in flames. The Indians were truly around. He reached the Peterson plantation and Nedi ran to him and clasped her body to his. Christmas saw some slave women slip out to stand in the shadows in front of their cabins.

'Massa Peterson taken Ijeyi to the slave market.' She breathed heavily.

He looked around her to the surrounding scene. Dawn approached. Lamps lights were still scattered around Louisville. He couldn't see Nedi anymore, even though she kept calling his name, even though she stood right there in front of him. He walked out of the plantation to the woods, and departed from his body. The energy came upon his spirit like a rush of cloud – it seemed like the power Orinya spoke of. But it wouldn't work if he remained in his body. The spirit emitted a cry of inconsolable anguish, floated into the air and swooped at speed in the direction of the slave market.

* * *

Christmas's spirit touched down in the crowded market. Wind swept dust into the sky. Children jumped in excitement. He looked around for Mr. Peterson. He floated through the crowd and scrutinised every naked child displayed for sale. He didn't find Ijeyi. He floated out of the marketplace gliding his invisible spirit through small layers of pregnant clouds. He caught sight of Mr. Peterson's buggy rattling across a narrow bridge. He touched down in front of it. Mr. Peterson stopped on sensing the arrogant wind coming against him.

Through Mr. Peterson's eyes Christmas could see the buyer from Georgia heading to Louisiana. Christmas in form of the wind swooped upon the buggy and pushed it into the river. Christmas soon soared away and flew over the Appalachian Mountains. He couldn't sense his son's presence anywhere around Kentucky. His spirit flew low over the Tupelo swamp and through the blue grass.

No hint of his lost son. He called for Orinya and rain came instead. He called for Abutu and he received silence. He saw the *enyo'nobi* bordering Georgia. He became the hurricane that came upon Louisiana in 1812, a year never to be forgotten.

PART SIX

BLACK JOHN

THE WAR OF 1812 FINALLY ended. Louisville hardly felt the war. Christmas thought of 1812 every single day. 1812 took Ijeyi away from his life forever. The same year, Nedi stopped being his wife. People suspected he flew, caught up with Mr. Peterson and left him with a perpetual mischief. The rumour went around. He didn't deny it. His spirit truly levitated. Some believed. Some didn't. They heard of flying negroes only in stories, only in the tales of the Igbos. It excited some negroes that this finally occurred in Kentucky. It frightened others, especially white slaveholders. Some white folks marched into the Preacher residence in the winter of 1812 and bundled him up. They gave him the whipping of his life. One of the men punched his face. He spat out a gory tooth. Another man put a string around his neck and tried in all his might to squeeze life out of him. Despite all the noise these white folks made in their barbaric acts, Mr. Preacher took time in coming out of the big house.

'He got to die. He would make other niggers fly like he does and they would chop off our heads if we don't end this,' one said.

Christmas didn't enjoy the status extended to him by this ability. But he appreciated the words Mr. Preacher put up for him. He still remembered how every sentence coming out the man's lips sounded.

'You all think Christmas really flew? You all think he really caused Mr. Peterson to lose his mind. I tell you this. Mr. Peterson, who has been spreading these lies about Christmas, has been out of his mind way before that day. Ask the folks in his plantation. We are talking of the same Mr. Peterson who murdered a wife and blamed it on his slave. This same Mr. Peterson murdered a slave man because of his lustful desire to take the poor slave's woman. Christmas cannot fly. If he could, he would go back to his home in Africa. I beg you all to stop spreading empty superstitions...'

He saw a white boy in the crowd of angry people and tears poured out of his eyes. The boy's stature appeared identical to Ijeyi's. Christmas felt he owed Mr. Preacher for the intervention. At the same time, he wished Mr. Preacher should have let them kill him. How could he live without knowledge of his son's whereabouts? He got tired of Orinya and Oda'nyaa's intrusions in his life.

Christmas couldn't give up on finding his son. His thoughts became a prayer. This new year of 1815 should bring back his son, he prayed. He fell asleep. The voices of Moses and Black John woke him but he avoided moving or opening his eyes.

'He sleepin' like a horse,' Moses said.

Black John giggled. 'You still believe the story about him flyin'?'

'Of course I does. Before them white mens brought us to America, we was special kind of people. They made us to forget who we is. Christmas remember this. He remember who he is.'

'Don't start this, Moses. I now think the story is garbage,' Black John said.

'That's what you believe. I got my beliefs,' Moses said.

Christmas opened his eyes and saw Moses heading to his room. Black John headed back out. He heard Mr. Preacher call from outside, 'Christmas!'

Christmas got up slowly and headed out.

'Why did Black John have to cook yesterday when it was your turn?'

'I done forget it my turn, Massa.'

'You have to stop forgetting things,' Mr. Preacher said. 'You spend too much time thinking these days.'

'I don't know what to do, Massa,' Christmas said and squatted in front of Mr. Preacher. He held onto Mr. Preacher's legs. 'You should have let them white folks kill me. I don't have to live without my son.'

'Christmas! Unhand my legs!' Mr. Preacher said angrily.

Christmas flinched and let his legs go.

'Don't ever touch me in that manner again,' Mr. Preacher said and left.

Christmas sighed and cursed underneath his breath. He felt like crying but the tears weren't coming. He couldn't sleep at night. He wandered around the neighbourhood in the dark. The constant shouts of soldiers singing songs of victory against the British and Indians remained in the air. He felt the energy Orinya promised him. The energy propelled his strength of levitation in spirit and in body. Profound excitement. He looked around and saw no one. He leapt up into the air. On reaching the height of the pine tree by the side of River Road, he thundered back to the ground. What was wrong? He tried to get to his feet but he couldn't. The lower part of his right leg burned. He dragged his body over the ground to the entrance of the Preacher residence. Moses approached to help him to the dwelling.

'What happened to you?' Moses asked.

Christmas said nothing.

* * *

The dying days of winter brought Christmas relief. The cold got brutal at a point. February. Christmas kept his distance from Nedi, but his spirit visited her each time he missed their son. He knew Nedi never stopped mourning Ijeyi. She thought about the day in December of 1812. Two men brought Mr. Peterson home all covered in blood. The day brought ruin to the Peterson plantation. Residents, reluctant in believing some Africans could fly, said Mr. Peterson's accident resulted from a sudden heart attack suffered by the horse harnessed to the buggy the white man rode on the day he sold Nedi's son, hence the buggy slipped off the narrow bridge into the river; however, the same horse still lives recovering from a fractured spine. Some of them said Mr. Peterson's buggy fell into the river and his head collided with a rock, yet Nedi couldn't see any fracture on Mr. Peterson's skull. The wounds were mostly on his face. The last of the stories Nedi chose to believe indicated that a flying Christmas, in body, collided with Mr. Peterson's buggy on the narrow bridge.

Mr. Peterson didn't come out of the mansion for days. Slaves heard him scream out of his nightmare. He shouted, 'Spare my life! Spare my life!' The kitchen women took food to Mr. Peterson and they came back unable to breathe properly because of the smell in the mansion. He wouldn't let Sus and the other slaves clean. Mr. Peterson, unashamed of his nakedness, turn out to be embarrassed about slaves seeing the faeces he left around his mansion floors. He ate so much, there were hardly any leftovers. Once, he came out stinking so bad and chose three males at random. He hung them on the pine tree and whipped them for speaking about flying negroes. No one on the plantation challenged this. Mr. Peterson encouraged all the plantation children to laugh whenever he whipped rebellious slaves.

Six of Mr. Peterson's slaves recently disappeared and nothing happened. The master noticed nothing. Life went on and the rest of the slaves kept their lips sealed. A week passed and more slaves left. Christmas wondered if Nedi could ever leave.

Mr. Peterson visited Nedi's cabin several times. During his last visit, he behaved like a child discovering a woman's body for the first time. She tried to push him away and he slapped her. Christmas couldn't make himself care anymore. Let the wretched white man continue to deposit his insanity in her. On this cold night, Christmas's spirit witnessed Mr. Peterson rush into Nedi's cabin with a whip in hand. He dropped the whip and took off his clothes. Nedi noticed how the man's wounds were becoming scars. A few on his back and on his chin. She kept staring at him until his sheepish smile faded. He picked up the whip and walked toward her. He stood in front of her and gazed at her chest. She seized the whip from his hand. She, like Christmas, couldn't believe Mr. Peterson's reaction. Fear apprehended the man. The memory of Ijeyi turned to rage within her. She lifted the whip and landed it on Mr. Peterson's skin. The white man roamed about the cabin like a rat. He screamed and fell. He got up and ran into an old cabinet which held a set of blackened pots. She continued to whip him in her rage until she became breathless.

The man managed to find the bolt on the door and ran out stark naked.

* * *

Christmas, on an errand to collect rent money on Mr. Preacher's behalf, went past Main Street. He noticed some slave families of the Peterson plantation with sacks whose bulge suggested they contained their belongings. He stared into the Peterson premises and saw Nedi in conversation with Ark. She looked exhausted and laughed desolately. Christmas saw a third person with them. He soon recognised the blue bright shirt of Black John.

Christmas completed his errand and headed back to the Preacher residence wondering about Black John's motives. He waited for Black John's return. Black John soon returned and Christmas waited patiently for him begin his story.

'I saw groups of negroes movin' out of the Peterson plantation and I thought I'd pass by and see why.'

'You heard somethin'?' Christmas asked.

'Massa Peterson's insanity too bad now,' Black John said. 'Every negro leavin' the plantation. The man don't remember nothin' no more. I heard he roamin' too.'

'Is Nedi and her children all fixin' to leave?' Christmas asked.

'She say she got nowhere to go.'

Christmas thought. Her son Ark, nineteen now, could fend for himself if his mama wouldn't leave. 'You see Sally?'

'No I didn't,' Black John said. 'Just Nedi and Ark. That boy Ark grown so tall.'

'I gon fetch Nedi and her children some food tonight,' Black John said.

Christmas didn't like what he heard, but he remained quiet. Every part of him missed her. He decided to attend the Quaker meeting for the first time since his marriage to Nedi. He entered the meeting room and witnessed an unfamiliar negro saying the prayer. Tallie stood next to the man.

Mr. Preacher made a brief announcement. He said they should be wary of some Quakers. 'I heard the devil has put it in the heart of a few friends that our Lord Jesus Christ wasn't born as God and waggishly they see no significance in his virgin birth.'

'Who is Christ to them?' another negro asked laughing.

The meeting continued into the evening.

* * *

Black John entered the room carrying a small sack. Christmas looked up from the bed. He managed to walk up to the big house earlier in the afternoon despite the pain in his leg. Black John sat on the bed, looked at Christmas and said, 'Taking some food to Nedi and her children.'

Christmas sighed. He didn't know why he envied Black John. He felt irresponsible. 'Black John, you shouldn't bother about her. She gon find a life for herself and her children.'

'She your wife, Christmas.'

'She ain't no more.'

He noticed Black John's fixed stare on him. Black John soon left, and Christmas thought about Nedi. He called Oda'nyaa's name in frustration. And out of the black river, she came to be with him.

'He's a good man,' she said.

'Who?'

'Black John,' she replied and lay beside him. 'Are you surprised Orinya hasn't visited in his arrogance?'

'He will come,' Christmas said looking away. 'And he isn't arrogant.'

'You know he is going to kill you if you keep letting him into your life.'

'Stop it, Oda'nyaa. If he is going to kill me in the future, I feel it is...' He stopped and looked deeply into her eyes. 'Why should I listen to you?'

'Listen to yourself, grown man. Why did you not say that last night or the night before? You don't want to know that he, Orinya, is a coward.'

'He isn't. He is the great alekwuafia, once an *Achadu* of Kwararafa country. One father of Oli'doma. One true son of Abutu Eje. One warrior and crocodile.'

'Let me try to convince you,' she whispered and took his hand. They travelled through the black river to so many years ago. They became the infertility of the ground in the Idoma settlement in Kwararafa. And Orinya in human form looked helpless, urging Ayi'doma to flee if the Bornu Empire chose to invade their villages. The raiders came in the night. Horses neighed. The blood of children flowed over the soil. Most of their women were taken, and Orinya needed to take the place of the captured *Achadu*.

The barren land witnessed Orinya run defencelessly into the forest with his kinsmen. 'That is your cowardly ancestor,' Oda'nyaa said.

* * *

He felt ashamed to have seen Orinya, his family's idolised hero, dashing for the bush. How could that be? The great ancestor. Christmas walked to and fro between the walls of his room, in quick angry strides. He thought of the likelihood of returning to Oli'doma. Oda'nyaa could be right. He should remain in Kentucky and have her all to himself. He thought of Nedi. His spirit found her in the Peterson plantation telling the children of the plantation a story that he, Christmas, once told her about Africa – about Onoja, a slave catcher, known to originate from Oli'gra. Onoja sold men and women to white people.

'On his own,' she said, 'he raided African countries like Ole'gbo and Oli'doma and caught thousands of slaves. He was a giant and possessed six fingers on each hand.' And Nedi went on, telling of how the giant became very rich from the slave trade and married many women. Christmas's spirit hung in the air Nedi breathed. He could taste the stale feeling of her mouth. She wanted to tell the children a second story but spotted Black John walking into the plantation.

'Children, I think Aunty Sus got more interestin' stories about Africa,' she said to them, and they all scrambled off in search of Sus.

'I brought food,' Black John said on reaching her.

'I hate that we becomin' a burden to you...'

'You can't say that, Nedi.'

'I'm just wicked,' she said and sighed. 'Why you do this, Black John?'

Black John couldn't look Nedi in the eyes. 'Ain't what you thinkin', Nedi.' They were sitting on the ground.

'Why?' she asked and moved toward him. 'I sees the way you look at me.'

'How about Christmas?' Black John asked.

'What about him?'

'You still like him?'

'If I tell you no, what you gon do?'

Black John remained quiet.

'You should take your food back.'

'Nedi, I swear to you. This ain't what you thinkin'. It never cross my mind that I... I likes you. This food ain't about winnin' your affection. I... I likes you but nothin' can be done about it. Christmas like a brother to me.'

Satisfied, Nedi smiled.

Christmas's spirit felt broken. Black John couldn't resist her. She wanted him.

* * *

Christmas fed the hogs, shut the doors of all the pigpens and limped to the shed. His leg deteriorated. Black John's affection for Nedi haunted his heart.

He saw a wagon drive into the residence. It parked in front of the big house and he could see Tallie leading three negro men to the house. Mr. Preacher hugged each of these men in front of the door before letting them in. They were clearly fugitives.

'Pretender,' Christmas muttered. Mr. Preacher's intent to impress his Quaker friends kept yielding results. Christmas felt glad about Esther's presence. She now handled most of the kitchen chores.

He noticed a bird flying low from a distance. It grew bigger until it became shadowy and transformed into the tall ghostly masquerade in a colourful burial shroud. Christmas's heart missed a beat.

'You have allowed Oda'nyaa back in your life.'

'Where were you when she came back?'

'I was right there to see if you would give in. The disappointment drove me further away.'

'Orinya, you intend to kill me on my return to Opialu.'

'Death isn't death as you think of it. It's a passage.'

Christmas looked away and said, 'You got to stay away.'

'You cannot twist destiny. I will always be around.'

'I want to fly with my body?'

'You can, but only at a predestined moment. Believe me, Ochigbo. The time is coming when you have to return to Opialu. Nedi's loss is a blessing. The death Oda'nyaa spoke to you about is a passage into the world of the ancestors, after which Olofu will continue our journey of *eche*.'

'And if I stay in America?'

'Oda'nyaa will keep using you. And soon she will kill you.'

'How is she going to kill me? Show me.'

The masquerade lifted his hand and they faded into the thin air and appeared as crocodiles gliding through the waters. From the bottom of the cold grubby river they saw Oda'nyaa's kingdom. The palace's floor of gold looked resplendently beautiful. There were two royal seats and Christmas, in the form of a crocodile, saw his future self sitting on one and Oda'nyaa on the other. There were mermaids before them, singing and worshipping. Through crocodile eyes, Christmas and his alekwuafia watched Oda'nyaa kneel before the future Christmas. She kissed his feet. All the mermaids bowed their heads. Oda'nyaa got up abruptly, stepped back and projected her hands forward. Her face turned furious with hate.

'I curse this moment,' she cried. 'I curse you to regret this moment. I curse all the times you have been born. I hence seize your ability to breathe in every black river.'

The crocodiles saw the kingly Christmas convulse. They watched the *alichebe* he wore fall to the floor. The future Christmas, once on the throne, now lay on the floor. His held his throat and gasped for air. Water began to take over the kingdom and every mermaid standing on legs possessed legs no more. Now, they possessed different coloured caudal fins beautifying the waters. Future Christmas continued to convulse. Christmas, in the skin of a crocodile, couldn't watch any more. The waters attacked against him and Orinya. The black river punished them by becoming pungent and overpowering. He longed for air to breathe but death seemed to grab him firmly.

'Stop it,' Christmas begged.

The waters threw him back to Louisville. He felt his body and panted. He stood up, looked around and walked a few steps. The pain in his leg vanished. Orinya, once again, brought him healing. He searched around for his ancestor, instead he heard Orinya's voice.

'You have to return to Opialu, where we have prepared a virgin for you to take as a wife.'

* * *

Christmas became the orange sun setting in the summer evening. He glared over the Peterson plantation and wept. Black John, there again, stared at the sparse cotton plantation. A lot occurred between him and Nedi in such a short time. He could enter her cabin freely.

'Everyone gone. We the only ones left now. Me and my children,' Nedi said.

'And Sus?'

'Her son, a free negro livin' in Lexington, done come fetch her.'

'Nedi. Best time to go. The man mad. You could claim he gave y'all freedom, you know. You know I can write now. I gon forge you a freedom certificate.'

'Where I gon go?'

'Come to the Preacher residence.'

'No. Not with Christmas there. You don't know what he gon do if he knowed about us.'

'Sure he ain't gon be happy.'

'You ought to talk to him if he good with you being with me.'

'That gon be hard.'

'If you want me, you got to do it,' she said.

'Nedi, we gon do this together. He ain't gon punch my face with you there.' He paused. 'Never seen Christmas kill a man. If what they say about him flying true, I'm sure headin' to the grave.'

'Let us do it together,' Nedi said.

He nodded. This seemed to make him smile. 'You gon share my room with Sally. Ark and me gon stay in the outer living room.'

'Too soon to talk about that. We might be in the grave by tomorrow,' Nedi said.

'Tell you the honest truth, I think he never done flied.'

'You sure, Black John? Mr. Peterson lost his mind because of Christmas.'

'That ain't true, Nedi.'

'How about Mr. Preacher?'

'I got to stop attendin' them Quaker meetings – just like Christmas done did when he with you,' Black John replied.

The sun sank into the dark yellowish clouds. Nedi arranged all her clothes and pots into a couple of sacks. She called Ark and Sally and they came. She informed them of her decision and wanted them to leave with her.

Ark didn't care. Sally became sullen.

'You gon remain in slavery all your life?' Nedi asked her daughter.

Sally didn't look at her mother.

'Many runaways hid in the Preacher place. You never know. Somethin' good might be waitin' there for us,' Nedi said. She got a third sack and tossed in some of Sally's clothes.

Ark and Sally packed up their stuff and went ahead of Black John and their mother. At respective ages of nineteen and twenty-one, the siblings didn't need their mother to make such decisions for them.

But it didn't take a lot for them to go with their mother's decision; Mr. Peterson's tyrannous whims always dominated their lives until now. Black John carried two sacks on his back. Nedi held one. They got to the gate and she stopped. She dropped the sack. 'I got somethin' in the big house I gon fetch,' she said.

Black John looked at the dead sun. 'Don't tell me you gon enter that mansion with that crazy man in there?'

'Wait,' she said and left.

He dropped the sacks.

Christmas's spirit swayed into the night from the buried sun and followed her. Nedi headed to her cabin, and found the whip she once used on Mr. Peterson. She sneaked out to the mansion and manoeuvred her way through the dark on entering. The house smelt horrible – like a ton of decomposing bodies. She found the stairs and softly climbed them until she found the door to his room. She entered. She noticed him sitting on the bed. She lit the candle beside him and showed him the whip.

'I was leavin' your worthless plantation and remembered I should return this.' She shoved the whip toward his face, startling him. She laughed.

'See what you is? One stinkin' vegetable with a big empty plantation,' she said and stepped backwards before releasing the whip on him. Mr. Peterson danced off his bed. The whip dug into his flesh. She continued to whip him. He jumped about until she flung the whip to the floor. He watched it coil. Her bitterness wouldn't die. She thought of Ijeyi every night. In handling the whip, she felt like the queen in one of the African tales Christmas told her. The white man made her children, all of them, fatherless.

She got back to Black John and said, 'Sorry I keeps you waitin'. I forget some my best spoons.'

'I heard someone bein' whipped,' Black John said defiantly and kept his eyes on her. She walked past him and dropped two spoons into her sac.

The closer they were to the Preacher residence, the closer Christmas's spirit, in humiliation, drew to his body. They entered the dwelling's living room and met Moses seated. Ark dumped his sack against the wall and sat down. Nedi headed straight for Black John's room.

'What is goin' on?' Moses said staring at his brother.

'They movin' in here since Mr. Peterson gon crazy,' Black John whispered.

'Ain't Christmas know?' Moses asked.

'He care?' Nedi asked on coming out of the room.

'How about the white man in this residence. He knows?' Moses asked again.

'I gon talk to him,' Black John replied.

Esther walked in. She got confused on seeing Nedi and her children. She stared directly at Black John, aware he took her food several times.

'Where you gon be sleepin' at?' his mother asked.

'The livin' room should be fine for me,' Black John replied.

'Is you alright to come to my room? I want to talk to you alone.'

Black John appeared reluctant. He gave Nedi a reassuring gaze before following his mother.

On shutting the door, she shook her head and said, 'You doin' somethin' with her apart from cookin' her somethin'?'

'Mama...'

'You gets me damn well. Don't lie to me, son.'

'Mama. I likes her way back before Christmas took her.'

'You gon betray a brother because of a negro woman who ain't even free?'

'Christmas no longer with her, Mama.'

'You done talk to him?'

'No, Mama.'

''Talk to him. For me, it gon be hard puttin' up with her. Massa Preacher ain't gon take it either.'

'I can try. I'm goin' to lose all my pay and work for free in the residence. What I done did for Moses, I does for anyone.'

The night, in its weakest state, consoled Christmas. Now in his body, Christmas heard the expected knock on his door. He let Nedi and Black John in. He didn't wait for them to begin. He forced a smile, avoided looking at Nedi and said, 'I'm happy for you, Black John. Treat her good. I should be checkin' them hogs soon.'

* * *

Christmas returned and met Moses standing in front of the dwelling. He noticed Moses's anguished smile and walked by without a word. He went up and saw Ark and Sally in conversation.

'The flyin' man!' Ark called.

Sally didn't look up. She now looked so much like Nedi in structure.

'Christmas, I need to talk to you,' Ark said walking toward him. 'Just to let you know me and my sister still respect you. We stand with you. If you don't want us here, we can go but we can't drag our mama with us.'

Christmas cleared his throat. He lacked words.

* * *

Christmas dreamt of Mr. Preacher hanging a suit in the wardrobe. A dog wailed outside. Massa heard his name. The voice belonged to Antonia. He dashed for the door and opened it. Mr. Preacher lost his footing on racing downstairs. He fell brushing his body against the stool beside the staircase. He heard a child's voice calling loudly, 'Father!'

Mr. Preacher looked around, and saw nobody. He heard the wrangling sound of the well-bucket from outside. His eyes settled on the wooden walker Harriet once used. The seat dangled. Christmas woke.

* * *

Christmas conveyed a load of dishes to the kitchen house. He went back to big house, and he overheard a statement made by Tallie. The negro arrived late for dinner but still enjoyed the roasted pork and gravy Mr. Preacher prepared.

'You don't have to act angry. Quakers all over America will praise you once they hear you took slaves whose master gone insane.'

'That is true,' Mr. Preacher replied.

Christmas nodded in disappointment and carried some used tumblers to the kitchen house. Black John and Moses were there. He didn't want to talk to them. He washed the dishes in silence and soon proceeded to the hog farm. Ark couldn't be avoided. The young lad vehemently tried to have conversations with him, particularly about levitation. Christmas searched for possible excuses and ways to walk away. He saw Ark's mother seated in Black John's room. He wondered why she always kept the door open. She tried to make eye contact with him but he eschewed her attempt. In difficult times like this, Oda'nyaa waited to provide him solace. In frustration he often embraced the mermaid. Each time he longed to forget Oli'doma completely, but couldn't. Their language of communication became lust. Affection with distrust.

He entered his room to meet her waiting in her *alichebe* which meant they were to go on a journey.

'You have to believe me when I say that destiny has its own way. I couldn't find your son. As I have said before, we can visit his future but not his present.'

His spirit floated out of the Preacher residence with her into the sky. Some Louisville residents marvelled at the sparkle of travelling stars lightening the sky. Christmas and Oda'nyaa shone with pride and verve. They finally got to the world of his son's future. They saw Ijeyi, now a man of middle-age, leading a wife and three children through the Lexington woods searching for refuge. War came, but it never felt like the wars Christmas knew. This war ate up cities and lives. Standing before the big iron gate were white men in blue uniforms. They welcomed Ijeyi and his wife and children. Ijeyi's locks were beginning to thin. The strands were long. They were longer than anything his mother could claim. Two of Ijeyi's children possessed locks similar to Ijeyi's at the time Mr. Peterson sold him. His wife, an octoroon, looked beautiful. They entered this refuge and for the first time they felt like free people.

Ijeyi's family soon settled into their clean and nicely arranged cabin. A bed and small cushions fitted the size of the room. The white soldiers played cards with the blacks and they joked about their women. Several days later, Ijeyi wore the blue uniform and held his gun in pride. He marched alongside other black soldiers to the Ohio border. They exchanged fire with white people in green uniforms. Many of the blue uniformed soldiers died. Many in the green uniforms died too. The stars were pleased Ijeyi returned home to his family at the refuge.

On Ijeyi's second assignment, along with about five hundred blue uniformed negroes, they were situated near Covington. Attacks from the opposition took many lives. Again, Ijeyi survived. Tragedy awaited him on his return to the refuge he made home.

All his children and their mother were driven out of the refuge along with other black children and women. But why? Ijeyi, and the other black soldiers, couldn't understand. Their boss indicated that a new law in place prohibited negroes from living in the refuge. Ijeyi found his wife and children living on the street in the cold night. They made a fire and kept themselves warm. Ijeyi could only hope for a better life, and henceforth refused to wear the blue uniform again. He lived with them on the street, eating the crumbs of bread thrown down by returning soldiers assigned elsewhere to fight. Once in the middle of the night, he and his family, and every negro on the street, narrowly escaped death. The blue uniformed men rushed out in defence sending the green uniformed soldiers back in the direction they emerged.

Ijeyi's last child caught the flu and shook terribly for days. Death didn't spare her. Ijeyi wept. His wife wept. The watching stars dimmed and almost vanished. Ijeyi buried the little girl's body in the woods.

One sunny Friday the refuge gates were kicked open and the blue uniformed soldiers rushed out calling to all women and children on the street. One white General approached Ijeyi, shook his hand stiffly and led him and his family back into the refuge.

The war went on and many blue uniformed men returned with a missing arm; many returned with a lost leg. The hospitals on the refuge grounds were packed with the wounded, and Ijeyi's frame could be seen among the surviving soldiers.

* * *

Someone knocked on the door.

Christmas sat up but made no effort to check. The person gently pushed open the door, and Christmas saw Moses.

Moses sat beside him and put a hand on his shoulder. 'We brothers, Christmas. Don't think I take Black John's side...'

'Stop,' Christmas interrupted him.

'I shouldn't?'

'Don't talk about them,' Christmas stammered.

'I got to, Christmas,' Moses insisted. 'I ain't no pretender. I sees wrong here and I point at it and say it wrong. I ain't ashamed to stand up to nobody and say he done wrong.'

'You wrong, Moses. But Black John ain't wrong. Nedi ain't wrong.'

'I can't believe you say this.'

'Leave them to live right. They happy.'

Moses sighed. He placed a hand over his forehead. 'You decided she never gon be yours again because you lost a son?'

Christmas nodded, 'You right.'

Moses got up and began to pace. 'Christmas, I knows you got this African religion and I knows you done flied and all that... I strongly believe you gon be interested in a revelation I got last night. You believe in spirits, Christmas?'

'I does.'

'I been with Antonia lately. I been with her in my dream. She said somethin'. Somethin' about to happen in America that gon free them black people.'

Christmas stared at him.

'You believe in the white man's God?'

'I don't know.'

'My mama believe in that God. I used to believe too. Tell me Christmas, how there be three gods in one God? That is what them white folks say, and they taught us to believe that too.'

'It true in the life beyond,' Christmas replied.

'Why you say that?'

'I believe them white people,' Christmas said. 'I, for instance, is three persons. I done reincarnated as an ancestor before. I now livin' as Christmas and I gon come back in the future again as a descendant of my very own self,' he explained.

Moses couldn't take his eyes away from Christmas. 'I believe you,' Moses said. He looked away before walking out quietly. Christmas knew Moses didn't say everything he came to say. Christmas stood up to close the door. He met Nedi's gaze from the living room. She looked away and continued knitting. Slowly, he closed the door and bolted it.

* * *

They met in the attic again. But this time, Moses acted differently. Moses hugged him, patted his back and said, 'Peace my black brother.' He smiled and proceeded to hug the fugitives.

'Y'all seem to likes my mama's food. She a good cook. That the only part of her that remain black till this day,' Moses said. They laughed.

'You see Christmas here?' He said to the fugitives. 'He a good man. My own blood brother took his wife, as white mens do to us all, takin' our mothers and sisters. They call that adultery. Christmas ain't broken. He still standin'. Y'all know he can fly. He done flied all over the deep South searchin' for his own son white people stole.'

'You found this son of yours?' one fugitive asked Christmas.

Christmas shook his head.

'He gon find him someday,' Moses said.

The fugitives randomly nodded their heads and continued to listen. One of them said, 'You got a strong heart, man.'

'White people go about doin' what the bible call wrong. They teach black people wrong thins'. My brother follow what them white people do. Mr. Preacher is the one who teach him that.'

'But it because of him we gon be free,' one fugitive interrupted Moses.

'He right,' Christmas said to Moses. 'It because of Mr. Preacher they gon find their way to freedom.'

'No white man innocent. A white man gon always be a white man,' Moses replied. 'I ain't sayin' y'all should refuse the liberty he offerin'. But look at it from another point. It was white people who got to Africa and got us all here. Stole our ancestors and got us here in a boat. Imagine you steal a chicken, as I likes to do, from white people. And you realise you wrong and return the chicken back to its owner. That ain't gon wipe away the mark of theft on you. You only got a moment of repentance, folks.'

Christmas watched Moses. The thirty-seven-year-old appeared to have lost weight. He kept thick sideburns.

'I got somethin' special for us all,' Moses said and got up from a wooden box, opened it and took out bottles of beer which he offered to the fugitives and to Christmas. 'I took from the white man who own this residence. Ain't call that stealin', Christmas?'

They drank and got to relish all Moses continued to say.

* * *

Months went by. Christmas saw Nedi from the distant farmyard. She didn't look like herself. A bit bigger, it seemed. She could be pregnant. This stung Christmas. He could make out Moses's voice singing loudly from the dwelling. Esther transformed the look of the premises. The fallen leaves under the trees were usually swept away these days. He walked to the corner of the big house and saw Black John and Mr. Preacher. They appeared to be having a private talk.

'Christmas,' Mr. Preacher called. 'Come join us.'

Christmas joined them.

Black John kept his eyes down.

'I was just having a word with Black John about Nedi. No one expects you, Christmas, to be happy.'

Mr. Preacher seemed like the devil in this situation, Christmas thought. He pretended to care.

'I wants her no more, Massa. I done told them to be happy together.'

'Christmas,' Mr. Preacher said putting a hand on his shoulder. 'You will have to live around this hurt.'

'I knows this ain't lookin' right but...' Black John fought back tears.

'Christmas ought to be weeping, not you Black John,' Mr. Preacher said.

Christmas bit his lower lip. 'I sees she pregnant.'

Black John nodded.

The infant yours?' He stared at Black John.

'I pray so, Christmas,' Black John said.

'What you have done, Black John, isn't a reflection of a committed member of the Friends' Society. But they can stay. I can permit the woman and her children to assist Esther with the chores and get some income off me. You and her would continue to stay away from Quaker meetings.'

'I appreciate this kindness, Massa,' Black John said.

Christmas couldn't sleep at night. He wondered if he acted well around Nedi and Black John. His jealousy got so strong, he wanted to kill someone. In a way, he felt Mr. Preacher took sides with Black John. His spirit became the angry fire travelling toward the big house. He couldn't control the rage. The snake of fire climbed up the wall of the big house and found the master bedroom window. Antonia's spirit, stuck to the ceiling, glared over Mr. Preacher's body. The white man remained asleep on his bed. The tentacles she possessed for legs moved slightly. Mr. Preacher's whole body trembled. He held his chest and he fell off the bed. The curtains in the room caught the fire.

* * *

Christmas didn't weigh the damage from his rage until the curtains caught fire. His spirit withdrew into his body in his room, and he ran out of his straw bed heading out toward the big house yelling at the top of his lungs, 'Fire! Fire! Fire!'

On reaching the door Antonia's sweet and ominous laughter hit him. He pushed it open. He got to the top of the stairs and saw the fugitives racing down from the attic. Through the space between the master bedroom door and the floor, he saw fire. Christmas kicked the door open and saw Mr. Preacher on the floor. The fire stretched toward him. Antonia vanished. Christmas jumped over the growing fire and rushed to the bed, dragging off the heavy quilt. He used it to whip the flames. One fugitive pulled Mr. Preacher out of the room. Moses stood still by the doorway and watched. Another fugitive got two pillows off the bed and started killing the flames climbing up the wardrobe from the curtains. He smacked the pillow repeatedly against the wooden wardrobe until the fire went out.

The room became extremely smoky. They heard Mr. Preacher coughing outside the room.

* * *

Christmas felt bitter. He felt Oda'nyaa controlled his life. He wondered if he could ever be happier in Kentucky. He pulled off his boots and placed his hat beside the bed. He caught the sight of Orinya's indigo and colourful attire.

'Why bothering me?' Christmas asked.

'I want you to know that you are making a mistake.'

'For rejecting you because you are going to be the cause of my death?'

'Because I know that mermaid. She is a liar. She has ruined many and I don't want her ruining you.'

'Better she ruins me than for you to kill me.'

'Death, Ochigbo, is inevitable. It is how and where you go after death that is vital, and I can assure you that the path I and your other ancestors intend for you isn't evil.'

'I can't believe you,' Christmas replied.

In the masquerade's attempt to convince Christmas, he showed him a tale of his ancient existence. The room became a world of the past, and he and Christmas became indistinguishable; they were one person. They became the sun and watched over Opialu. They saw Orinya Ogah in human flesh and Oda'nyaa eating a bowl of *Onihi* Orinya's sixth wife prepared. This occurred many years after the great migration from Kwararafa country.

In his old ripe age, the goddess Oda'nyaa returned to be his youngest and most beautiful of wives. The other wives saw no happiness all through her presence in the household. Oda'nyaa lived like the queen. She ate with Orinya all the time and watched the other wives clear the bowls. She told Orinya's wives what she and Orinya wanted to eat, and held on to the spot beside him most nights so that the other women felt condemned.

On a cloudy day during sunset, Oda'nyaa invited a strange man to the house in the absence of Orinya. She shared Orinya's bed with this man. The other women of the house feared her and couldn't open their lips. Days later, she repeated this in Orinya's absence again. But this time, with a serpent from the land of the dead.

'This is the woman you want to trust over your own self?' Orinya said.

They soon returned to the small room with the straw bed by the corner.

Christmas cleared his throat.

'You must know that there're a lot of pathways to your destiny. Each has a different adventure and call. An eventual destination is always death which makes your chosen pathway more vital in the journey of life.'

'What are my pathways?' Christmas asked.

'Between myself and Oda'nyaa, you must choose. No one has that *ofu* over you.' And with that, the thunderous voice of the tall ghost died.

* * *

The next morning Christmas saw Mr. Preacher in front of the big house and walked up to him.

'Thank you, Christmas. I could have died if not for you.'

'Massa, we ain't lettin' you die and leave nobody. How you feelin'?'

'Feel a little pain in my chest.'

'You gon be fine, Massa.'

'I pray so. I turned fifty this year. No longer a young man, Christmas.'

PART SEVEN

MOSES

IN 1822, FORTY-EIGHT-YEAR-OLD Christmas hovered in circles above Moses's sleeping body. He searched Moses's mind and dug out a secret. This mind possessed a waiting pit of great fire designed for Mr. Preacher. Christmas in his spirit saw no difference between himself and Moses since he too connived with his alekwuafia many times to harm the white man. The night spirit released a sigh before sinking deeper into Moses's dream world. In the dream, Moses saw himself slide into a shallow but wide river. In the river were many black people he never knew. He joined a line of people waiting to be immersed in water by a woman. He dragged his legs through the waters and left bubbles behind. It got to his turn. He recognised the woman waiting to immerse his body in the water. Antonia glared at him. She looked sturdier. He noticed how she whispered to the others before him and push their bodies down into the water. She whispered to him, 'You are one black messiah among many. Don't fail.'

Her hands were warm. She immersed his body in the water. He didn't feel himself being lifted back up. He tried to rise but lacked strength. The warm fingers were traps. He struggled. Time passed. He needed air. He shook his head below the water, searching for breath. Water rushed into his head through his nostrils and mouth. He woke. Christmas's spirit rose out of Moses's body.

A sheet of paper wavered over the floor in the room. Still breathing hard, Moses got up, lit a candle and picked up the dirty looking sheet. The writing, sketchy and barely visible, came from a different world. The writing seemed to be in blood instead of ink. It came from Antonia.

* * *

Many fugitives often passed through the Preacher residence. Some were unlucky and never made it to freedom. Many made it. Two brothers, Paul and Saul, arrived on New Year's Eve. Christmas climbed up to the attic, and saw Moses shaving a fugitive's hair.

'What is goin' on?' Christmas asked.

'Get a seat Christmas, and Saul gon shine your head,' Moses said. 'Blackness is our thin' to show off and it good for white people to see our heads shine.'

Christmas didn't know why he agreed but felt excitement stirring.

'See somethin' I done showed them boys,' Moses said gesturing at one of the fugitives. The fugitive passed on the piece of paper to Christmas.

He looked at the grubby piece of paper and read the words.

Messiah
You must fight for us. In this torture we learn to write and I have written this in the pit I now dwell in. The pit so full of black people. They kill and dump us here. So much suffering here. Don't let them win.

A.

'You knows who wrote that, Christmas?' Moses asked.

'Antonia?'

'I always knowed your magic strong,' Moses said. He looked at Paul. 'I never told nobody but Christmas knowed it was the dead woman who wrote it.'

A fugitive started to shave Christmas's head. The sheet faltered between Christmas's fingers.

'Look at it well. I'm the black messiah. I'm to save them black people.'

Christmas, curious, felt a portion of his hair shaved.

Moses handed the fugitive he just shaved a little mirror. 'I done seen them runaways come here to hide like scared chickens. We all got hands to resist slavery. White folks can't just wake up one day, go to Africa and steal people and not suffer the punishment for the wrong. We gon fight, Christmas. I gon be goin' back to the countryside, with our fugitive friends here. They ran from there. We gon all go back and slain that massa in the middle of the night.'

One of the fugitives nodded in agreement.

'And we gon come here and get rid of our own, Christmas,' Moses said. 'Mr. Preacher gon die.'

Christmas stopped the shave. He stood up. 'Moses, I ain't gon lie that I never wish Massa dead. I wish he dead many times, but think this with me: how we gon survive in Kentucky? Where we gon live. Where we gon earn somethin' small? How we gon eat, Moses?'

'He bought you and me. Please don't act no fool. We Africans. Before they done took us in Africa, we was farmers and hunters. We never beg no white man to survive. The words I speak is for our ears alone,' Moses said looking straight at Christmas. He showed Christmas his hands and continued. 'Whoever betray my words gon be killed by these.'

Christmas sat back and sighed.

Moses continued, 'If we all died for this, other black messiahs gon continue from where we stop. They all over America. Black messiahs. Fighters.'

'Mr. Preacher seem like a good white man,' Paul said.

'How dare you call that monster a good man!' said Moses in anger. 'This same white man be tried if caught in Africa for dividin' families. Look how he got my mother away from me for all the years, and when she back, she different. She ain't my mother no more. How dare you say that white man good when he got Antonia pregnant and got her killed. He keeps us all here makin' us believe them lies that we free. Without us, he can't survive. He no good man.'

* * *

The two fugitives were in the stable looking at the horses, comparing them to their master's horses. They came to agree no horse can beat the Kentucky breed. Moses insisted horses were horses. They selected horses to use on the day they intended to slay white people. They looked over Louisville, a place growing in population. Buildings sprouted up everywhere. A new three-storey building stood across the road. The place used to be a vast amount of cow pasture. There were many post offices with the closest situated on the east side of Third Street.

'I got to go to Lexington to bury an axe in the snow,' Moses told them. 'It is a ritual that gon help us defeat every white man we gon face.'

Christmas felt consumed by guilt in his heart. His eyes were on the white horse born the last time Mrs. Preacher set foot in the house.

'Can't the axe be buried here in Louisville?' one of the fugitives asked.

Moses unbolted the gate and let two horses out into the fields. He watched the horses chase each other. 'What ought to be done can only be done in Lexington.'

The clouds became pregnant with rain, and Moses departed. Christmas started to worry. At dinnertime Christmas stayed quiet, but listened to the fugitives talk about the women they left behind. He turned down their request to partake in a card game.

He got back to the dwelling, and saw Small John kicking a pig-bladder around the living room.

'Small John, if you want to play that, you do it out in the dark,' Christmas said shuffling the quadroon's blond hair.

Small John picked up his toy and ran into Black John's room. Christmas smiled. He remembered the year of the boy's birth. 1816. He returned from the hog house one foggy evening to the news about Nedi going into labour. His eardrums almost shattered. He could remember how Ark took advantage over everybody's distraction and sneaked a negro girl into Esther's room. Esther, being the midwife, never learned of the occurrence on her straw bed until this day. Christmas remembered Black John's reaction on seeing Small John for the first time. He wanted the baby to be his. Black John strode toward the room he now shared with Nedi. Esther held the quadroon baby by its legs and slashed the cord using a knife. Black John fell to his knees and cried.

* * *

Christmas along with the fugitives were being surrounded by patrollers with long guns. A few inches away, he saw the gory dead body of Moses on the ground. Christmas woke. His spirit remained troubled even though the tragedy turned out a dream. The winter night got colder. Christmas fed the fire in his room with more wood. He sat on the stool and placed his palms over his face. He did not believe Moses's reason for going to Lexington. To bury an axe? In his panic and frustration, his spirit became the flakes of snow blown into Lexington's thin air by the night wind. He could see Moses waiting behind a set of whitened trees watching a small cottage constructed of uneven and blackened planks. The snow whorled all over the place. Moses kept watching the house. A man and a woman returned in a wagon with shaky lamplights. The horse trotted smoothly. The wagon wheels left marks on the snowy ground. The snowflakes recognised the thirty-eight-year-old woman. Miss Emily Margaret Thatch. Christmas didn't feel like the flakes of snow anymore. The wagon's driver untied the horse and led it toward the stable. He saw Moses bring out the axe from underneath the red cloak he wore and sneak toward the house. How could he, Christmas, save the woman? He couldn't. Moses reached her.

The woman, unpacking some items from the wagon, didn't notice Moses behind her. He grabbed her from behind and placed the edge of the sharp axe against her throat. She couldn't make a sound. Moses dragged her back toward the set of trees, and did it. He killed the woman he last saw eighteen years ago. An elderly woman holding an infant came out of the house. The man in the stable ran back. Moses began to run. The flakes of snow slowly settled over the splash of blood on the ground.

Christmas panted strenuously on his return to his room. Moses truly buried the axe in the woman's throat. Christmas's heartbeat quickened. The fireplace gave off intense heat. He thought of his dream – how some patrollers surrounded him and the fugitive brothers. He left the dwelling for the big house, went up to the attic and woke the fugitive brothers.

'Y'all must leave now or face somethin' worse,' Christmas whispered.

'You askin' us to betray Moses?' one of them asked.

'Moses done killed somebody in Lexington. He be leadin' patrollers here.'

Saul got off the pallet on which he lay and said, 'I ain't goin' to no jail.'

They packed their belonging and sneaked out of the house. Street dogs barked loudly. Christmas found his way to Mr. Preacher's room.

'Massa, you gon die. You got to leave before he return,' Christmas said in great alarm, sending Mr. Preacher scrambling off the bed.

Confused, the white man yelled, 'Who? Who?'

'Moses gon kill you.'

'Where is he?'

'On his way from Lexington.'

Mr. Preacher sighed. 'What did he go to do there?'

'To kill Miss Emily Margaret.'

'You knew about this and didn't say?'

'He say he gon kill me.'

Mr. Preacher began to pace. 'Who else knows about this? Black John?'

'No, Massa.'

'Who else knows?'

'The two fugitives, Massa.'

'Where are they?'

'They gone.'

'Get two horses ready. We have to leave for somewhere safe.'

On their way to the patrol station, dawn skulked in. They came across a cart of slave catchers, and, surprisingly, the fugitive-brothers were bundled inside and forced to sit among other fugitives. They looked dejected and eyed Mr. Preacher contemptuously. Mr. Preacher ducked his head, and Christmas looked away. The dirt road waited ahead.

* * *

Christmas and Mr. Preacher waited in great trepidation at the patrol station. Christmas rocked himself into a light nap on the bench they were offered and his spirit stole back to the Preacher residence. Some patrol officers and their horses were all over the residence. Black John looked through the tiny window of his room.

A patroller whistled. The rest of the patrollers began to gather in several groups. Christmas saw Moses through the eyes of the sky walking toward the residence. On seeing the patrolmen, he spun around and began to run. A group of patrollers followed on foot. Two on horses. A larger number stayed behind but aimed their guns in the direction they saw Moses running.

The patrollers on horses caught up with Moses just before a jewellery shop and one of them tried to kick him down. Moses resisted and contoured his body to maintain his balance. He got the axe out and swung it at the officer kicking at him. The sharp edge of the axe stuck the officer's face, and blood splattered over his horse. The patrolman fell, and the other officer stopped the chase, got out his gun and shot twice. Moses fell. The sky shuddered. Someone wailed. Christmas sensed the presence of a vengeful spirit. Antonia wavered like a candlelight in the wind. Esther, horrified, ran to Moses and grasped his body.

* * *

Mr. Preacher and Christmas finally left the patrol station. On reaching the residence, Christmas sighted Black John approaching in a furious manner. They didn't anticipate an attack. The pull, fierce and quick, brought Christmas down onto the snow. The horse Christmas fell from galloped away. Black John started punching Christmas and screaming, 'You betrayin' nigger!'

Mr. Preacher jumped down from his horse and dashed toward Black John. He grabbed Black John by the shoulder and tossed him aside.

Black John hesitated before finding his feet. 'Don't touch me again, Mr. Preacher.'

'Black John, We need to talk,' Mr. Preacher pleaded.

'This betrayin' nigger caused my brother trouble. You knows what this gon do to my sixty-seven-year-old mama? She dyin' too...'

Christmas sat up and wiped the blood from the side of his mouth.

'They call you a flyin' man, Christmas,' Black John said in deep anger. 'I ain't no fool to believe that. You disgust me.'

Mr. Preacher gestured at Christmas not to say a word.

* * *

The shops were all closed – the drug stores, the Vienna Bakery, even the flower shops. Christmas, Mr. Preacher, Black John, Esther and other Louisville residents, mostly white, arrived early to follow the proceedings. Two patrolmen dragged Moses, covered in bandages, toward the scaffold. Four other patrolmen with three other residents confronted the patrolmen holding Moses. A tussle resulted between the confronting patrolmen and the ones with Moses. The confronters managed to take full-charge of Moses, and the crowd roared.

The assailants, now with Moses, headed in another direction, leaving the scaffold behind. They found a tree, knotted a rope and heaped some woods and coals underneath the tree. They tied the rope to a branch. They fixed the knot around Moses's feet and pulled. Moses's body dangled. Water ran out his nose. The crowd cheered the patrollers. Mr. Preacher cautioned Black John to remain calm. Christmas squatted, tears rushing from his eyes. He prayed to his alekwuafia for an intervention, to free Moses from this cruelty and to take him to a place of safety. Black John gnashed his teeth in silence. The people lit the fire underneath Moses. The fire excited them and they let the rope slide down slowly bringing agony upon Moses's body.

Moses tried hard to twist his burning body. He wanted to bend his upper body toward his legs, so he could try to free himself but the melting belly fat around his waist hindered this. Moses called his mother's name. He called for Black John. He screamed. They wanted him to die slowly hence they didn't let the fire take full control. They dragged his burning body upwards. Moses gained energy from the air and raised himself with great effort. He overcame the hindrance over his waist. His hand got hold of the knot around his legs. He tried to untie himself but the men dropped him down, on the fire. Moses writhed in agony. They lifted Moses away from the fire, placed him on the ground and battered his body with burning logs. Two men invited by the assailants used machetes to cut off Moses fingers in four blows. Christmas shivered. The gory fingers lay over the patchy snowy ground. A woman in the crowd fainted. They pulled Moses back up using the rope. He went crazy. He pulled his burning body up again to untie the knot around his feet but could only smear the ropes with blood.

* * *

'Why they kill him like that?' Black John cried over Christmas's shoulder. Small John walked into his mother's embrace. Ark and Sally seemed to lack words.

'America bad under President Munroe,' Nedi said.

Black John stopped crying. Silence. He cleared his throat and began, 'I always thought that you, Christmas, gon kill me because of Nedi. You never done that. But I tell you...' He paused and swallowed. 'Moses's death hurts so bad. I don't know if I can forgive you for rattin' on him like that. I swear I was gon kill you.' He couldn't continue.

'I loves Moses too,' Christmas said.

'Don't tell me that, Christmas,' Black John responded. 'I gon keep hopin' them black messiahs like him come save black folks.' He sighed and looked at Nedi. 'I loves you Nedi. I loves you.'

'My man, I loves you too,' Nedi replied.

'Mr. Preacher should pay for this,' Black John lamented. 'He should die for this.'

'If he die, Black John, where you gon go? How you gon live?' Christmas said.

'How Tallie and the other free negroes in Louisville survive?' Black John replied.

They heard someone's footstep on the staircase outside the dwelling. The door opened and closed. Mr. Preacher walked in. 'You all should leave this...'

'We ain't your slaves no more,' Black John stood up to challenge Mr. Preacher. 'You don't tell us what to do! You should give me back all them money you held back for Moses's rent now that you and your white folks done killed him.'

Mr. Preacher took off his hat and walked up very close to Black John. 'I know you blame me and Christmas for your brother's death. I feared for my life, and what resulted wasn't of my making. I didn't compel anybody to live here. I gave you all options because I know how terrible this land is to negroes. Moses grew to hate me, and I do not blame him for that. He understood what white people in this land of America represent. For you, Black John, to become like your brother,' he shook his head, 'is unacceptable. I would be forced to harm you.'

'I'm gon stay here and...' Black John began.

Christmas touched him. 'Black John, I beg you not to say no more.'

'I came to request that you all leave this dwelling,' Mr. Preacher said. 'I got word from Tallie that an angry mob from Fayette County are on their way here to cause hurt. I would say some of them were neighbours of the late Emily Margaret. You all should go and stay in the woods until dark.'

* * *

The cold increased. Black John suggested they make a fire, but Nedi feared it might draw the attention of the Lexington people. Esther stayed quiet covering herself with the red quilt with yellow stripes she brought along. Small John gathered some large leaves and spread over the earth for him and Sally to lay on. Ark wandered further into the woods, and Christmas, desiring some warmth from the fire, got his spirit to transmute into fire. His body indeed felt the warmth, but in the spirit he could hear voices. What he heard became a vision. People came in numbers. They rode in circles. Their echoing voices were like the night. They screamed like wild birds in front of the big house. Mr. Preacher came out with a gun slung over his shoulder.

'You must be Mr. Preacher?' the man likely to be their leader asked. His voice echoed all the way through the woods against Christmas's ears.

'Yes,' Mr. Preacher replied.

'The nigger who murdered the Lexington woman lived here, we are told.'

'He was answerable to the law, not the mob,' Mr. Preacher replied, a calm echo.

'We reckon he had accomplices and we have come for them,' the man shot back. His horse got unsettled, expressing its agitation.

'That is wrong. Please leave my residence at once.'

'We are going nowhere until you hand the murderers to us.'

'I'm asking politely. Please leave,' Mr. Preacher said pulling his gun which hung from his shoulder and aiming it at the man.

'Henry, we didn't come for him,' one of the assailants advised.

'Any white man who loves niggers is also a nigger,' Henry said. He walked toward Mr. Preacher.

'Stay away, young man,' Mr. Preacher warned.

The man spat on the ground, turned around and headed for his horse. He soon headed out of the residence along with his faction.

* * *

Christmas's spirit flared up and became uncontrollable. He watched himself, aggravated by anger, tearing down the three-storey brick building, burning freedom papers, their clothes and beds, devouring broken walls and bricks. Around this destruction, he saw the Lexington horsemen and hungered for their lives.

Christmas desired to consume Mr. Preacher's mansion. He desired to end Mr. Preacher's life, but he hesitated. And through the eyes of the fire he saw Mr. Preacher firing his long gun at the horsemen. They fled, and the big house remained.

* * *

They returned deep in the night. Esther, at the forefront, held onto Small John's hand. The boy coughed. She stopped and wrapped her quilt around him. Ark walked alongside Sally. Nedi's wail alerted them. They saw the misfortune awaiting them. Their dwelling, burnt to the ground, seemed to be dispensing a lot of smoke into the air. The roofing sheets, blackened by the cruelty of fire, glared upwards.

Mr. Preacher emerged, and cleared his throat before speaking. 'They came here to cause us trouble,' he said sadly. 'I was on watch but didn't realise their presence until they set the dwelling on fire. They plotted to burn the mansion too. The patrollers have been here and are in search of the crooks.'

'What this hate for?' Esther grieved.

Christmas knelt. '*Eche!*' he muttered.

* * *

The feeling in the big house felt different. The clatter of Small John, and the intensity of his voice. Mr. Preacher now allowed the Society of Friends to meet in his living room since the dwelling existed no more. The big house became a full house, and he needed to show his fellow Quakers his transformed nature.

Christmas returned from the farm. On this noisy morning, he could hear Small John having an argument with Nedi. She wouldn't let him go out of the residence to mingle with other negro boys his age.

'You different,' she always said to him. 'Not for bein' a quadroon, but for bein' a slave.' Kentucky law still considered him a slave.

The boy accepted the restriction, headed toward the stable and began kicking the pig-bladder around.

Christmas stepped into the hallway and saw Mr. Preacher peering into the room Nedi, Black John and Small John shared. The white man, now fifty-seven, seemed to indulge in this. The particular door stayed slightly ajar during most part of the day. Nedi, unclothed, failed to notice anything. This didn't shock Christmas, but he felt offended. The so-called righteous and humble Quaker perished in lust. Christmas watched Mr. Preacher approach the door. The white man pushed it further, entered and shut it. Christmas heard Nedi call out once. Not in panic. Only once. Some silence followed. Christmas walked to the door to open it, but stopped. She failed to object. Moreover, Nedi wasn't his anymore. Why should he, Christmas, care? If they were still together, the pathetic white man wouldn't be alive.

Christmas proceeded to his new abode in the attic and sat on a wooden stool. He wondered if he could protect her dignity. He thought of what he could do.

For the rest of the week his spirit kept hovering around the big house monitoring Nedi's carnal relations. Sometimes he got entrapped in lust. Nedi stayed in Black John's company most of the time, and not Mr. Preacher's. But he dug up something else. Mr. Preacher seemed fond of Esther. They were greying considerably and matched each other.

In one of Christmas's restless nights, his spirit found Mr. Preacher and invaded his mind. The white man tried to do some writing in his journal but the words weren't coming. He heard Esther whistling. The whistling soon faded into a sob. Mr. Preacher left his study for the lobby. Esther held the piece of cloth meant for cleaning the stair-rails. Mr. Preacher approached her and touched her on the shoulder. She shivered and wept the more. He pulled her into his embrace. Christmas reflected upon his affection for this woman.

'My son die bad,' she said to Mr. Preacher.

'I'm sorry, Esther,' Mr. Preacher replied.

She continued to sob. The front of his shirt stuck to his chest with her tears.

'My Moses. My Moses,' she went on. She let the cloth in her hand fall and held Mr. Preacher around his waist. She desired comfort. The clock ticked. A horse outside neighed. Esther kept sniffing. The white man pulled her away and stared into her eyes.

Mr. Preacher said nothing, but kept his arm around the back of her shoulder.

'Thank you, Mr. Preacher,' she said, wiped her eyes, picked up the cloth and left for the staircase.

She placed a foot on a step and glanced back at the white man.

'Wait,' Mr. Preacher said and went to her. He pulled her to his body and placed his mouth on her lips.

She remained still. He took his lips away, and she sniffed. Again she said, 'Thank you, Mr. Preacher.'

* * *

Christmas's spirit monitored Mr. Preacher's affair with Esther. She woke in the middle of the night on Mr. Preacher's bed and sat up. Mr. Preacher opened his eyes, touched her hand and squeezed it.

'I got to go,' she said.

'Stay till dawn,' he pleaded, and she lay back.

Toward dawn, Moses's spirit walked into the room. The spirit stared around before focusing on Mr. Preacher. Christmas's spirit felt disturbed. Christmas knew Mr. Preacher felt the presence of Moses. He attempted to open his mouth to scream but couldn't. Mr. Preacher tried to take his hands off Esther but couldn't. He shut his eyes for a moment and opened them. Moses walked away through the walls of the room. Voice and strength came back. Mr. Preacher started to choke and Esther woke.

'Mr. Preacher, you alright?'

'I... I saw him right here... Moses,' he said.

Esther held him in terror. Mr. Preacher feared for his own life. She cried. She loved Moses. Christmas wept and left them for his abode. Now in his body in the attic, he could hear loud laughter of some men. The noise came from the living room. It seemed too early for anyone to visit. He climbed down the attic and entered the living room. There were three young men all with Ark. They stared in his direction. They were the Preacher sons. All grown now.

'Is that you, Christmas?' Marcus, now thirty-two and solidly built in stature, asked.

'It is me, ole Christmas.'

'Everybody in Louisville has changed,' Hugh, still thin and now twenty-two, added.

'Ark here is giving us all a good laugh. He thinks our old man found himself an old mistress,' Simons said, and they all began to laugh again until they heard their father's footsteps coming down the stairs.

'Oh! My sons! Look how grown you have all become. Must have travelled during the night,' Mr. Preacher said, elated.

* * *

A group of white Quaker men started to visit Mr. Preacher and his sons, sometimes thrice a week.

Marcus soon got tired of their constant visits. 'I wasn't born to be a Quaker. I am not interested in using the words 'thee' and 'thou' to nobody,' he said to his father and walked out of one meeting.

Simons, Hugh and their father kept meeting with the Quakers in the weeks that followed. Simons soon followed in Marcus's steps. Unlike Marcus, he didn't get angry. He just stopped showing up whenever they came. Hugh's interest surprised Christmas. He never expected Hugh to get involved in the Society, but he did.

* * *

Christmas completed his evening chores in the kitchen house before heading for the big house. He took out one of the straw beds in the attic and slid the pallet underneath the remaining straw bed.

He heard someone's footsteps coming up to the attic.

'How you doin', Christmas?' Black John said on entering. 'Surprised I'm here to see how you was?'

'No... Not so bad. The house too full.'

'I reckon they be here all summer. The first thin' Massa Marcus say to me when he saw me – why y'all black folks still livin' like slaves?' Black John sat on the chair in front of the bed.

'What you says?'

'I says, livin' outside this residence was livin' in hell.'

'And what he say?'

'He says, as usual, come live in the north. Come to New York.'

Christmas sighed. 'I likes Hugh. He grown to a fine gentleman. Still so white.'

'He got some of Antonia's looks.'

'He far better-lookin',' said Christmas. 'He becomin' a Quaker man.'

'I never likes the strange manners of those folks,' Black John said. 'You gon play cards? Massa Simons been wantin' us to join them in the livin' room.'

'Ain't keen but don't want to disappoint nobody.'

In the living room, Christmas, Black John, Marcus and Simons got deep into the game of cards. Marcus often ran his fingers through his long curly hair. Mr. Preacher read the *Kentucky Observer*. Hugh, seated beside him, tidied his fingernails.

'Any news on that Denmark Vesey fella?' Marcus asked looking at his father. 'That negro was capable of wiping out all of the South.'

'The paper mentioned he has been hanged,' Mr. Preacher said and put the newspaper aside.

'History would certainly be in the books if he succeeded. Certainly, the bloodiest insurrection in America,' Hugh said.

'The negro took his time like the world was waiting for him. White folks in the north were safe, anyway,' Simons added on playing a card.

'This man y'all calls Denmark Vesey...? Where he from?' Christmas asked picking a set of cards.

'I think North Carolina,' Hugh said.

'South Carolina. He is from Charleston in South Carolina,' Marcus corrected.

'Father, I understand Christmas and Black John are free but I can't help wondering why they can't begin a life of their own,' Simons said.

'I asked Black John the same question on our first day here,' Marcus added.

'They are employed here and all have a life of their own,' Mr. Preacher replied.

'Massa right. Nowhere in Kentucky as good as here,' Christmas said. He remembered how Mr. Preacher entered Nedi's room. Christmas imagined Nedi's bare body in the arms of the white man.

'Growing up in New York we heard of southern white masters lashing negroes they kept in their household, and I was only glad to learn that father wasn't that way,' Simons said.

'I used to be like that,' Mr. Preacher said.

'But you are certainly guilty of using negro women, father,' Marcus said.

'Stop it Marcus,' Simons said looking up.

Silence.

'Matters of slavery shouldn't be ignored,' Marcus said.

'It is sensitive especially with Hugh and Black... John here,' Simons said.

'Father needs to pray tell what the hell he does with the negro women that live here!' Marcus insisted.

Mr. Preacher stared at Marcus. Christmas looked at Black John. Black John stood up and began walking away.

'You don't walk away like that, Black John,' Mr. Preacher said stopping him. 'It is disrespectful.'

'My brother done died because of you, Mr. Preacher. I beg you, please let me be. I don't want to know what you makin' my mama or Nedi do.'

'You don't talk to our father like that! He didn't rape your mother or even your woman,' Simons said looking straight at Black John.

Black John looked away, and walked out of the lounge.

'Some things better left unsaid, Marcus,' Mr. Preacher said.

Marcus sat up, nodded his head, got up and left too.

'I'm sorry, father,' Simons said.

'There was no need for such conversation,' Mr. Preacher said and stiffly took his leave.

Simons followed, leaving Christmas and Hugh. Silence.

'What you see yourself as?' Christmas asked.

'You mean as being a negro or white folk?' Hugh replied.

Christmas shook his head. He watched Hugh light a pipe and puff out some smoke.

'All my life I thought I was white. As I grew older I began to notice the difference between my brothers and I. Mother said she wasn't my real mother. She said my real mother was a terrible black woman.'

Christmas sighed.

'Tell me, Christmas. Was she bad? She is the reason I hate to think I'm a negro.'

'Antonia ain't bad... But she stubborn. She done whatever she wanted. She worshipped Mr. Preacher. She said whatever comes to her mind and did whatever she can to hurt folks who hurt her. She a good woman. She no fool. Slavery all that is evil.'

'She killed Harriet, and mother will never forget Harriet.'

Christmas walked up to him. 'Moses ain't dead because he a bad person either. Slavery all that is evil.'

'How would you react if you were Antonia, Christmas?' Hugh asked. 'If you were in her place and in love with your own owner?'

'I don't know.'

'Would you like to return to Africa?'

'I don't know,' Christmas answered.

'To answer your question,' Hugh began. 'I see myself as a spirit. My body is just a house. The spiritual world is all that matter. It controls this earthly world. In the spiritual world, we have no race. No white man. No black man. We are all equal.'

'I believe that too,' Christmas said, a bit more interested.

'You can't be conscious of your spiritual self except you carry the inner light in you.'

Christmas sighed. He wanted to hear something different, something related to his Idoma beliefs.

'Don't get me wrong, Christmas. I'm not preaching religion to you. I'm not my father. I hate hypocrisy. I'm not interested in the use of 'thee' and 'thou'. Those words I will never use. How can you not talk to everyone in the same manner?'

'I got my own beliefs,' Christmas said.

'Can you share your beliefs with me?'

Christmas laughed. 'I believe there's another world where all my ancestors done go after they dead. I believe Abutu Eje is the first man of my great tribe. His father was a leopard who impregnated a beautiful woman.'

'Why are you living a world of lies?' Hugh asked. 'Remember my question. Think on it.'

This reply offended Christmas but he could only smile.

* * *

Christmas seeped into his master's mind. The night became extremely windy and tree branches outside broke noisily. Candle flames within the house flickered. Mr. Preacher, seated behind the desk, started to scribble a letter. He worried over his children's reaction to his relationship with Esther. He ended up with a pile of crushed papers in the bin. What reason could he give the Society of Friends for his exit? Could he say God led him? He indeed followed a leading. Everything in him pushed him to leave the Society. He began to write again and narrated all the occurrences between himself and the two negro women living in his house. This resulted to two pages. He couldn't give them this, he concluded. Covetousness and fornication were his sins. He took out another sheet and began to write again. He indicated he wasn't comfortable with the doctrines the Hicksites were suggesting in Quakerism. He stated how he couldn't stand the division and misunderstandings emanating between the liberals trying to alter Quakerism; and to make it worse, they left the evangelicals to fight the terrible war of slavery alone. He again tore up the letter, and Christmas felt sorry for him.

Back in his own body in the attic, Christmas thought of his son. Oda'nyaa emerged and sat on the bed gazing at him.

'I think you and Orinya lie always. You two keep lying to me.'

'You beginning to believe the black son of Mr. Preacher.'

'Prove to me he is wrong. Show me Ijeyi now if you are not a "lie" in existence.'

'There're some things destiny is in control of. Ijeyi being sold is a result of destiny having its way,' she replied.

'Destiny,' he muttered. 'Orinya also says it is my destiny to die in Oli'doma.'

'The question becomes this – is he telling you the truth?'

'You have said that before. That is not important right now. What must I pay to have Ijeyi back in my lifetime?'

She stood to her feet. 'I will tell you.'

He watched her ghostly form turn her back to him. He gazed at her legs. These legs weren't real but were vital for her to be with him.

She turned around and said, 'How about I give you an opportunity to strike back at the cause of the loss?'

He thought of what he could possibly do to the mad Mr. Peterson at this hour of the night. He could gouge out his eyes and cause his brain to melt out of his head.

She smiled. 'Shall we go?'

He nodded in agreement. She placed her hands on his shoulders and she became the night. He became a shadow. Trees shook in the wind. Oda'nyaa finally transformed to a woman in slave clothing. Her hair, tangled in locks like Nedi's.

Oda'nyaa banged on the door of the mansion in the Peterson plantation several times. Mr. Peterson opened, and she went in. The door shut. Soon, she reeled out and staggered toward the dead cotton fields. The emaciated white man, fully bearded and dirty, emerged following her toward River Road. Christmas saw Oda'nyaa beckoning Mr. Peterson. The white man followed. Two stray cats ogled and howled. Mr. Peterson soon began to stagger. Christmas's shadow followed.

The white man chased Oda'nyaa on the bank of the black river she led him to. In the form of the night shadow, Christmas ran toward the river and dived into it. He felt the water burn. He metamorphosed into the warrior his people in Oli'doma were known for. He became a crocodile sliding through the waters to catch up with the man. On reaching an easy spot to catch Mr. Peterson, the crocodile leapt up high and reached him. The beast dragged Mr. Peterson into the river.

Oda'nyaa metamorphosed into a crocodile and joined Christmas. They sank their teeth into the skinny flesh. They tore his limbs and fed on the flesh. They drank the blood, which washed down the meat until they were full. They cracked the bones underneath the river and spared the head.

On Market Street the following day, the bell rang to warn residents of dangerous crocodiles in black Kentucky rivers. This actually occurred; not lies in his head. Hugh couldn't be right.

* * *

Christmas led Tallie and the two other white Quaker men to the living room to meet Mr. Preacher. From there Mr. Preacher led the men into the tea room.

'We hear that thy sons are still here,' one of the visitors said.

'Yes. They are out hunting,' Mr. Preacher replied. 'Hugh has been building himself in the faith. He attends meetings in the Hammond residence.'

Christmas filled the tea kettle and placed it on the table.

'Did ye hear about the killin' in the river?' Tallie asked.

Christmas paused on his way out of the tea room.

'Crocodiles they say,' one of the overseers added.

'Here in Louisville?' Mr. Preacher asked.

'Ate a whole man leaving just the head that was found floating this morning.'

'Oh dear God,' Mr. Preacher replied. 'Any chance the dead was identified?'

'A butcher swore it was Mr. Peterson of the Peterson plantation, but the patrollers are still asking people questions.'

'Oh goodness, that fella lost his mind years ago,' Mr. Preacher said.

Christmas, back in the tea room, served tea to each of the men.

Mr. Preacher glanced at him. 'You heard the story about Mr. Peterson, Christmas?'

'I heard he dead, Mr. Preacher,' Christmas replied.

'Poor wretch,' Mr. Preacher said.

'Mr. Preacher,' one of the men began, 'we got thy letter, and as our practice directs, Mr. Timothy and myself were delegated to come visit thee and perhaps...'

'I have requested to leave the Society and I don't see any possibility of becoming one of ye again,' Mr. Preacher replied. 'Just as my letter reads, I am of a mind to keep a mistress which is unacceptable in Quakerism.'

'We got to work around this as God leads, Mr. Preacher,' Tallie added.

'Any marriage in my life again is adultery, and I will be killed by my own guilt if I pray for Fiona to die. As a Quaker man I cannot divorce as ye know.'

'We can try to resolve thy marriage again.'

'It has been tried before. It failed. Ye know nothing can be done. I would rather not speak about my decision henceforth,' Mr. Preacher said.

Two of the men emptied their teacups and left disappointed. Tallie stayed back.

'Even if thou ain't gon be part of the Society, thou can still have a relationship with God.'

'Tallie, that would be between myself and the Lord.'

'Quaker brethren in neighbouring states have warned fugitives to avoid your residence since the Moses incident. But if any runaway shows up, I am at your service,' Tallie said and he stood up to go.

'I will count on thee if necessary, Tallie.'

Christmas saw him to his horse outside.

* * *

The news of Mr. Peterson's passing soon circulated and Black John danced with Nedi over it. Nedi, although reluctant in dancing, loved the news.

'They say a crocodile done ate the white man, leavin' his head floatin',' Black John said and released Nedi. She sat on a stool, and he continued to dance. 'It gon be liberty for the woman I love! Liberty for her children too! Hooray! It gon be Preacher and his sons next.'

'Don't wish that on other white folks,' Nedi said. 'What a cruel way for a white man to die. Mr. Peterson deserves death but not like that.'

'Ark, come dance with me,' Black John called out on seeing Nedi's boy come into the living room. 'Your mama ain't talkin' no sense.'

'Ark, don't,' Nedi objected.

'I wasn't gon dance like a clown,' Ark said.

Black John stopped and asked, 'Why?'

'Mr. Peterson horrible,' Nedi began. 'But Ark ain't that cruel to celebrate his own father dyin'.'

'She right,' Esther said walking by.

'I never got no father, people,' Ark said, his face in disgust.

'Let's talk about somethin' different,' Black John said. 'What it gon cost me to have Nedi dance with me again?'

Christmas wondered if Black John ever knew of Mr. Preacher being with Nedi.

'You want to know?' Nedi asked. 'You gon roast me a chicken and them creamy salad leaves before we gon go merry-makin' on Sixth Street. There I gon dance with you'

'I gon do anythin' for you, Nedi,' Black John said.

Friday night came. In jealousy, Christmas watched Black John and Nedi leave for the dance. He got into the attic and noticed some blue and red reflections. He looked around and saw Orinya sitting on the floor with his back against the wall.

'Orinya, I...'

The masquerade raised a hand to stop the words. 'I have only brought some news from Opialu.'

Christmas's heart ran faster.

'I know you don't wish to hear from me but I remain by you. Oda'nyaa wouldn't tell you this. It is bad news. *Adou* passed on to the ancestral land. Abah your brother will bury him any moment.'

Christmas found the straw bed and sat, with his palms over his face. He asked, 'How is my mother?'

'She left the world before he did. Three years now.'

'You were quiet about that?'

'She was a woman.'

Christmas sighed. Orinya left and his reflections in the room faded. His thoughts were back to the days of childhood. He cried and his tears spilled over the brick floor. The tears penetrated the floor, went down deeply and became the soil being dug in Opialu. He saw Abah and some of his step-brothers lay his father's casket into the ground. He heard the drummers' music and saw the young women dance. He smelt *onihi* and *njangada* soup.

Christmas lay on the bed in the attic and closed his eyes. He saw himself lying on the dirty playground filled with youths all asleep. He sat up and saw carts with greatly designed wheels all over the place. Their hooting sounds were like the sound of a trumpet.

'You!' someone called.

He turned around and saw Olofu of the future.

'What are you doing here?' Christmas asked, surprised because the Olofu he saw some time back wasn't this grubby; wasn't this small and couldn't even talk.

'I should be the one asking you what you are doing here in my world!'

'You are the one talking!'

'You are not talking to me in person.'

'Who am I talking to?'

'My spirit.'

'Your spirit... Hmm.'

'Destiny is wicked. Couldn't give me my voice. Our alekwuafia made it possible that I talk only in spirit.'

'Where is your body?'

'Elsewhere.'

'Where is this place?'

'Africa,' Olofu replied.

'Why is your spirit in this realm?'

'To talk to other spirits of young people. All of them sleeping there,' he said and pointed, '...are spirits embodied with lips all mute. They come here and our spirits chat away. What we can't do in the real world.'

Christmas pointed at a crowd ahead. They were filling an area like a market place. 'Are those people real people or spirits?'

'Real people,' Olofu replied.

'*Adam* dead,' Christmas said.

'In my world you are already dead,' Olofu said.

'But I'm you.'

'Not yet,' Olofu refuted.

'Tell me something. Between Oda'nyaa and Orinya, who...'

'Orinya is real, but everything about Oda'nyaa is a passing enjoyment,' Olofu interrupted.

'I saw you and her kissin' and...'

'She is only a distraction,' Olofu said.

'Orinya gon kill me,' Christmas said.

'Destiny is better than lies or empty happiness. If he kills you, he is taking you somewhere.'

'Hmm... I know,' Christmas said. 'You really as smart as you talk in spirit?'

'True... I'm better than you,' Olofu replied teasing.

Back in his Louisville bed his body remained asleep. But his spirit continued the journey. He went in search of his father. In the ancestral land a gathering of elderly fathers were seated in front of huts made of gold. The thatched roofs shone like marble. These ancestors laughed and one of them said to Christmas, 'Orinya has taken your father back to Opialu. If you leave in time you will see them.'

Christmas began his journey, first transforming into the heavy clouds before becoming rain. He rained upon Opialu. The village looked different. War crept in and he could see burnt houses around. Being the wet earth, he felt the trotting feet of horses. They were horses from Hausa-land and their riders were people of a strange religion. They came with books and beads hung around their necks.

He heard one shout, 'Ayi'doma must turn away from their ancestors and worship the real Allah.'

The man wore a thick white robe almost blackened by dust. He used the same kind of cloth to wrap around his head. His beard, covered too. Where was Orinya? Where was his father? Where were the people of Opialu? The earth sniffed around. His people were all hiding for their lives. He perceived a crowd coming from afar to fight these Hausas. A lot of noise came from the horde. They sounded like bees but weren't bees. They were tsetse flies, a great group of Opialu insects. His father, Ogwuche, and his greatest of ancestors, Orinya, were in the form of this multitude of tsetse flies. The Hausas dreaded these insects, and the entire troops of the Hausa army began to flee. The insects caught up with them and stung them. The Hausas were all overpowered by sleep on war grounds. And the people of Oli'doma came out of their hiding to chop off their heads.

Christmas woke in the middle of the night. He tried to sleep again but couldn't. He remembered his ancestors' presence in form of tsetse flies. He sat up.

He thought of his mother. He remembered her movements in the small kitchen house before dinner. He remembered the smell of her soups. How Ochi'Oche's father haunted their neighbourhood each time *Eje* and *Agbou* were about to be served. The man came, swallowing each time. And he ate and licked all his fingers. He always laughed a satisfying laugh: 'Kakakakaa'. Mother mimicked the laughter in his absence. Sometimes, he, Ochigbo, did the same. Even their father enjoyed mimicking the laughter. It brought joy to the evening stories that followed. Ogwuche Ogah, Christmas could swear, enjoyed his mother's food more than the food cooked by his other wives, but he sustained peace in his household and never allowed jealousy or strife live for a second.

* * *

Christmas couldn't sleep in the middle of the night. He thought of Black John and Nedi. His spirit became the night and found the dancing ground. A number of lamplights were spotted. Black John couldn't dance and raise his legs to the rhythm like Nedi did. Negroes clapped and sang alongside the sound of the harmonica. Nedi swayed her matted locks in a spectacular manner. The jealous night cursed Black John. Every other dancer stopped dancing to stare at Nedi and Black John.

'Why be with a woman better than you is?' a man asked, and a woman beside him slapped him across the face.

A group of men by the corner laughed. Black John fell over in exhaustion, panting. Another man took leave of his wife and dragged off Nedi. He danced with Nedi to the increasing cheer of the crowd.

Black John stood to his feet, found the woman serving liquors and asked for more.

'Ain't givin' you no more. Look at you. As drunk as a hog.'

'What you say? Ain't drunk.'

'You ain't even good enough for your woman.'

'She my wife,' he said. 'She ain't just my woman.' And he staggered off to join a group of men. Nedi stopped dancing and more cheers went up the air.

Black John joined a group of men. He heard one of them mention a familiar name. Denmark Vesey.

'Heard about that nigger. We ought to be proud of him,' Black John began. 'May be dead but his spirit ain't.'

More people gathered around him.

'My brother got this spirit of the messiah and they cut him down. We niggers too dumb to know the spirit we carry sometime. I can make black people rich and free in America when I find me some strong black folks,' Black John went on.

A few negroes cheered and encouraged him to keep speaking. Being the night, Christmas breathed evil upon Black John right there. Some folks mocked him. They said his words were empty. 'How you gon kill a chicken when you can't stand a woman dancin'?' a woman in the crowd asked.

The merry-makers' excitement soon turned to horror. A group of white men with muskets sprang into the crowd and negro men and women began to run. Some negroes didn't see the white men in time and suffered bruises from the butts of the muskets.

Nedi fled but Black John stayed and continued to talk.

'You knows me. I got the messiah spirit. Dare to shoot me! You can't. Bullets gon go back to y'all. Try it,' Black John challenged them, pulling off his shirt.

'Shut the trench you have for a mouth,' one of the white men said.

'What you gon do?' Black John replied.

The white men cocked his musket, levelled at Black John's chest, and without a word of warning a shot rang out. Black John fell. Christmas thought of being with Nedi again. The white men pounced on Black John. They stamped on him. They hit him on the jaw, nose and head with their muskets. He couldn't even shield his face. The night felt the shattering pain in Black John's shoulder. He clutched his gory face and tried to stand. He fell again. Christmas's spirit slipped back to his body lying in the attic of the Preacher's mansion.

* * *

Someone banged on his door. Christmas opened the door to see young Master Marcus holding a rifle and behind him, stood Nedi, in tears.

'Come on, Christmas. Black John is in trouble. We need to go and fetch him.'

Christmas followed them to the stable and they untied two horses. Christmas mounted Mr. Preacher's white mare and pulled Nedi up on the back of the horse. This closeness stirred him despite the worrying situation.

'Them white mens come from nowhere and started whippin' negroes using muskets,' she began. 'I so scared they gon kill him.'

'No way they gon kill him, Nedi,' Christmas said, unsure of his own words.

They couldn't avoid the puddles before them. The mud-splattered horses endured and journeyed through the darkness. They couldn't see anyone in the merry-making ground on Sixth Street. They spotted about four broken lamps with flames still alive scattered in different corners.

'There.' Nedi pointed.

The horse Marcus rode neighed. Marcus released a bullet into the sky and some people were spotted sprinting out of their hiding places. Marcus and Christmas rode toward the body, gored on the ground. Nedi dashed for Black John's body. She lay upon it crying. Marcus checked around the vicinity for anyone else. Some horsemen, about five in number, were seen approaching from a distance.

'Nedi, watch out!' Marcus warned.

Christmas helped Nedi up. The horsemen reached them. They were patrolmen. Some of them held lamps.

One of them climbed down. He looked at Black John's body and said, 'Is that the negro, Black John?'

'Yes. He is of the Preacher residence,' Marcus replied.

The patrolman walked to the body and gave it a kick.

Black John moaned.

'He is alive.'

In tears Nedi embraced Christmas.

'We are taking him with us,' the patrolman said.

'Why?' Marcus asked.

'We heard he has been causing trouble. Declared allegiance to Denmark Vesey. We need to keep Louisville safe from rogues like this. Get him over here,' another patrolman on horseback said.

Nedi sat stock still, a figure of desolation on the cracked ground. She wouldn't stop weeping.

* * *

Hugh, now a devoted Quaker, often prayed loudly in a strange language. Marcus and Simons busied themselves hunting wild possums. Mr. Preacher isolated himself even more, shouting and calling Esther's name in the night. Moses's ghost kept visiting. Ark hired himself out to scrub a white woman's store, and met other negroes. He fell in and out of love affairs. One time he came home asking Christmas to help him decide whether to go with a free negro girl or a slave girl. Christmas, careful in giving advice, allowed Ark to point out the one he loved better and encouraged him to go for her. The rooms in the big house became too small for Small John. He now climbed over the fences and raced along River Road with other children, despite being warned not to mingle too much until Doctor Fruitvale saw him. Measles recently became the most frightful disease among children in Louisville.

Christmas and Nedi experienced their awkward moments. Once he helped her hang Small John's clothes on the line, and their bodies touched. He knew she felt the same way he felt. He knew she still held a place for him in her heart. He longed to help her. He helped her with fire in the kitchen. One time he helped her salt the pork Mr. Preacher sent down from the hog house. On washing their hands afterwards, he found himself doing what he normally did ten years ago – drawing her body to his. She pushed him away.

The next day she came to meet him at the hog farm.

'Been long since Ijeyi was sold away, Christmas.'

He nodded.

'We can't pretend that life gon ever be fine between us.'

'You right, Nedi.'

'I gon wait for Black John. I loves him still.'

Her words hurt.

'Difference is he in prison,' she added.

'And you gon wait?'

She nodded.

'You ain't gon pay no man of my kind time until he free?'

She nodded again. For all her words, it didn't end there. Some nights later he got woken by a tap on his door. He staggered up and went to open it. She stood in the dark. His wife. The one Black John never married. He let her in and bolted the door. He lit the candle and watched her disrobe in front of him.

He looked away, headed past her and sat on the brick floor.

'Ain't you gon touch me?' she asked.

His spirit became a butterfly flying through the night all the way to the dungeon on Fifth Street. Black John, with iron bars around his neck, looked up. Tears came down his cheeks.

She advanced toward him.

'Stop Nedi. He… he, Black John, still loves you. He gon come back soon and you two gon bury all the lost time.'

'How you know that?'

'I just know.'

'You loves me no more?' she asked.

Christmas said nothing. He watched her cover herself. She unbolted the door and left. He stared at the shut door and remembered how Mr. Preacher went into her room to have her. The pain of that day didn't hit him until now. The white monster truly touched the body he, Christmas, couldn't touch no more.

* * *

In Mr. Preacher's heated dream, the moon shone brightly on Louisville. Christmas, still angry, metamorphosed to an angry horse in his ancestor's presence. Old man Orinya rode him in a reckless manner. Mr. Preacher ran in tremendous fright on sighting them from the balcony of the big house. The white man possessed the strength of a much younger man. Mr. Preacher looked back and could only have seen an oldie on a horse. Orinya gaped in silence at his target. Mr. Preacher ran into the fields before heading back toward the hog houses. He jumped into the pigpen unsettling the animals.

He soon ran out of the pen. Orinya chased him to the spot the dwelling once stood. Right there, he fell to his knees, breathing hard. He couldn't run anymore. Orinya came down the horse Christmas became. On the darkest hour of the night, Orinya faced the white man.

'Wretched hypocrite,' he said and looked at the horse. 'Ochigbo, what should we do now?'

Mr. Preacher pleaded, 'Please, let me be.'

Christmas, being the king of the night, decided. He made his declaration through his horse mouth, 'Let the white man see *ikwu*.'

Mr. Preacher turned his face around locking eyes with Christmas in his animal body.

Orinya struck. Orinya lashed out at Mr. Preacher's chest with his rickety fingers. This sent Mr. Preacher spiralling on the ground. The ancestor followed Mr. Preacher's rolling body until it stopped. He knelt beside Mr. Preacher's trembling body on the ground and finished his work by bringing down an enormous blow on Mr. Preacher's chest. Christmas felt the blow. Mr. Preacher's eyes glazed over.

The blow stilled his heart for all time. Mr. Preacher never woke from the dream. Instead Christmas sat up on his straw bed in the attic. The smell of death took hold of the residence.

* * *

Christmas's spirit became a gentle wind and tipped a spoon off the edge of the stool in Esther's room. Esther woke up looking weak. Christmas floated into her mind. She wanted to begin the day's cleaning, a routine that kept her strong. She remembered assuring the white man of her presence before dawn. She never saw any of her grandchildren, if she got any. But felt glad about her bond with Small John. In a certain way, the boy filled the void Moses left.

Esther traced her way to the master's bedroom. She saw the white man's body lying on the floor beside the bed. She gathered her thoughts together and walked toward it. She touched him and knew. She swallowed. This seemed to be life after all. To experience the deaths of people – enemies and friends; children and the elderly. Once again, death snatched away life. This white, waggish man only started to mean something to her. She remembered Moses. She remembered all her dead children. And even the lost ones. She remembered Antonia.

'Rest well,' she muttered softly staring at Mr. Preacher's body.

* * *

Mr. Preacher's body lay on the door frame, pulled off the wall by Christmas and Marcus. Hugh seemed to be the most composed of the brothers in the tea room. Tallie and other black Quakers were around. Esther sobbed and said a few words. She spoke about him being a good father. She spoke about him being good husband whose marriage didn't last because of the many burdens his heart carried.

'Massa was a great thinker. Massa himself don't understand all that gone wrong in his own life,' she concluded and started the song, *Lord Lord*:

> *Lord Lord*
> *Hmm hmm*
>
> *Lord Lord*
> *Hmm hmm*

'Slavery is evil and my father used to have a hand in it,' Hugh began. 'I apologise on his behalf to every negro in this residence.'

They all sang again. They carried the body to a spot beside Harriet's resting place. Marcus requested a tombstone.

'Ain't a practice amongst members of the Society of Friends,' Tallie said.

'My father didn't die a Quaker!' Simons sounded furious.

'Father wouldn't want a tombstone,' Hugh intervened. 'Harriet never got one.'

Mr. Preacher got buried without a tombstone.

PART EIGHT

HUGH

IN HIS WILL, HE STATED this: *...should I pass away suddenly, let the ex-slaves and their loved ones be allowed to stay in the residence for at least three years.* Three years went by, and his sons could sell the big house and share the income since none of them desired to make a future in Kentucky. The negroes in the residence weren't looking forward to the moment in 1825.

'When they gon kick us out,' Ark asked.

Christmas thought of what to say. 'You never know. They might just want to keep us here forever.'

'Only Hugh got the heart to keep us here,' Nedi said.

Christmas nodded his head in agreement.

Not long after Mr. Preacher died, rumour circulated in the township about Hugh. He went about praying for the neglected sick, and people, crippled and begging on the roadside, began to walk.

'He still going about using the Quaker God to cure people?' Ark asked.

'Last time, about a week now, one negro woman in the neighbourhood swear that he make a blind negro man see right in front of her,' Nedi said.

'If that be true he sure could have woke Mr. Preacher when he died,' Ark said.

It got windy in the afternoon. Christmas, now fifty-one, watched Small John and some other children tail the tallest person in Louisville. Tall Porter ambled past River Road. The teenager appeared comfortable with the attention created. Sally entered the residence with a man tailing her. Christmas, sure this might be the man she kept a secret, nodded at them. Nedi, seated on a stool, always hoped to see this day. The day indeed came. Like Sally, the man appeared to be around thirty-one.

'Mama... and Christmas, this is Philip, the man I done agreed to marry. He a free man,' Sally said smiling at Nedi.

'Good day, ma'am. Good day, Uncle Christmas,' the man said.

Christmas nodded.

'How long you been a free man for?' Nedi asked.

'Was born free. My mama born free in the north. My father was a slave here in Kentucky. He free now and I live with him.'

The man's mannerisms showed his profound respect for people. Nedi, only forty-five with her locks greying each day, appeared pleased. Sally deserved this young man.

'We gon jump the broom at his father's,' Sally said.

'Why such hurry?' Nedi asked.

'Don't want no one stealin' her from me. We come ask your blessins' ma'am,' Philip said.

'As long as you treat her real good,' Nedi said and frowned.

'Someone gon become a grandmother soon,' Christmas teased.

Sally giggled.

'You ought to be askin' for my blessins', Philip, after all I done did for you – How I never told on Sally for sneakin' out to be with you,' Ark said.

'She a grown girl,' Christmas interrupted.

'If it be right, I grown too,' Ark said. 'Time I go find me a woman.'

'Shut that mouth,' Sally said to Ark. 'Every negro girl I knows on River Road been with you.'

'That ain't true. Ark still an infant,' Nedi said.

'You call a twenty-somethin-year-old man an infant, Mama?' Sally asked.

'Ain't Ark twenty-somethin'?' Philip asked.

'If my memory right, he twenty-nine,' Christmas said.

'Born the same year George Washington became President,' Nedi added.

'You look young to have them grown children,' Philip said to Nedi.

'Should be same age as your mama,' Nedi said.

'My mama forty-three,' Philip said.

'Nedi little bit older,' Christmas needled, good-humouredly.

The night of the ceremony came, and they all were dressed in their best clothes. Christmas in his bright red shirt and best pair of pantaloons. Nedi in her white blouse, now too tight. One of the many hats Mr. Preacher left in the world suited Ark. Small John cried and wanted to go with them. Esther pulled him into the room and shut the door.

* * *

Christmas found a comfortable chair and sat. The premises consisted of a cottage and a cluster of trees scattered over the hard ground. People danced in a wild manner. They jumped and clapped. Raised dust. They all cheered the new man and wife. Philip's father, a game master, appeared loud. Many of his hunter friends in attendance got drunk. Christmas noticed how Philip's father, a short man, a little bald, made a series of advances toward Nedi.

'Waited too long for Black John. I gon wait to the end. Tired of gettin' to love again and again,' she said afterwards.

'But he more handsome, Mama,' Ark said.

'What I gon do with a handsome man? I don't even think he handsome.'

'What makes you think Black John is any different?' Christmas asked siding with Ark.

'Even if he ain't different, I gon be with him till the end. So many mens is too much pain for any woman,' Nedi replied.

They headed back to the Preacher residence leaving the newly married to dance with their friends.

* * *

In the morning, before Marcus and his brothers left for the court house to deal with issues regarding their father's debts, they called for Christmas.

'We are going to give you and the other negroes living here eight months to find work and some place to live,' Marcus advised. 'We are running expenses and will be decreasing the income you all get. You are aware there has been little work to do here since father's passing.'

The news stung, but Christmas maintained silence.

'We are not being needlessly cruel, Christmas,' Simons began. 'Hugh is to start his engineering study at the Rensselaer Polytechnic in New York, and he needs some money from this property for sustenance. Marcus and I would be returning New York too. Time is limited, and as Marcus says, expenses are high.'

'Talk to the others, Christmas,' Hugh managed to say. 'They all listen to you.'

Marcus and Simons headed outside. Meanwhile Hugh drew closer to Christmas and placed a hand on Christmas's right shoulder. 'It's so fortunate that I have older brothers who want the best for me. At the same time, it is unfortunate that I cannot influence their decisions. Most of the income generated from the other houses we own in Louisville now goes to our mother. There will be a way, Christmas.'

'Hugh,' Simons called from outside.

'Be there soon,' Hugh responded and looked at Christmas in the eye. 'That boy of yours that was sold way back... I want you to know he would be free. He would be happier in life than you are.'

'How you know this?'

'I'm a praying man, Christmas. You and the others are likely to keep staying here. I am not going to the school in New York. Something is going to happen and I have little control over its outcome,' Hugh replied, and left Christmas worried.

Christmas followed and watched the brothers saunter away on their horses. He found Nedi and her children in front of the kitchen house. Ark acted like Philip's father, trying his luck with Nedi.

'Mama dance with nobody cause we there. I tell you Christmas, the man ain't bad lookin'.'

'More handsome than me?' Christmas asked.

'A little bit, I would say,' Ark replied laughing.

'I never see you dance with any of them pretty girls either,' Christmas said.

'Ain't see no pretty girl. They all too old.'

Christmas laughed.

Esther, standing there, seemed a little agitated.

'Used to be Sally. Everyone ask when she gon marry. Now she done married and everyone ain't lookin' at nobody but me. Don't try to put me on the spot, ole man,' Ark said.

'Ask your mama how ole I was when we jumps over the broom?' Christmas teased.

'Much younger than you is, Ark,' Nedi said.

'Y'all leave Ark alone. He gon get himself a woman when he ready,' Esther reluctantly added.

'I gon find me a woman too,' Small John said.

Esther smacked him on his behind. 'What you knows about womens?'

'He grown, Esther. Let him be,' Christmas said and got on his feet.

'I ain't gon let him spoil like them dead mice,' Nedi said. 'He just nine.'

Christmas broke the possible news of their impending eviction and decreased wages. He said nothing about his conversation with Hugh. Silence dominated fleetingly before someone entered the house. They all heard the door slam to a close. Christmas knew the sound of each of the Preacher brothers' steps. It couldn't be any of them. The person seemed to know the house well. The steps stopped briefly before continuing. A negro with patches of grey hair entered the lounge. The man, in a thick black coat, held a sack. His face spoke of anguish. He opened his arms to them. And opened his mouth to speak. The man lacked visible teeth. Christmas recognised Black John. Esther threw herself at her son.

'I free for the second time in my life. Ain't goin' back to that dungeon no more,' Black John said. He left his mother to cuddle Small John. 'You big now!'

Nedi embraced him and cried.

He pulled her away from his body and brushed her greying locks with his fingers. 'Been a long time, bee pie,' Black John said. 'Nedi. You agin' so good.'

She swayed her body into his embrace again, and they held tight to each other.

'Let me embrace my only livin' brother,' he whispered to Nedi.

He hugged Christmas like a bear. They patted each other on the back and laughed.

'You ain't goin' no jail no more,' Christmas said.

* * *

The clouds appeared dark and heavy. Gunshots were fired into the air to celebrate Quincy Adams's inauguration. Christmas returned from the farm house and noticed five horsemen galloping toward the Preacher residence. His heart skipped. A cloud of birds exploded out of a distant tree. The horsemen encircled Christmas, and one familiar voice among the men spoke.

'This is the one they call Christmas.'

One of the other horsemen alighted, confronted Christmas and forced him to lie on his stomach. The young man placed Christmas's hands behind his back and started binding them using a rope. Christmas lamented in pain. His tapered bones weren't of a young man anymore. The man with the familiar voice alighted and took off his brown hat. Christmas recognised Master Gill. A large man in the middle of his fifties. The white man, now with a terrible scar by the side of his nose, approached.

'Damn it, Massa Gill,' Christmas lamented. 'What you want from me?'

'Go look for the others. There should be Black John and his mother,' Master Gill said to two of his men, and they headed toward the big house.

Gill squatted before Christmas and said, 'My brother died and left me only slaves. Gave his goddamn houses to his sons.'

'I'm a free man,' Christmas went on.

Master Gill looked around before he viciously kicked Christmas in the mouth. 'I didn't come here to listen to trash.'

Christmas spat blood and struggled over the ground. He shook his legs and tried to loosen the rope holding his hands together.

Two of the men that headed to the big house returned with Black John and Esther. Black John kicked dust into the air. They forced him down onto his knees in front of Master Gill.

'Don't hurt my mama. Don't touch her,' he yelled.

They made Esther kneel. Gill went toward Esther and struck her across the face. Christmas looked away. This quietened Black John. Only the devil could do this – hit a seventy-year-old woman.

They pushed Esther and Black John to the ground and bound them with ropes. The Preacher brothers emerged with their Kentucky rifles pointed at Master Gill and his men.

'No, no, no,' Master Gill said on seeing them. 'I'm only here to claim what is rightfully mine.'

'You will listen to every word we say to you,' Hugh said. 'You have no right to come here and treat folks this way. We know who you are.'

'Now don't go pointing guns at us,' drawled Master Gill. 'We have legal rights to make claims, same as you do. Your father did leave me these niggers.' He gestured at the negroes.

'You are a cockcomb, Uncle Gill,' Hugh said cracking the rifle.

Master Gill raised his hands in surrender and gestured at his men to do the same. 'I want proof that these negroes are free people.'

'Nedi,' Simons called.

Nedi, watching in horror from behind the oak tree, appeared startled and confused on hearing her name.

'Nedi, you know where to find their papers?' Simons asked.

'I look in them rooms,' she said and started to head toward the house.

'Mine in my shoes,' Christmas yelled after her with his face still facing the ground.

Christmas remembered how the fire consumed all the original freedom papers. The current ones were redone by Mr. Preacher prior to his death. Nedi soon came back.

The Preacher brothers still held their rifles pointing at Master Gill and his men. Christmas, Black John and Esther were still on the ground with their hands bound. Christmas noticed Simons gesturing with the gun at Nedi to show all the papers to Master Gill whose hands were still up. Nedi showed them to him.

'I have seen them. You boys better let us go now,' Master Gill said.

'Get going, Gill,' Marcus said.

Master Gill and the other men standing, mounted their horses, and rode away leaving dust in the air.

Hugh dropped his gun, walked toward Christmas and untied the rope around his wrists. Christmas untied Black John's and Esther's hands.

'The rope done wound me,' Esther moaned.

* * *

Oda'nyaa came through the walls. Christmas sat up in bed. She sat beside him and began by cuddling his lap. Her fingers walked up to his chest and were about to unstrap his shirt. He pushed her hand away and stood up. He walked away and stopped in front of the wall. She represented his destruction. He could never escape death. She couldn't alter his wish. He desired to see Opialu before death. He wouldn't let her stop him. She approached him from behind and held him around the waist. Her touch, pure and exceedingly stirring, interrupted his thoughts.

'I will fly back to Opialu. Orinya is right. Death is only a passage into the ancestral land and sure, I will reincarnate,' he said.

She let go of him and walked toward the straw bed. 'This is your destiny, Ochigbo. America. Tell me how Opialu is better than this place?'

'I want Opialu to be home again. I would go before I die in this body. I don't want to die like Moses, here in America, in a land that is not of his ancestors. I must go back.'

'Not as long as I continue to live,' Oda'nyaa said.

'Your death is near?' Christmas said.

'Don't threaten me, human. You know nothing about death,' she said raising her voice.

'I know more than you think. I know your death is possible and it would be more than a thousand deaths of real people because your kingdom would perish. I know you fear death. Me, I am not afraid of death no more.' Sweat trickled down his body.

'This is your country now.' Her voice became softer. 'You have mastered their language. *Aa kela* like them now…'

'I don't belong. I must die where I belong.'

'Who said death was near for you?' she asked.

'I am not less than fifty any more. I know I have lived more than half of my life.'

A loud scream echoed within the big house. Clambering sounds and blows shook the house. Christmas, in spirit, travelled out of the room, and saw Gill's men raiding the house. The night made it impossible for the Preacher brothers to reach for their rifles in time. This time, Gill and his men bound the three brothers and forced them to lie on their stomachs on the floor in the lounge. The negro women of the house screamed in terror. Black John hid in one of the kitchen pantries. Christmas, in spite of the occurrences, wanted Oda'nyaa to see his point. The noise in the lounge continued. The neighing of horses and the loud thuds of vehement feet.

Oda'nyaa got distracted by the noise. A royal staff appeared in her hand and she went toward Christmas and touched him with it. Both of them became snakes and slithered out of the attic through a hole in the room.

* * *

He sneaked back to the attic a lone snake, tired. Oda'nyaa truly slurped his energy. Even though aware of the situation in the residence, he decided to rest. He lay down and felt a shadow over him. He opened his eyes in the dark. Massa's face. A troubled look on a wrinkled face. The image stayed briefly.

Christmas went downstairs in the morning. Ark and Nedi were rearranging the house. The lounge seemed like a boar's playground. The cushions, still displaced. The piano, shattered.

'They done took Hugh,' Ark said.

'Massa Gill and his men?' Christmas asked.

Nedi nodded her head. 'Massas Marcus and Simons gone searchin'.'

Hugh truly foresaw his capture. Marcus and Simons came home by midday. Their quest for the day brought no result. Christmas's heart stopped briefly.

'I will have to go to the Deep South to search for our brother,' Marcus began. 'Gill has evidence Hugh was born a slave and we have no counter-evidence to claim otherwise.'

'But he white,' Ark tried to argue.

Nedi touched her son's shoulder.

'Hugh was born by a slave woman, and Christmas would be the only one here who can remember that clearly. The law still maintains that any person born of a negro slave woman is a slave. Uncle Gill took this advantage over our father who is no more with us today, and the law is strongly on his side.'

Marcus paused and swallowed before he continued, 'Simons will stay here to manage our affairs. I will go to Mississippi. We have word that they are taking him there.'

'What a terrible man Gill be,' Christmas lamented. He wouldn't die in this crazy place. Surely heading back to Oli'doma.

* * *

Before sunset, Christmas took Marcus to the harbour using the wagon, and the journey down south began. Days passed and weeks became months. Summer came. No news came from Mississippi. Each time Christmas asked if Massa Simons heard something, Simons either mumbled meaningless words or said nothing at all.

* * *

Christmas pulled off his boots and sat on his straw bed. The night got windy. His ancestor visited.

'Ochigbo, I'm glad you have made up your mind to return. When the strength comes, you will know. You will feel it in body, spirit and mind. Every bit of you will levitate over the great black ocean.'

'Why can't I be given this gift now?'

'Abutu Eje will determine the right moment. It is not now.'

Christmas stayed silent. Orinya left. He tried to sleep but couldn't. He kept thinking of Hugh. Christmas thought of the young man's foretelling about Ijeyi. His spirit sprang out into the night. He looked at the full bright moon, and muttered a prayer to Orinya. 'Help me find Hugh.'

Silence.

In dissatisfaction and anger his spirit swayed into the sky and headed for Mississippi. He hovered over Mississippi before dawn and his instincts became difficult riddles. He couldn't find Hugh. A place kept coming into his vision, but this place belonged to the future. He landed there. Orinya's indigo reflections gave the swamp a resplendent appearance.

'Help me find Antonia's boy, Orinya,' Christmas pleaded. '*Ko chow.*'

Orinya, whose wings folded into his burial shroud, said, 'There's little we can do when destiny is on course.' He pointed to the swamp in front of them. 'That would be his freedom. He would be free in the swamp. But the future holds that.'

'Orinya, do something. *Do something.*'

'Destiny is stronger under these circumstances, I repeat.'

'Allow me see this future,' Christmas asked and sighed.

The masquerade didn't refuse this time. They first became dark coloured waters. They transformed to the greenish and watery mud in the swamp. They felt a great number of fugitive slaves dragging their feet through the muddy water. Christmas saw Hugh, a leader, amongst the free. At least the future spoke of his freedom. He saw Hugh hunting wild hogs and fishes. He saw Hugh's face grubby with suffering and his body scarred with slavery.

* * *

Night sneaked in quietly. Ark and Christmas made a fire beside the big house.

'Always feel my light skin is privilege but it don't mean nothin',' Ark began.

Christmas thought briefly before encouraging him. 'It still a privilege,' he replied. 'You don't know nothin' about me. If you knows my story, you gon keep thankin' God.'

'Christmas, I just hates myself right now. I wish you was my father.'

'Don't say that. The mulatto, the octoroon, the quadroon, all gon be the bridge between black and white folks in America.'

'What you mean?' Ark asked placing more wood in the fire.

'Peace. The bridge is peace. A time comin' when America gon appreciate this.'

Ark looked up.

'Reconciliation always be the way forward. Gon be after negroes take America and put them white folks in this place that we negroes currently is.'

'You sayin' there gon be war?'

'In some way,' Christmas replied.

'Look at what done happened, Christmas. Never knowed Hugh was born of a black woman. He whiter than me. He so white yet look at what done happened to him. I feel mulattos, quadroons and octoroons pay twice for a cause that wasn't their fault. I speaks as one quadroon, Christmas. I sees mulattos and quadroons bein' whipped no different from the black negro. Me, as a quadroon, is black. I feel we pay for wrongdoins' of the white man. I talks to negroes outside this residence. If I'm sure about one thin', I knows no negro trust no quadroon or mulatto negro.'

'I understand,' Christmas said putting a hand on Ark's shoulder. 'You can trust me. You be thankful you still have your folks around. Your mama. Sally.'

'I wish to kill a white man before all black folks free in America.'

'You no different from me, Ark. I done some really bad thins' in America I ain't proud about.'

Silence. A pop and wan sound that ended like a sizzle followed.

'I gon head down the street,' Ark said.

'You sure it ain't too late for that?'

'Ain't goin' too far, Christmas.'

'How about I come along?'

'I be fine,' Ark said.

* * *

From the attic, Christmas heard a loud bang on the mahogany door downstairs. He rushed downstairs, opened the door and saw Tallie almost walking away. The man, now a little bent due to age, entered the house and took off his coat.

'I got to talk to you and all the other negroes,' he said, his voice cracklier. His movements seemed slower too. Christmas followed him to the lounge. They met Master Simons playing the new piano brought home to replace the one Master Gill and his men destroyed.

Master Simons stopped and stared. 'Greetings, Tallie.'

'Mr. Preacher, I'm sorry about all that happened. We been prayin' for Hugh to be found. There's somethin' else very crucial that thee must be aware of. It about Nedi and her children,' Tallie said and turned to Christmas.

'Please fetch them.'

Christmas left wondering. The residence still mourned Hugh's capture. Marcus hadn't returned. Christmas returned with Nedi, Ark and Small John.

'Where your daughter?' Tallie, already seated, asked Nedi.

Nedi became anxious. 'She done married a free negro named Philip, and they stay together on Green Street.'

'We ought to fetch them. Y'all must stick together. A great-grandniece of Mr. Peterson is in Louisville and she out to get y'all once owned by Mr. Peterson. She already made the Peterson plantation home with her husband, and done paid people to catch folks who were in servitude under Mr. Peterson.'

'We will have to start keeping watch,' Simons added and sighed.

* * *

The next night, Christmas and Black John went out in the wagon to fetch Sally and her husband. She hugged Black John. They hadn't seen each other since the latter's release from the dungeon. The young man, Philip, took off his hat and bowed to them. To Christmas's surprise he remained calm and humbly soft-spoken on understanding the gravity of the threat against his marriage.

* * *

The communication among the negro residents became whispers. They became cautious in their movements even within the residence. In the attic on one of these days, Christmas searched the future. He saw the birth of Ijeyi's great grand-daughter, Girl Carolyn. A continuation of life. Destiny indeed separated him from Ijeyi. The same destiny allowed the dissemination of his lineage. Girl Carolyn's mother, a tall and slim negro woman with bold lashes, entertained no husband. Girl Carolyn came out crying very loudly. Christmas felt proud. He became the air the infant breathed. He stayed still and watched a midwife cut her umbilical cord.

He looked at the sky and cried, 'Enough. Enough! I done seen enough and got to return to my country, Oli'doma.'

He stepped out of the house. The cold night stayed still. He walked over the patchy lawn onto the street. The moon vanished briefly. 'Enough. Enough,' he repeated.

A crackly old voice shouted from one of the houses in the neighbourhood, 'Shut that trench you have for a mouth.'

Christmas ignored the person. He called on his alekwuafia. 'Tell Abutu Eje to give me my strength of flight now. I want to return at this moment; I'd like to return from this place.' The night remained silent. He swayed his body into the sky but landed on a rock that left his arm bleeding. He sat down. He struggled in pain to stand but fell. He wept and lay on his back.

He wept until his spirit became the night of the far future. He became the space Olofu flew to. Girl Carolyn, now a young beauty, flew to this same space from America. The night rocked them.

'Who are you?' she asked.

'Olofu.'

'Girl Carolyn.'

'I know your name. In my world, I cannot speak. I'm dumb.'

'How come you speaking here?'

'It's an ability that I can't use in the physical world.'

'We related?'

'Yes. I have a forefather who was your forefather. He was a slave in your country.'

'They said they named him Christmas,' Girl Carolyn said.

'We know him as Ochigbo.'

'I see why we meet.'

The night felt proud, rocking them like babies.

'I am troubled. My country is crumbling,' Olofu said.

'Where is your country?'

'Come and I will show you what is going on.' He took her hand and they levitated to a beautiful street. She got lost in wonder. Christmas's spirit enjoyed the journey. The houses on the street reflected riches and splendour. Beautiful white mansions and carved fences.

'These are the houses built for selected kings of the new country that Oli'doma is forced to cede to. Soon my country will be no more. These kings coming to rule over Ayi'doma are of the Ole'gbo and Hausa countries. White people are forcing this on us,' Olofu explained.

The night's heart broke.

Girl Carolyn swallowed hard. 'Is everyone in your country black, just like you?'

Olofu nodded

'Who are the white people you talk about?'

'Some of them come from your country. They are very few. But they don't stay.'

'I wish it was the same in my country. Come see.' She dragged him and they floated away. The night released a refreshing breeze which remained in their company. The night saw her wishes. She imagined America black. She wished those long carriages without horses could take only black people. She wished black people could seat in them comfortably. She wished for a different America. In her current world, white people sat in carriages and black people stood. White people chose their own white kings in America.

'How come white people choose your kings?' she asked Olofu.

'I don't know,' Olofu replied.

* * *

Master Marcus came back with no fortunate news. The Preacher residence remained quiet. On this day, Christmas and Black John led Tallie and two other white Quaker men of the American Colonisation Society into the big house. Death couldn't be differentiated from Hugh's kidnap. The young man just started life and knew nothing about slavery.

'We will continue to look for Hugh,' one of the Quaker men said. 'Our friends in Mississippi are still searching. We will not give up the dream of seeing every negro free in this country.'

'Hugh doesn't understand slavery. He heard his mother was a slave and that was all,' Simons lamented. 'It's going to be hard for my brother.'

'He never understood why our mother wasn't his,' Marcus added.

Tallie stood and walked toward Simons. He sat next to him and placed a hand on his shoulders. 'We gon keep prayin' and deployin' more searches down south.'

Antonia paid for her crime with her life, Christmas thought. Hugh, a white man born of a black woman, paid again, for the atrocity.

The white Quaker man yet to speak glanced at Black John and said, 'Tallie recently brought to our attention that members of your family are at risk of being taken back as slaves.'

'Christmas used to be married to Nedi. She now engaged to Black John,' Tallie clarified.

'We understand the woman in question has some children whose presence in Kentucky is quite concerning, since Mrs. Brightline has placed various adverts calling out for anyone with any information on any of Mr. Peterson's slaves,' one of the visitors added.

This got Black John uneasy. He adjusted himself in his seat.

'Yes. Nedi has three children, currently living in this residence,' Marcus said.

'Are there other negroes who live here?'

'My mother, Esther, and Nedi's son in-law, Philip,' Black John added.

'Mrs. Brightline, as ye know, is out to get Nedi and her children,' Tallie began looking at the white men. 'She done recaptured some twelve negro mens, seven womens and nine children. Some of the children she got was born after their mothers left the Peterson plantation.'

'We suggest that every negro in this residence move to Tallie's home, and that has to be tonight. I would be surprised if no neighbour is already giving Mr. Brightline some useful cognizance,' one of the visitors said.

'Why should I go along?' Christmas asked.

'I was about to talk about that,' one of the white men pointed out. 'The final destination wouldn't be Tallie's home. Christmas, you have a choice to refuse the proposal. I'm sure Black John can make the decision on behalf of Nedi and her children. It's an opportunity that comes once in a lifetime. A move back to Africa at no cost. We would pay for all the travel expenses.'

Christmas's heart skipped.

The Preacher brothers looked at each other.

'Africa,' Black John repeated.

'Yes Africa. Liberia, the land of freedom,' one of the men replied. 'We understand how hard it is for a negro even as a free man to live in America. Negroes can have lives of their own in this settlement of Liberia.'

'How far it gon be from Oli'doma?' Christmas asked.

'Oli'doma?' One of the white Quaker men seemed confused.

'It is the country that Christmas comes from,' Simons explained.

'I never heard of that place,' one of the visitors said.

'This gon give Nedi and her children freedom forever,' Tallie added.

'Why not take us all to the north?' Black John asked.

'America is America. Slave catchers hunt fugitive slaves illegally in the north. Liberia is the best chance right now. I can falsify papers for you folks to board the ship,' one of the white Quakers said.

'Black John, this is something you must think about,' Marcus advised. 'I told Christmas the other time you all got to leave this residence before the end of 1825. Time is fast running out. The opportunity could come at no better time. If you would like to go, let Tallie know. Simons and I are in talks about the future of this residence. This is a chance I recommend you consider.'

Christmas couldn't think about it. He thought of his ability to levitate. He wondered what Orinya might suggest. Liberia may be very close to Oli'doma.

* * *

Christmas couldn't answer most of the questions Black John, Nedi and her children asked about this place called Liberia.

'They got them oil lamps there?'

'Heard lions roam about Africa.'

'Liberia same as Africa?'

'Them speak English?'

Christmas kept their hopes up.

'As long as I and my children and grandchildren never gon cross path with any of them Peterson's folks, I'm fine with it,' Nedi said.

Sally put her hand on her husband's shoulder and beckoned at him to speak.

He said, 'If it gon be the best for Sally, I gon go too. No free man likes his wife a slave.'

All eyes seemed to settle on Ark.

Silence.

'Ark?' Black John called.

He didn't respond.

'Ark?' his mother called.

'I ain't goin' to no Africa,' Ark finally said. 'I was born in America, and the only place I knowed is America. I ain't goin'.'

'You got to go somewhere, Ark.' Where you gon go?' Black John asked quietly. 'Massas Simons and Marcus ain't lettin' no negro live here no more. Ain't even safe.'

'He gon head back to the Peterson plantation,' Nedi said sarcastically.

'Where Christmas gon go?' Ark asked.

All eyes fell on Christmas.

* * *

Christmas folded his pairs of pantaloons, shirts and socks into the sack. He tossed his quilt into the same sack. He cleared up everything he owned in the attic, and decided to lie on the straw bed one last time. He closed his eyes, and felt Orinya's shadow over him. He smelt the masquerade. He felt the touch of his alekwuafia. Orinya dragged Christmas's spirit into the continent of Africa. And they ran through the dark and through the bright morning. They ran through rice fields and banana plantations.

It felt different. The trees and grasses were of different species. The landscape appeared fuller and greener. Liberia's forests possessed slimmer trees unlike the forests in Oli'doma. Huts were sparse and weren't like the ones in Opialu. Liberia frightened him even with Orinya by his side. He felt lost in a strange land, and terror became his voice. He called out for help. Their spirits burst into a crowd of people. They were indeed spirits among people. They were black people like himself but they spoke languages he didn't understand. None sounded like Idoma. He didn't know this place.

'Is Oli'doma close by?' he asked Orinya.

'No,' Orinya replied.

He opened his mouth to speak again and found himself on his straw bed. The candle burnt gently. He wouldn't go to Liberia.

Tallie soon arrived in a carriage. Christmas went along with the other negroes in the Preacher residence, all carrying their belongings. They arranged their sacks in the carriage and took their seats. The carriage began to move.

'Made up your mind about Liberia?' Black John asked Christmas

'Ain't goin'. Liberia ain't Oli'doma.'

Nedi glanced at Christmas before staring at Ark.

'Ark says he ain't goin' too,' Small John said.

'At least I got myself a companion. Only trouble now is where to stay,' Christmas said.

The carriage stopped briefly and continued.

Ark got up and moved across to sit beside Christmas.

* * *

They were made to squeeze into a room amongst other negroes, about twenty, already waiting for the ship heading to Liberia.

'This Liberia them white folks talk about, I heard negroes die on the sea even before they reach there,' one of the new faces they met said.

'Mosquito bites, they say, causes it. Sea mosquitoes kill travellers a lot,' another said.

This brought fear on Nedi. Esther slept most of the time. Black John didn't care.

'They say it land of gold. Where black people gets so rich, the natives think of negroes as white folks,' one negro said and people laughed in the blink of hope. Esther, now awake, heard this.

The day finally came. At the harbour, Christmas and Ark stayed with Black John, Nedi, Esther, Small John, Sally and Philip, until Tallie arrived with one of the Quaker men arranging the trip. Christmas didn't expect the separation to be like this. He since accepted Ijeyi's loss. He and Nedi were separated but they still saw each other – a privilege soon to be lost. He never regretted his role in the death of Mr. Preacher. The death took away the sense of loss in Nedi. He remembered how the white man, consumed by lust, went into her room.

At the harbour, ships floated in circles. White sailors gave orders and negro workers unloaded cargoes. The white man handed them their respective papers. Ark and Christmas refused theirs as anticipated.

'Nedi, you and your children must act confidently, for the papers aren't real. Don't draw attention no matter what. There will be a stop-over in New York. Try to stay together. We have gone against the policies because we cannot prove you and your children are free. Go under God's guidance.'

Time came for them to leave.

'Look after them, man,' Christmas said on embracing Black John.

Nedi hugged Ark in tears. 'You so stubborn. Come if you can. To visit. I pray your reasons gon serve you well.'

Christmas embraced Nedi. He felt her tears rush over his shoulder.

She said, 'One fine man in my life I never understood. I gon miss you. Please take Ark as yours. He can't be Ijeyi but you got to love and look out for him as a son.'

Black John sighed on hearing this and led Esther and Small John away toward the ship.

'Our love was real, Christmas. If you ever find our son, tell him I loves him. That I never gon forget him,' she said and wiped away her tears. She hugged him again before leaving to join Sally and Philip.

Christmas watched the ship sail away. He and Ark waved. 'Let us get goin', Ark. You gon tell me why you stayed back.'

PART NINE

ARK

MID-SUMMER IN 1831. Christmas and Ark found work in market slaughterhouse in Frankfort, Kentucky. They moved here eighteen months ago. Frankfort, vast in nature, appeared hilly. It held sparse houses and few people. The markets weren't rowdy. People were quieter. Negro women outnumbered the men. Christmas and Ark were usually the only males amongst the population that walked from the market in the evenings. They lived in the home of Mr. Desmond and his wife. Christmas remembered the first time Tallie brought them to the house. He and Ark could afford to share a room. They didn't pay much for it. Mr. Desmond and his wife aged gracefully. The husband seemed to be stronger than his wife. He did most of the cooking even though slow. Mrs. Desmond spent most of the time on her bed. She found it difficulty walking and wouldn't leave their bedroom unless her husband came around to support her.

Thirty-five now, Ark kept a full beard to disguise himself. Mrs. Brightline, certainly aware of Nedi and her children's departure to Africa, searched no more. Ark, on some days, returned to the house late into the night. He never announced his real name to any Frankfort resident. Instead he took the name "Mark". Ark worked during day and travelled on most nights to see his woman. Christmas knew of these secret journeys to Louisville. Only a woman could drive a man to make such sacrifices.

Ark's movements woke Christmas. Ark appeared distressed. Christmas couldn't go back to sleep. Ark fought back his tears and remained quiet. Christmas offered him some leftover potatoes but he pushed the food away.

'I done did everythin' for Memory,' Ark complained.

'What you mean?' Christmas asked.

'I loves Memory. I be honest with you. She the reason I refuse to go to Liberia.'

Christmas smiled. 'You could find lot of other "Memories" in Africa.'

'None like she is, Christmas,' he said. 'Memory done agreed to one thin'. She gon run away with me to the north,' Ark replied and lay on the pallet.

'You done talk about this slave girl before?'

'She the one.'

'Uhm...' Christmas said.

'Mrs. Brightline ain't lookin' for you no more. Kentucky is alright for you now, and because of her, you gon leave?'

'Mrs. Brightline could still find me someday. And I do like Memory to see freedom.'

Christmas remained awake. The candle flame remained still. Ark soon slept. Christmas thought he saw Massa Preacher. He sensed a strange presence in the room. Moses's voice spoke.

'Is you tryin' to scare me?'

'Is you scared?'

'Should I be scared of you?'

'You, an African, ain't scared of nothin',' Moses said. 'I come ask you to do me a favour.'

'Hmm.'

'A greater messiah than I is gon need your help. He gon fight against them white people.'

'You ain't givin' up, Moses.'

'I beg.'

Christmas sighed.

* * *

They didn't attend the meetings presided over by a younger white man in the Desmond residence. On Saturdays Christmas helped Mr. Desmond in milking his only cow. He endured listening to Mr. Desmond's reflections of Mr. Preacher's time in Frankfort in 1795.

Ark vanished again, of course to see his woman. Once the milking ended, Christmas headed for his room, and his spirit felt a profound urgency to become blood. The blood of white people. He lay down in the colossal room and became blood. In a vision he saw cruelty take hold of Southampton County in faraway Virginia. Through a dark channel, Christmas travelled into his vision.

The man Moses's ghost spoke of saw the moon's rage take life out of the sun. The blood Christmas became saw this too. He endured being underneath a white man's skin soon to be slain by one of Nat Turner's men.

Nat swiped a knife and spilled out blood from a white pregnant woman. Christmas desired to speak.

'This ain't the way, brother. It sure wouldn't end well.' The thin blood spoke in a distinct accent.

Along with his accomplices of six well-muscled men, Nat turned around in shock.

'God done prepared me for this day and I rebuke you, whoever you is,' Nat replied. He turned to his men and said, 'We go. Still much more to do.'

Nat split his allies, more than forty of them, assigned to various murders. Blood kept flowing. Blood of women. Blood of children.

In the massive room in the Desmond household, Christmas sweated profusely. The killings in Virginia went on. Being blood, he spattered out of the skin of more white folks. Being blood, he gushed out of slit throats of men.

Nat and his men wouldn't give up. They marched on through the night to locate an armoury they intended to break into to acquire guns and more swords with great anticipation to finish off the white folks. Right there in front of the armoury, white soldiers encircled them with guns. Christmas, dissolved in blood inside each of these soldiers, saw the need to save Nat and his men. He owed Moses something. Something he himself couldn't explain.

Christmas decided to boil, and so he did. He became bubbly and steamed through a soldier's body. This soldier trembled and his horse started to shake violently; Nat, his men, and the rest of the white soldiers became confused. The ferocious horse threw the soldier to the ground, and right there, the man blew up, with his limbs and organs littering the ground. Blood splattered into the air and over the faces of Nat, his men and the rest of the soldiers still holding onto their guns. The dead man's horse galloped off. The man's severed head rolled on the hard ground. In fright, horses reared up, neighing

The remaining blood of the shattered white man coagulated and began to swell. The remains swelled into a big black boar, and Christmas felt his spirit in this wild hog. Christmas dashed for Nat and his men. At once, these men became hogs. The white men started to shoot. The hogs bolted in diverse routes.

* * *

Before dawn in Frankfort, several dozen men surrounded Desmond's home with claims that a runaway slave of Mrs. Brightline of Louisville resided there. Christmas, awakened and pushed out of the house, could remember being surrounded by dead hogs. Somehow Nat remained alive. Christmas saw the hog Nat became, limping away in the dark. He feared for Ark. Awakened residents started to gather and whisper. The moon shone over Frankfort.

'Christmas here is a free man,' Mr. Desmond said to the ringleader of the mob.

'You sure there isn't no thirty-five-year-old male that goes by name Ark or Mark in your residence?'

'No,' Mr. Desmond said. 'The free negro in front of you doesn't look thirty-five either.'

The slave catchers carried out a thorough check of the house before leaving. Mrs. Desmond hobbled out of the room. She reached for her husband's shoulder for support. Christmas could see the great desire in her to scream.

Morning came. Mr. Desmond entered the room Christmas and Ark shared. 'Do you know where Ark is?'

'No.' Christmas sighed.

'I don't think Frankfort can contain you two anymore now that Mrs. Brightline knows he is still in Kentucky.'

'As soon as I gets knowledge of his whereabouts, we gon be on our way.'

'I'm certain Mrs. Brightline's men will visit us again,' Mr. Desmond said. 'Ark shouldn't have neglected the opportunity to live in Liberia. There was no better opportunity.'

* * *

The following night, Ark came back. The quiet sound of the door alerted Christmas.

He stood still in front of the closed door and said, 'We leavin' for the north, now.'

'We?' Christmas whispered.

'Memory is with me,' Ark replied. 'I knows Mrs. Brightline knows I'm still in Kentucky.'

'What happens to me?' Christmas asked.

'You should keep workin'.'

'Hell no. I'm goin' to the north with you. Kentucky ain't for me no more.'

'You ready?' Ark said. 'She waitin' outside.'

'I am.'

'On so many nights, I wait for her master to go to sleep so I can be with her,' Ark said. They collected a few belongings together. 'Imagine how I feel all the time knowin' that the woman I loves was in bed with her damn owner. Me, waitin' each time for her to meet me after tendin' herself to the cruel ole massa. If I listens to my heart, that man be dead long time.'

'You strong, Ark,' Christmas said. 'It was one reason I couldn't keep your mama no more.'

'I owe you a punch for that,' Ark said. 'We got to be quick, ole man.'

* * *

She approached them in the dark. And Christmas said to Ark, 'You gon marry a woman who walks like your mother.' She reached them and smiled at Christmas. She looked skinny. She reminded Christmas of the first time he saw Nedi walking Sally and Ark in Louisville. The three of them walked all night using the map Mr. Desmond gave Christmas. Sometimes they relied on fallen branches of trees to cross over deep puddles. They were suspicious of the traveling white men they passed. At dawn, they were welcomed into a black home in Covington whose residents spoke so well of Cincinnati but warned them about slave catchers fronting to be Quakers. One of such people got more than a dozen fugitive slaves heavily drunk in Cincinnati, got all of them in a convoy of wagons and transported each of them to their respective owners in Lexington. They told another Cincinnati story – how free negro men were captured, blindfolded, bound and sneaked into a ship heading for the South to be sold.

They continued their journey the next night. The stories they heard in Covington unsettled Memory. They soon ran into trouble. Some dirty looking men on horses surrounded them. Christmas wasn't sure if these men were slave catchers. They came down from their horses and pulled out their guns.

'You fugitives?' their leader asked.

'I swear I ain't. I'm a free negro from Jefferson county and these are my children,' Christmas said.

The man's eyes fell on Ark and Memory. His beard, so full and long it touched his chest. He turned to his men and said, 'They got a really comely negro woman. Who amongst you hasn't had a woman recently?'

One of his men stepped forward. A robust man slightly shorter than Memory. The full-bearded man beckoned at Memory and said to the robust man, 'She's yours.' The robust man took hold of Memory and dragged her away heading toward some tall shrubs. Christmas expected Ark to stay calm. But he shook. It began quietly but he lost it. Ark couldn't hold it anymore. He flared, and raged, 'You cannot touch her.' Ark dashed toward Memory. But the full-bearded man cocked the rifle over his left wrist and gunned him down. Smoke rolled into the air. A bird squeaked somewhere.

Christmas heard Memory scream. He saw Ark coil on the ground, covered with dried leaves.

'How dare you lie to me? She ain't this nigger's sister. You a slave,' the bearded man said to Christmas. He approached Christmas and stood before him.

'I'm a free man, and I got my paper to prove it.' Christmas noticed the robust man pushing Memory further behind the back of the shrubs. Their figures soon faded.

'Let me see it,' the bearded man demanded.

Christmas got the paper out his pocket.

The man wouldn't take it. 'Open it.'

Christmas opened it. And the man stared. 'Why did you lie to me that they were your children?'

'He is my son,' Christmas stammered.

The man spat on Christmas's face and beckoned at his men. One of them brought down the edge of a rifle on the side of Christmas's neck. Christmas fell. They mounted their horses and started to leave. Christmas's eyes fell on Ark's body. He failed Nedi. He could easily kill the men but his spirit felt weak. He couldn't protect her son from America. He picked up his document from the ground.

Memory came back, her clothes tattered and wet. She rushed over to her dead lover's body and wept. The louder Memory's sobs became, the more tears he shed. At night he dug a hole with a massive tree branch and buried Ark. Memory sat before the fire and remained quiet until Christmas spoke.

'We got to continue the journey,' he said.

She shook her head. She didn't want to.

'It was his dream that you see freedom.'

'Ain't no freedom in America,' she said.

'You right,' he said resting his back against a tree.

'They say you fly and you couldn't protect us,' Memory said.

He sighed.

'I never believe it,' she said. 'Lies. You never flied. You weak as any other negro. Like Ark. Bein' born in Africa mean nothin'. I always told Ark it ain't true that you flied.'

Christmas closed his eyes. He couldn't say a word. Sleep came, and he became the cloud staring at Virginia. He saw many black men and women's bodies littering the ground. Vengeful white men moved across counties burning houses and cabins of negroes. Christmas shook himself awake and saw Memory asleep beside the burning fire.

* * *

A strange laughter woke him. He recognised the laugh. It belonged to Oda'nyaa. He looked around him and saw no one. He couldn't see the mermaid. He couldn't see Memory either. The morning sun shone brighter. The fire died. He sprang up and walked through the woods in search of Memory. He met a flowing stream and hoped Memory wasn't naked washing herself there. He felt relieved on seeing the sweet smelling black stream.

He took off his clothes and waded into the water. He continued to wash himself. He heard Oda'nyaa's laughter again and looked up. He saw nothing. Christmas cupped some water in his palm to pour over his heard. The laughter came again. He looked in the direction it came from and saw Memory.

He scrambled to get out of the water. He got on his pantaloons and headed toward the spot. She hung lifelessly from a tree. He screamed loudly in Idoma, *'Odi yaa la'America?'* He stood looking at the body. How the soiled rope moved her corpse and her protruded tongue dangled; how her blouse danced to the breeze. He climbed up the tree and gently untied the rope letting her body fall. He buried her beside Ark's resting place.

Toward the evening, he continued the journey. Christmas soon reached the Ohio black river. He remembered the fugitive woman he and Massa helped here. He remembered how she walked over the water. This time, the water lacked frozen cakes. Just pure flowing water. He saw the north across the Ohio black river. He entered it and started to swim across. Minutes passed. He lost strength, but endured. His greying beard got soaked. He got across finally and threw himself onto the land. He lay on his back, felt breathless and closed his eyes.

He opened his eyes and turned his head to the side. A dead body lay next to his. He sprang up and saw many other bodies of men and horses. He recognised the full-bearded man among the dead. He saw the robust rapist lying in a pool of his own blood. A wrecked boat lay by the curve of the river. Fear gripped him.

'I was ruthless,' a voice said.

Christmas turned around and saw Orinya walking away.

'Come back. Come back.'

Orinya didn't. His colourful burial shroud soon faded into the air.

* * *

Cincinnati, unlike Louisville, seemed populated. Christmas understood the reason fugitive slaves lasted a long time in the city without being caught. Some negroes amongst the black population spied against their own race. They reported to the authorities once they were able to identify a fugitive. Negroes could be seen playing games heart-to-heart with white folks. Whites could be seen in loud arguments with blacks. This surprised Christmas. He joined a group of homeless elderly negroes by the side of the rowdy fish market. Christmas and his new companions devoured the raw fish leftovers on sale each day.

On this day the fish sellers, unable to sell everything, threw fishes at them. Christmas and his new friends became like street dogs fighting amongst themselves. They soon were satisfied and rested on the bare ground underneath their grubby quilts.

Christmas studied the men around him. They were between seventy and eighty years of age. Christmas's physical strength distinguished him from these men. He walked upright. His grey beard wasn't different to theirs. If white people were way right about his age, he recently turned fifty-seven. But he felt like a man over sixty. He made a friend named Drunken-Chai. The old negro man claimed he got emancipated forty years ago and lived a good life in

England selling books. Drunken-Chai spoke of his desire see Africa one day.

'They denied me the Liberia opportunity because of my age. They say I'm too ole and got no family.'

'I got the opportunity but I say no to them. I'm from Opialu in the country of Oli'doma. We called the crocodile people. Nothin' like the people in Liberia,' Christmas said.

'Why they call y'all the crocodile people?'

'We used to belong to the great nation called Kwararafa. A group of Hausas came into the country and took our women and children. This happen long ago. The number of my people that survived fled to Oli'doma as crocodiles.'

Drunken-Chai retold it to the other men. 'He a crocodile man from Africa,' he often started before adding some of his own stories to the tale.

Underneath his quilt, Christmas thought of Ark. He thought of Nedi and wondered how he could break the news to her. His spirit, a blur in the haze, travelled to Africa, to Liberia. The spirit became the soil farmed by the locals. Christmas saw a youth whipping the locals and giving instructions. The lad wasn't impressed with the work of villagers. Christmas felt awkward about this. This youth wasn't white. How could this happen in Liberia?

From a closer look, the young lad seemed to be on the fairer side - a quadroon. It didn't matter. A quadroon born of a slave woman ain't different from a negro. The lad wore boots. But the field-hands wore nothing other than the leaves covering their private organs. Christmas recognised Small John. A young boy grown too big for his age. Probably fifteen years old now. This seemed to be the lifestyle of free negroes in Africa. Becoming like the white man.

* * *

One clear winter night, Christmas and all the other elderly negro men clung onto each other to fend off the snow. They covered themselves with fish smelling quilts. An elderly woman approaching, stopped and looked at them closely.

'Drunken-Chai,' she called.

Drunken Chai stood to his feet. 'Oh... so long.'

They hugged, each falling over a heap of snow.

Christmas and the other men stared. They anticipated some good news.

'Ain't believe them folks that said you made this place home, Drunken Chai,' she said. She looked at Christmas and the others. 'I suppose they your friends?'

Drunken Chai nodded. On this same cold night, the woman led them to the Ohio Home, a new building owned by the Methodist church. Christmas found a home here. The Ohio Home people gave him a small room. A pallet occupied a quarter of the entire space. He liked it.

* * *

The new people of the Ohio Home were kind to Christmas at first. The white people, unlike the cruel ones Orinya killed, were generous. They provided adequate food. There were more elderly negro men and women here. They shared everything – sausages, diary, soda soaps and even umbrellas.

One cold morning, an elderly black woman pulled one of the workers with her, and confronted Christmas. Christmas, alone sipping a cup of tea, noticed their quiet hostility. An elderly negro man watched him from the passageway. The women dragged out seats and sat. They ignored his smile and this baffled him.

'Mama Alicia has reported you to me, Christmas, but I would like to first of all hear your side of the story,' the white middle-aged woman, known to be Rose, said.

'Side of the story?' Christmas asked. 'I got no story.'

'You crazy son of a whore done raped me right beside my husband,' the old woman said.

Christmas spat out his tea and got to his feet, grabbing a napkin from the table to clean his pantaloons. 'This woman sick, Rose. Don't waste no time.'

'Mama Alicia, can you repeat your story? What you said to me before we came here,' the white woman said.

'I was too scared to resist. My husband was damn scared too.'

The old woman narrated what sounded like mere dirty and waggish talk.

'Can you leave me and Christmas to talk for now?' Rose requested looking at the elderly woman. She walked away to meet the man watching from the passageway. Rose looked at Christmas and said, 'I'm sorry Christmas. We take matters like this seriously here. We are part of the Church of God. I'm not saying I believe it. She may be sick and making up stories.'

'I'm never like that, ma'am,' Christmas said.

'I would take your word.'

'Why do you do what you do?' Christmas asked. 'Helpin' black folks?'

'I do it for God,' she replied. 'I have a husband but we are yet to have children of our own. I'm delighted in my work for now. I hope to have a child one day and become a housewife.'

Christmas nodded.

A month passed before Rose confronted him again. Rose, Drunken Chia and Drunken Chia's woman waited for him in the yard. They watched him hang a washed shirt and a pair of pantaloons over the line. He soon went to them. Drunken Chia's sudden punch blinded him for a moment. Rose tried to hold Drunken Chai back from doing more harm. His frail looking woman spoke, 'Nigger pushed me into his pallet last night.'

'What!' Christmas shouted. 'What I gon do that for?'

Somebody laughed. They all turned around but saw no one. Christmas's heart raced. He sensed Oda'nyaa's presence.

'I gon wait for my shirts and pantaloons to dry before takin' my leave,' Christmas said. 'Whatever I say ain't gon change nothin'.'

Sunset came, and the cold wind started to settle in the dark. Christmas left for the bank of the black river in Cincinnati. He looked over the river and called, 'Oda'nyaa! Oda'nyaa, I know you hear me. You are a fool to do all these bad things to me. I used to think your ancient age signified wisdom. Now I know it doesn't. You are just a fool. Just a lying selfish slut.' The torture couldn't prevent his departure. 'You don't know that you are pushing me further to Opialu,' he went on to say.

* * *

He lay on the bank of the black river in Cincinnati to sleep. Deep into the night, some of his good friends in the Ohio Home woke him. Despite their thin frames and fading strength, they attacked him. Some stamped on him. Their punches were like infant strokes against his jaw. One of them scratched his face with his calloused fingers, and Christmas let out an involuntary moan and kicked out. The man fell hard on a heap of snow, and the others drew away.

The fallen one struggled to his feet and ran in the direction they came from. The others followed.

Christmas felt blood trickling down his chin. He lay down again and wondered. Oda'nyaa, indeed miserable and frustrated, seemed to revolt. She couldn't stop him from going to Oli'doma. He felt embarrassed and angry over the allegations. In the cold and in profound shame he metamorphosed into a stray dog. He explored the heaps of rubbish on street corners. He enjoyed the lightness in his movement, with his long tongue hanging out. He remained this way for days. He sensed something very unusual one particular night. In his privilege of possessing the most incredible sense of smell, he found the purest form of life somewhere in a heap of dung. He dug out a lifeless mulatto infant. Sniffing at the heart, he sensed it still possessed life. He carried the infant, locking it between his dog teeth and gently ran to the set of cottages in front of the Ohio Home. He dropped the infant in front of the house he often saw Rose retire to. He barked. Someone unlocked the door. The dog sat watching. A man came out before Rose did. They were angered at first until they caught sight of the naked and freezing mulatto child under the rays of the moon. Rose rushed to pick up the infant. The dog took to its heels.

In the months to come, he remained a dog eating from rubbish heaps. He played in the black river one day until dusk. Back on the land, he shook his body, and headed to his sleep place. Four negro boys appeared to be waiting for him.

'Come on, whiskey,' one of them said offering him a piece of dried meat.

He sniffed at the hand, and one of the boys behind him brought down a beer bottle on his skull. The bottle shattered. He wailed and jumped. The boys laughed and kept a safe distance. They attacked him again, this time, all throwing kicks. The dog snarled viciously. He watched them become still. They withdrew. He ran off bleeding from the side of his head. He soon became human and noticed a scar on the side of his head. Christmas found himself a lone man again awaiting the strength of levitation.

He taunted Oda'nyaa. He wanted to tell her that her strategies against him were useless; that he would certainly go home to Opialu. He walked into her territory in the black river, but lost his way amongst mermaids with caudal fins. Some ignored him. Some found his legs funny. He hated this.

The river became dark and all the mermaids vanished. His ability to breathe under water ceased, and water gushed into his nose and mouth. He fought it, blowing and kicking, climbing up in a rush to find the surface. But the journey became endless. Death seemed to have a grip on him. He woke and found himself on the Cincinnati black river bank. His alekwuafia stood before him.

'Where is my strength? I'm ready to go back to Opialu.'

Orinya stayed silent.

'Answer me. Is the strength coming?'

The masquerade's wings sprouted.

'Where are you running to? Answer me!' Christmas got to his feet and kicked the loose snow in remorse and anger.

Orinya's figure faded away. Christmas went hungry and felt displaced. Children, negroes and whites, laughed at him each time they went by. Some looked afraid of him and they kept their faces straight. Snowflakes added whiteness to his aging beard.

One bracing moment, his spirit became snow and he watched himself sit at the side of the road. Truly, he appeared mad and frail. He saw himself talk to himself. He heard himself laugh to himself.

He felt himself punching the air and waving at the vultures devouring a dead bull. The cold streets once again became his dwelling place.

On a cold morning in 1831, he felt the strength Orinya spoke about come on him. He felt the desire to fly in his spirit, body and mind. He dropped the pile of stems in his hand. He expected to see Opialu soon. He laughed. Christmas looked around him, the land on which his seed sprouted and got lost among the weeds. He couldn't claim anything. He couldn't remain a sad old man. Abutu Eje truly provided strength. Christmas swayed his body into the sky. In anticipation, he attained great speed with his vision becoming wide.

* * *

The creatures he encountered in the clouds bowed. They possessed skins different to the white man's and to the negro's. Some blue. Some green. They were like shadows and were ceremoniously dressed in robes that weren't of this world. They wore crowns of different sizes. Their women were easily distinguishable. Their reflections gleamed.

The journey took long. He rocked his floating body to sleep. He floated into the future through his spirit. In this future he walked into Girl Carolyn's wedding. He sensed sadness in the air. Olofu wept over the wedding from his small chamber in Africa.

She married a white man. According to the late Moses Preacher, the white man and a thief ain't different. Christmas didn't care. He wanted to dance with Girl Carolyn in her long white robe but he couldn't. She didn't even know him. But she knew the name, Christmas. So his spirit danced on his own enjoying the feeling. His body remained asleep in the comfort of the sky.

Oda'nyaa threw her mighty net from the black ocean up to the sky. The net tickled his body at first and he laughed in his sleep. It felt too prickly and took his breath away. He awakened to the problem. He opened his eyes only to see the net bringing him right down. His body whipped the golden platform upon which Oda'nyaa's seat dwelt. The potent power behind his capture left him brutalised. He could hardly stand or even reason. Darkness almost took hold of his life. He raised his head and saw a lot of mermaids. Oda'nyaa's throne lit up the entire kingdom. Her gaze wouldn't leave his body.

'Let me go, mermaid!' he managed to say.

The other mermaids chortled.

'That is what you call me now?' Oda'nyaa said laughing. 'I am no more your damsel. No more your queen. No more your love. No more your life. But a mermaid!'

The other mermaids chanted in reverence to their queen, 'You are his damsel. You are his queen. You are his love. You are his life.'

Oda'nyaa wore a cobra over her neck and advanced toward him in confident strides. A gentle mermaid, positioned on the left side of the throne, smiled giving Christmas hope.

'Do you prefer Echanyaa to me?' Oda'nyaa asked on noticing his stare. 'You can have the both of us...'

The other mermaids giggled.

'Or you can have us all!' Oda'nyaa said.

'Let me go,' he pleaded.

'Go where?'

'Opialu.' He sighed.

'Why do you want to go to that place?' Another mermaid asked

'We would rather have you here. You're safe here,' Oda'nyaa said.

They all laughed again.

'Put him in chains,' Oda'nyaa ordered.

Two mermaids approached him and lifted him off the golden floor. He struggled but they dragged him firmly to a corner. They chained him to two pillars.

* * *

In allegiance to Oda'nyaa, the mermaids led him to the chamber of mirrors forcing him upon the royal bed beside the naked Oda'nyaa with legs apart. He remained defiant. The mermaid, Echanyaa, stood by the entrance and watched closely. The look on her face steeled his resistance. A kind of hidden hope rested somewhere within Echanyaa's gaze. Oda'nyaa permitted the mermaids to take him away. He couldn't give in.

They chained him to the golden pillars again and Oda'nyaa whipped him. Jeers and laughter filled the water world. He stared at them. The mermaids wore dazzling legs. Echanyaa seemed different. The fair skin. The broad gorgeous lips. Alluring brow. She looked tall. Her curves glinted like fire in the dark. Deeply seductive even in little movements. She walked with shoulders high and held a confident and tranquil gaze. She remained quiet and sustained an elegant poise.

The ocean went to sleep and snored loudly, that Christmas felt a severe ache go through his head, like a sword. His heartbeat slowed. He watched Oda'nyaa and the other women transform into their mermaid bodies and leave. Some in purple form, some in orange.

Oda'nyaa came to him afterwards alone. She came to taunt him. He felt very weak and sore in the cruel chains.

'You want to go to Opialu.' She laughed. 'Why do you want to do that? Home is America. And in America you are betrothed to me and me alone.'

'Let me go,' he pleaded.

'Will you be with me as before?' she asked. 'You go back, and you die. You will be killed,' she said

'Kill me.'

'She can't do it!'

Oda'nyaa turned around and locked eyes with Orinya, Christmas's very own alekwuafia.

'Where have you come from?' Oda'nyaa asked.

'From the sky,' the masquerade said and drew out a sword from his side.

'What are... you going to do?' Oda'nyaa stammered.

'Stop you from keeping him,' he said.

'Do it!' she challenged the masquerade. 'And I will cease his ability to breathe in my kingdom.'

'You cannot do that!' Orinya spun his sword swiftly, thrice on both his sides, and turned his back on them. He back-flipped three times in quick succession, and landed by Oda'nyaa's side. He pushed the sword through her belly and pulled it out. Oda'nyaa could scarcely comprehend what death really meant to her kingdom. The snore of the ocean went still. The accusatory voices of the mermaids waking up in devastating anger filled the black ocean. Oda'nyaa fell into a pool of her blood. The trembling tides caused the moon to burn terribly, and the ocean poured over the golden floor. A great flood of mourning followed, and the mermaids poured in, in numbers.

Orinya stared at Christmas. 'You will have to do your part.' His wings sprouted, he threw his sword against the flooding floor and leapt up into the sky. His colourful burial shroud lightened all around him.

'You can't leave me here,' Christmas lamented.

The mermaids saw their fallen queen in blood. Their mourning got louder. In anger their voices were deafening. One of them, clasping Oda'nyaa's gory body, met Christmas's eyes. She raised her blood-soaked index finger at him. Christmas tried to shake himself loose. The chains clattered. The tides quietened but the ocean continued to pour in. The women's feet were transforming into caudal tails. They formed a circle around him and hopped toward him in vengeful anger. Fear became Christmas's shield. Their mourning became warring chants. Echanyaa leapt out of the circle of mermaids, and pushed herself to shield Christmas against her kind. This appeared useless. The scorn and chants got stronger. Echanyaa's eyes fell on the floating sword the masquerade left behind. She squatted, picked it up and pushed it into her body. Every mermaid felt the pain she felt. They screamed like Echanyaa, and fell in the same way she fell. They bled. The black ocean flooded the queen's chamber.

He started to drown in the infuriated waters. This signified death. The water grew around him and ran into his nose and eyes and ears. The water broke the pillars securing the chains and set him free. The black ocean in its own might brought him to its surface. The great leopard man once again provided the strength to levitate. Christmas vomited the water in his belly. He thrust himself upwards. The clouds embraced him again. He kept his body afloat and headed for Opialu.

He fell asleep during the journey and dreamt. Echanyaa came to him in the form of a cloud creature. She opened her lips and kissed him. It felt magical. The kiss signified freedom.

PART TEN

OYICHO

SITTING ON HIS BAMBOO CHAIR, Ochigbo watched his four-year-old son run around the compound. Oyicho, born in Ochigbo's late years – at sixty-six, climbed up a cashew tree. Ochigbo chose the name 'Oyicho' which meant 'child of the sky'. The overwhelming feeling of the sky remained with him to this day. He landed in Opialu and prospered. Chief Ona Abutu didn't just bless him with a daughter for a wife, but gave him land, on which he now owned three huts. He remembered how he glided through the sky from America; He didn't want to think of those moments. Onwowo emerged. She held an incredible resemblance to the mermaid, Echanyaa. The red beads around her waist dangled as she approached with a plate of kolanuts. The tiny white dots and designs on her face gave her an alluring look. Her enormous hips seemed to slow her intense movements. She knelt, and her womanly smell poured over him. She never visited his dream all through his life in the white man's land.

He broke the kolanuts and fed her a piece. Her smile exhibited her love for him. He gave thanks to his alekwuafia and to Abutu Eje before eating a piece. She turned around to leave. He admired her behind until she entered her hut.

He thought of how they met in the physical world. He landed from the sky in Opialu upon her roof and tore through it. He nearly collapsed on her body. She screamed loudly that her father, brothers and uncles surrounded the hut with machetes. Her screams were deafening. He never heard anything so loud. Sleep cleared from her lovely eyes, and his alekwuafia's spell fell on her. She covered her mouth using a hand. She became his gift. Christmas knelt and thanked his ancestors in prayer.

He emerged out of the hut in his white man's clothes. Her family members all drew back and couldn't attack. The chief priest of the village arrived on time to announce his return.

'He isn't a wizard,' the chief priest claimed. 'I saw it in a vision. He is an Ogah son of Opialu who has returned from the white man's land.'

Opialu residents arranged a great ceremony in his honour, and a number of masquerades joined in the merriment, dancing amongst men. Orinya, present with these masquerades in his colourful burial shroud, led the troop parading through the village.

* * *

Still sitting on the bamboo chair, Ochigbo kept having reflections of the past few years. Oyicho ran to him, and he lifted the boy onto his lap. He heard chaotic voices coming from afar. He dropped his son and stood to his feet. He felt more comfortable in the wrapper around his waist than the sleeve shirts and pantaloons he wore in the white man's land. He looked over the little hill in front of his compound and sighted his brother, Abah. The man along with a few cheering youths, marched into Ochigbo's compound. Abah Ogah obviously enjoyed depriving him of peace. Abah monitored his wife each time she visited the stream, Ochigbo learned. Abah always watched his compound from the high rocks. This brother told the village that he, Ochigbo, possessed no blood of his. Abah promised to prove himself right using the last drop of his blood.

Ochigbo owed Abah nothing. His dream to see Opialu before death wasn't a crime. Abah could go on telling inhabitants that he wasn't Ochigbo. Abah could go around telling people Ochigbo since died in the white man's land. Ochigbo could tolerate all the empty words but not Abah coming into his compound to challenge his existence. Abah appeared rigidly thin and muscular. His wrapper, knotted at the back of his neck, left his hands bare but covered his chest downward to his knee.

'You cannot keep lying to Opialu,' Abah said.

'Leave,' Ochigbo replied quietly.

Abah continued, 'I challenge you to a fight. There's always an Ogah who is the greatest.' Abah lifted his right hand up toward the sky to receive lightning, stunning Ochigbo. Abah opened his palm and lightning sprang out of it to hit Ochigbo.

Ochigbo fell and yelped in fright. Onyowo came out of her hut and picked up her son. She glanced at Ochigbo but ran back into the hut with the child. The group of young men laughed and jeered. They cheered in Abah's support. Abah flung more lightning at Ochigbo. Ochigbo lamented. The sound of thunder spattered over the ground. Ochigbo eschewed subsequent throws of lightning using his levitating ability. Abah didn't hesitate before striking more lightning at greater speed. Ochigbo got struck by the lightning on levitating to a height greater than the Iroko tree by the corner of his wife's hut. He fell upon his wife's hut which collapsed – yet again. He heard his wife cry; he heard his son whimper.

'He is not an Ogah. He is not my brother.' Abah laughed in mockery. 'Last time any Ogah son flew was in the days of Orinya. Not this day.'

Ochigbo squatted. He stared at Abah, the hero of the Opialu youths. Ochigbo's spirit left his body, and became his own brother's blood. Abah's blood started to boil and his body began to shake. The heat gripped him. He fell to the chaotic alarm of his own supporters. The youths encircled him, tried to touch him and calm him, but his body felt too hot. Steam ascended out of his body. It occurred. Abah exploded and infinitesimal pieces of flesh and blood streaked at his followers. Abah's existence on earth ended. All the youths froze, staring at Ochigbo in deep shock. He remained in the same squatting posture. One of the youths staggered into a run, and the others followed, leaving Abah's remains in Ochigbo's compound.

A strange voice screamed from afar, and Orinya landed from the sky onto the compound in full force, raising dust. Ochigbo raised his head to look.

'You should have allowed me to deal with this on my own,' the masquerade said.

'He was going to kill me,' Ochigbo said.

'You don't kill your own blood.'

'You should have stopped me before now,' Ochigbo snapped. 'You should have stopped the fight.'

'You will die now!' Orinya said and drew out his sword. He rushed in thudding strides toward Ochigbo.

Ochigbo's eyes settled on the fallen hut. His wife, covered in blood, nursed his wounded son. Ochigbo raised a leg in defence before the masquerade got to him. He jabbed his knee against his alekwuafia's side. Orinya fell and his sword rolled out of his hand. Ochigbo dived for it, grabbed it and held it in defence. The masquerade got up and rushed forward. Ochigbo swung the sword and stuck Orinya thrice. Ochigbo, sure the edge of the sword chopped into the ancestral body, held the weapon firmly. Orinya seemed to have no sense of pain. In their struggle for the sword, it fell again and Ochigbo felt a child's hands grab him from behind. He couldn't see the face of this person. Orinya got hold of the sword and pushed it right through Ochigbo. Ochigbo tried to move but couldn't. The hands left him. He fell to the ground. He strained his eyes to look at the person behind him. He saw his future self, Olofu.

'You cannot fight yourself,' Olofu said.

'What are you doing here?' Ochigbo asked.

'I came to end this. You were at war with your own self.'

'Why Olofu?' Ochigbo asked.

'It is time, Ochigbo,' Orinya said gazing at him.

* * *

In death, he took a step into the past inheriting the eyes of the sky. He saw himself alive again with Onyowo still carrying Oyicho in her womb. On their way to the stream, he cuddled her hand and held her from behind, desiring to have a feel of his unborn child's silhouette in her belly. In death, he took the greatest of strides into the future and saw Ijeyi in the blue uniform of an American soldier. His son, born in America, survived a war and returned to Louisville. Ijeyi looked tall like an Ogah son. He appeared bulky. His beard gave him an intimidating look. Ijeyi stood before a tombstone engraved with the name 'Christmas'. The sky got confused and Oda'nyaa's voice echoed from a distance.

'I won after all,' she said. 'You died in Cincinnati, and one of your master's sons brought your remains back to the Preacher residence.'

'Crazy lying mermaid.' Christmas laughed. 'I returned to my beloved country, Oli'doma.'

'Let's see if the world will believe you or me,' she said.

'You dead,' he said.

'And you?' Oda'nyaa asked. 'Do you think you are still alive?'

He thought of her question and remembered Hugh's words – that he, Christmas, lived in a world of lies.

Acknowledgement

Black River: An account of Christmas Preacher, a slave freed would not have been completed without the reliable and generous support of the Auckland University of Technology's creative writing programme. Paul Mountfort as the chair of the programme was able to guide and direct me to places I never thought I could reach. James George as a mentor was the surprise craft-master who kept offering simple tips and approaches that were able to solve issues I thought were impossible to solve. I say thank you to all the other lecturers (both ex and current). Great stories emerge because of what they do. Pip Adam, a creative writing tutor at Massey University, was also a mentor – she was always calm in meetings, knowing where the work was headed. I say thank you to Zana Bell, who was the inspiring writer I travelled with on my recent PhD Journey at the Auckland University of Technology. I say thank you to Anna Gailani and Elizabeth Ardley for the editing and proofing of this work.

I appreciate my dear wife, Tega Ojabo, for looking after the kids, Kyle Ojabo and Leona Ojabo. They were the greatest of gifts I had during the time I was writing this novel. I say thank you to my parents, Leo Ojabo and Cecilia Ojabo, and to my siblings, Daniel Ojabo, Enuwa Odinya, Victor Ojabo and Ebo Ojabo – for being there. I acknowledge my in-laws, Margaret Oghene, Rukevwe Obayiuwana, Kesiena Oghene, Dafe Oghene, Basirat Olaitan, Risikat Gbadamosi, Tom Odinya, Richard Obayiuwana and Nanbyen Ojabo. I also acknowledge all my beautiful nieces all around the world – Shekinah Odinya, Gabriel Odinya and Makayla Ojabo. I cannot finish without acknowledging God. He is my everything.